THE BIG-TOWN ROUND-UP

THE BIG-TOWN
ROUND-UP

BY

WILLIAM MacLEOD RAINE

 This book, while produced under
wartime conditions, in full com-
pliance with government regula-
tions for the conservation of paper
and other essential materials, is
COMPLETE AND UNABRIDGED

WILDSIDE PRESS

CONTENTS

THE BIG-TOWN ROUND-UP

THE BIG-TOWN ROUND-UP

FOREWORD

THE driver of the big car throttled down. Since he had swung away from the dusty road to follow a wagon track across the desert, the speedometer had registered many miles. His eyes searched the ground in front to see whether the track led up the brow of the hill or dipped into the sandy wash.

On the breeze there floated to him the faint, insistent bawl of thirsty cattle. The car leaped forward again, climbed the hill, and closed in upon a *remuda* of horses watched by two wranglers.

The chauffeur stopped the machine and shouted a question at the nearest rider, who swung his mount and cantered up. He was a lean, tanned youth in overalls, jumper, wide sombrero, high-heeled boots, and shiny leather chaps. A girl in the tonneau appraised with quick, eager eyes this horseman of the plains. Perhaps she found him less picturesque than she had hoped. He was not there for moving-picture purposes. Nothing on horse or man held its place for any reason except utility. The leathers protected the legs of the boy from the spines of the cactus and the thorns of the mesquite, the wide flap of the hat his face from the slash of catclaws when he drove headlong through the brush after flying cattle. The steel horn of the saddle was built to check a half-ton of belting hill steer and fling it instantly. The rope, the Spanish bit, the *tapaderas,* all could justify their place in his equipment.

"Where's the round-up?" asked the driver.

The coffee-brown youth gave a little lift of his head to the right. He was apparently a man of few words. But his answer sufficed. The bawling of anxious cattle was now loud and persistent.

The car moved forward to the edge of the mesa and dropped into the valley. The girl in the back seat gave a little scream of delight. Here at last was the West she had read about in books and seen on the screen.

This was Cattleland's hour of hours. The *parada* grounds were occupied by two circles of cattle, each fenced by eight or ten horsemen. The nearer one was the beef herd, beyond this — and closer to the mouth of the cañon from which they had all recently been driven — was a mass of closely packed cows and calves.

The automobile swept around the beef herd and drew to a halt between it and the noisier one beyond. In a fire of mesquite wood branding-irons were heating. Several men were busy branding and marking the calves dragged to them from the herd by the horsemen who were roping the frightened little blatters.

It was a day beautiful even for Arizona. The winey air called potently to the youth in the girl. Such a sky, such atmosphere, so much life and color! She could not sit still any longer. With a movement of her wrist she opened the door and stepped down from the car.

A man sitting beside the chauffeur turned in his seat. "You'd better stay where you are, honey." He had an

idea that this was not exactly the scene a girl of seventeen ought to see at close range.

"I want to get the kinks out of my muscles, Dad,"
the girl called back. "I'll not go far."

She walked along a ridge that ran from the mesa into
the valley like an outstretched tongue. Her hands were
in the pockets of her fawn-colored coat. There was a
touch of unstudied jauntiness in the way the tips of her
golden curls escaped from beneath the little brown
toque she wore. A young man guarding the beef herd
watched her curiously. She moved with the untamed,
joyous freedom of a sun-worshiper just emerging from
the morning of the world. Something in the poise of
the light, boyish figure struck a spark from his imagination.

A *vaquero* was cantering toward the fire with a calf
in his wake. Another cowpuncher dropped the loop of
his lariat on the ground, gave it a little upward twist as
the calf passed over it, jerked taut the *riata*, and caught
the animal by the hind leg. In a moment the victim lay
stretched on the ground. In the gathering gloom the
girl could not quite make out what the men were doing.
To her sensitive nostrils drifted an acrid odor of burnt
hair and flesh, the wail of an animal in pain. One of the
men was using his knife on the ears of the helpless
creature. She heard another say something about a crop
and an underbit. Then she turned away, faint and indignant. Three big men torturing a month-old calf — was
this the brave outdoor West she had read about and
remembered from her childhood days? Tears of pity and
resentment blurred her sight.

As she stood on the spit of the ridge, a slim, light figure silhouetted against the skyline, the young man guarding the beef herd called something to her that was lost in the bawling of the cattle. From the motion of his hand she knew that he was telling her to get back to the car. But the girl saw no reason for obeying the orders of a range-rider she had never seen before and never expected to see again. Nobody had ever told her that a rider is fairly safe among the wildest hill cattle, but a man on foot is liable to attack at any time when a herd is excited.

She turned her shoulder a little more definitely to the man who had warned her and looked across the *parada* grounds to the hills swimming in a haze of violet velvet. Her heart throbbed to a keen delight in them, as it might have done at the touch of a dear friend's hand long absent. For she had been born in the Rockies. They belonged to her and she to them. Long years in New York had left her still an alien.

A shout of warning startled her. Above the bellowing of the herd she heard another yell.

"Hi-yi-ya-a!"

A red-eyed steer, tail up, was crashing through the small brush toward the branders. There was a wild scurry for safety. The men dropped iron and ropes and fled to their saddles. Deflected by pursuers, the animal turned. By chance it thundered straight for the girl on the sand spit.

She stood paralyzed for a moment.

Out of the gathering darkness a voice came to her sharp and clear. "Don't move!" It rang so vibrant with crisp command that the girl, poised for flight, stood still and waited in white terror while the huge steer lumbered toward her.

A cowpony, wheeled as on a dollar, jumped to an instant gallop. The man riding it was the one who had warned her back to the car. Horse and *ladino* pounded over the ground toward her. Each stride brought them closer to each other as they converged toward the sand spit. It came to her with a gust of panicky despair that they would collide on the very spot where she stood. Yet she did not run.

The rider, lifting his bronco forward at full speed, won by a fraction of a second. He guided in such a way as to bring his horse between her and the steer. The girl noticed that he dropped his bridle rein and crouched in the saddle, his eyes steadily upon her. Without slackening his pace in the least as he swept past, the man stooped low, caught the girl beneath the armpits, and swung her in front of him to the back of the horse. The steer pounded past so close behind that one of its horns grazed the tail of the cowpony.

It was a superb piece of horsemanship, perfectly timed, as perfectly executed.

The girl lay breathless in the arms of the man, her heart beating against his, her face buried in his shoulder. She was dazed, half fainting from the reaction of her fear. The next she remembered clearly was being lowered into the arms of her father.

He held her tight, his face tortured with emotion. She was the very light of his soul, and she had shaved death by a hair's breadth. A miracle had saved her, but if

would never forget the terror that had gripped him.
Naturally, shaken as he was, his relief found vent in
scolding.

"I told you to stay by the car, honey. But you're so
willful. You've got to have your own way. Thank God
you're safe. If ... if ... " His voice broke as he thought
of what had so nearly been.

The girl snuggled closer to him, her arms round his
neck. His anxiety touched her nearly, and tears flooded
her eyes.

"I know, Dad. I ... I'll be good."

A young man descended from the car, handsome,
trim, and well got up. He had been tailored by the best
man's outfitter in New York. Nobody on Broadway
could order a dinner better than he. The latest dances
he could do perfectly. He had the reputation of knowing
exactly the best thing to say on every occasion. Now he
proceeded to say it.

"Corking bit of riding — never saw better. I'll give
you my hand on that, my man."

The cowpuncher found a bunch of manicured fingers
'n his rough brown paw. He found something else, for
after the pink hand had gone there remained a fifty-
dollar bill. He looked at it helplessly for a moment,
then, beneath the brown outdoor tan, a flush of anger
beat into his face. Without a word he leaned forward
and pressed the note into the mouth of the bronco.

The buckskin knew its master for a very good friend.
If he gave it something to eat — well, there was no harm
in trying it once. The buckskin chewed placidly for a
few seconds, decided that this was a practical joke, and

ejected from its mouth a slimy green pulp that had recently been a treasury note.

The father stammered his thanks to the rescuer of the girl. "I don't know what I can ever do to let you know . . . I don't know how I can ever pay you for saving . . ."

"Forget it!" snapped the brown man curtly. He was an even-tempered youth, as genial and friendly as a half-grown pup, but just now the word "pay" irritated him as a red rag does a sulky bull.

"If there's anything at all I can do for you —"

"Not a thing."

The New Yorker felt that he was not expressing himself at all happily. What he wanted was to show this young fellow that he had put him under a lifelong obligation he could never hope to wipe out.

"If you ever come to New York —"

"I'm not liable to go there. I don't belong there any more than you do here. Better drift back to Tucson, stranger. The *parada* is no place for a tenderfoot. You're in luck you're not shy one li'l' girl tromped to death. Take a fool's advice and hit the trail for town *pronto* before you bump into more trouble."

The rider swung round his pony and cantered back to the beef herd.

He left behind him a much-annoyed clubman, a perplexed and distressed father, and a girl both hurt and indignant at his brusque rejection of her father's friendly advances. The episode of the fifty-dollar bill had taken place entirely under cover. The man who had given the note and the one who had refused to accept it were the only ones who knew of it. The girl saw only that this splendid horseman who had snatched her from under the very feet of the *ladino* had shown a boorish discourtesy. The savor had gone out of her adventure. Her heart was sick with disappointment and indignation.

CHAPTER I

CONCERNING A STREET TWELVE MILES LONG

"I like yore outfit," Red Hollister grumbled. "You're nice boys, and good to yore mothers — what few of you ain't wore their gray hairs to the grave with yore frolicsome ways. You know yore business and you got a good cook. But I'm darned if I like this thing of two meals a day, one at a quarter to twelve at night and the other a quarter past twelve, also and likewise at night."

A tenderfoot might have thought that Hollister had some grounds for complaint. For weeks he had been crawling out of his blankets in the pre-dawn darkness of 3 A.M. He had sat shivering down beside a camp-fire to swallow a hurried breakfast and had swung into the saddle while night was still heavy over the land. He had ridden after cattle wild as deer and had wrestled with *ladino* steers till long after the stars were up. In the chill night he had eaten another meal, rolled up in his blankets, and fallen into instant heavy sleep. And five minutes later — or so at least it seemed to him — the cook had pounded on the triangle for him to get up.

None the less Red's grumbling was a pretense. He would not have been anywhere else for twice the pay. This was what he lived for.

Johnnie Green, commonly known as "the Runt," helped himself to another flank steak. He was not much of a cow-hand, but when it came to eating Johnnie was always conscientiously on the job.

"These here New Yorkers must be awful hardy," he ventured, apropos of nothing. "Seems like they're night birds for fair. Never do go to bed, far as I can make out. They tromp the streets all day and dance at them cabby-rets all night. My feet would be all wore out."

Stace Wallis grinned. "So would my pocketbook. I've heard tell how a fellow can pay as high as four or five dollars for an eat at them places."

"Nothin' to it — nothin' a-tall," pronounced Red dogmatically. Hollister always knew everything. Nothing in the heavens above or the earth below could stump him. The only trouble with his knowledge was that he knew so much that was n't true. "Can't be did. Do you reckon any o' them New Yorkers could get away with five dollars' worth of ham and aigs? Why, the Runt here could n't eat more 'n a dollar's worth."

"Sure," assented Johnnie. It was the habit of his life to agree with the last speaker. "You're damn whistlin', Red. Why, at the Harvey House they only charge a dollar for a square, and a man could n't get a better meal than that."

"Onct in Denver, when I went to the stock show, I blowed myself for a meal at the Cambridge Hotel that set me back one-fifty," said Slim Leroy reminiscently. "They et dinner at night."

"They did?" scoffed Johnnie. "Don't they know a fellow eats dinner at noon and supper at night?"

"I ain't noticed any dinner at noon for se-ve-real weeks," Hollister contributed.

"Some feed that," ruminated Leroy, with memories of the Cambridge Hotel still to the fore.

"With or without?" questioned Red.

"I reckon I had one li'l' drink with it. No more."

"Then they stung you," pronounced Hollister.

"Mebbeso, and mebbe not. I ain't kickin' none. I sure was in tony society. There was fellows sittin' at a table near us that had on them swallow-tail coats."

Johnnie ventured a suggestion. " Don't you reckon if a fellow et a couple o' plates of this here cavi-eer stuff and some ice cream and cake, he might run it up to two bucks or two and a half? Don't you reckon he might, Clay?"

Clay Lindsay laughed. "You boys know a lot about New York, just about as much as I do. I've read that a guy can drop a hundred dollars a night in a cabaret if he has a friend or two along, and never make a ripple on Broadway."

"Does that look reasonable to you, Clay?" argued Red. "We're not talkin' about buckin' the tiger or buyin' diamonds for no actresses. We're figurin' on a guy goin' out with some friends to eat and take a few drinks and have a good time. How could he spend fifty dollars — let alone a hundred — if he let the skirts and the wheel alone and did n't tamper with no straight flushes? "

"I'm tellin' you what I read. Take it or leave it," said Clay amiably.

"Well, I read there's a street there twelve miles long. If a fellow started at one end of that street with a thirst he'd sure be salivated before he reached the other end of it," Stace said with a grin.

"Wonder if a fellow could get a job there. They

would n't have no use for a puncher, I reckon," Slim drawled.

"Betcha Clay could get a job all right," answered Johnnie Green promptly. "He'd be top hand anywhere, Clay would."

Johnnie was the lost dog of the B-in-a-Box ranch. It was his nature to follow somebody and lick his hand whenever it was permitted. The somebody he followed was Clay Lindsay. Johnnie was his slave, the echo of his opinions, the booster of his merits. He asked no greater happiness than to trail in the wake of his friend and get a kind word occasionally.

The Runt had chosen as his Admirable Crichton a most engaging youth. It never had been hard for any girl to look at Clay Lindsay. His sun-tanned, good looks, the warmth of his gay smile, the poise and the easy stride of him, made Lindsay a marked man even in a country where men of splendid physique were no exception.

"I'd take a li'l' bet that New York ain't lookin' for no champeen ropers or bronco-busters," said Stace. "Now if Clay was a cabby-ret dancer or a Wall Street wolf —"

"There's no street in the world twelve miles long where Clay could n't run down and hogtie a job if he wanted to," insisted Johnnie loyally. "Ain't that right, Clay?"

Clay was not listening. His eyes were watching the leap of the fire glow. The talk of New York had carried him back to a night on the round-up three years before. He was thinking about a slim girl standing on a sand spit with a wild steer rushing toward her, of her warm, slender body lying in his arms for five immortal seconds, of her dark, shy eyes shining out of the dusk at him like live coals. He remembered — and it hurt him to recall it — how his wounded pride had lashed out in resentment of the patronage of these New Yorkers. The younger man had insulted him, but he knew in his heart now that the girl's father had meant nothing of the kind. Of course the girl had forgotten him long since. If he ever came to her mind as a fugitive memory it would be in the guise of a churlish boor as impossible as his own hill cattle.

"Question is, could you land a job in New York if you wanted one," explained Stace to the dreamer.

"If it's neck meat or nothin' a fellow can 'most always get somethin' to do," said Lindsay in the gentle voice he used. The vague impulses of many days crystallized suddenly into a resolution. "Anyhow I'm goin' to try. Soon as the *rodeo* is over I'm goin' to hit the trail for the big town."

"Tucson?" interpreted Johnnie dubiously.

"New York."

The bow-legged little puncher looked at his friend and gasped. Denver was the limit of Johnnie's imagination. New York was *terra incognita*, inhabited by a species who were as foreign to him as if they had dwelt in Mars.

"You ain't really aimin' to go to New York sure enough?" he asked.

Clay flashed on him the warm smile that endeared him to all his friends. "I'm goin' to ride down Broadway and shoot up the town, Johnnie. Want to come along?"

CHAPTER II

CLAY APPOINTS HIMSELF CHAPERON

As he traveled east Clay began to slough the outward marks of his calling. He gave his spurs to Johnnie before he left the ranch. At Tucson he shed his chaps and left them in care of a friend at the Longhorn Corral. The six-gun with which he had shot rattlesnakes he packed into his suitcase at El Paso. His wide-rimmed felt hat flew off while the head beneath it was stuck out of a window of the coach somewhere south of Denver. Before he passed under the Welcome Arch in that city the silk kerchief had been removed from his brown neck and retired to the hip pocket which formerly held his forty-five.

The young cattleman began to flatter himself that nobody could now tell he was a wild man from the hills who had never been curried. He might have spared himself the illusion. Everybody he met knew that this clean-cut young athlete, with the heavy coat of tan on his good-looking face, was a product of the open range. The lightness of his stride, the breadth of the well-packed shoulders, the frankness of the steady eyes, all advertised him a son of Arizona.

It was just before noon at one of the small plains towns east of Denver that a girl got on the train and was taken by the porter to a section back of Clay Lindsay. The man from Arizona noticed that she was refreshingly pretty in an unsophisticated way.

A little later he had a chance to confirm this judg-

ment, for the dining-car manager seated her opposite
him at a table for two. When Clay handed her the menu
card she murmured "Thank you!" with a rush of color
to her cheeks and looked helplessly at the list in her
hand. Quite plainly she was taking her first long journey.

"Do I have to order everything that is here?" she
presently asked shyly after a tentative and furtive
glance at her table companion.

Clay felt no inclination to smile at her naïveté. He was
not very much more experienced than she was in such
things, but his ignorance of forms never embarrassed
him. They were details that seemed to him to have no
importance.

The cowpuncher helped her fill the order card. She
put herself entirely in his hands and was willing to eat
whatever he suggested unbiased by preferences of her
own. He included chicken salad and ice cream. From the
justice she did her lunch he concluded that his choice
had been a wise one.

She was a round, soft, little person with constant
intimations of a childhood not long outgrown. Dimples
ran in and out her pink cheeks at the slightest excuse.
The blue eyes were innocently wide and the Cupid's-bow
mouth invitingly sweet. The girl from Brush, Colorado,
was about as worldly-wise as a plump, cooing infant or a
fluffy kitten, and instinctively the eye caressed her with
the same tenderness.

During the course of lunch she confided that her name
was Kitty Mason, that she was an orphan, and that she
was on her way to New York to study at a school for
moving-picture actresses.

"I sent my photograph and the manager wrote back that my face was one hundred per cent perfect for the movies," the girl explained.

It was clear that she was expecting to be manufactured into a film star in a week or two. Clay doubted whether the process was quite so easy, even with a young woman who bloomed in the diner like a rose of the desert.

After they had finished eating, the range-rider turned in at the smoking compartment and enjoyed a cigar. He fell into casual talk with an army officer who had served in the Southwest, and it was three hours later when he returned to his own seat in the car.

A hard-faced man in a suit of checks more than a shade too loud was sitting in the section beside the girl from Brush. He was making talk in an assured, familiar way, and the girl was listening to him shyly and yet eagerly. The man was a variation of a type known to Lindsay. That type was the Arizona bad-man. If this expensively dressed fellow was not the Eastern equivalent of the Western gunman, Clay's experience was badly at fault. The fishy, expressionless eyes, the colorless face, the tight-lipped jaw, expressed a sinister personality and a dangerous one. Just now a suave good-humor veiled the evil of him, but the cowpuncher knew him for a wolf none the less.

Clay had already made friends with the Pullman conductor. He drifted to him now on the search for information.

"The hard-faced guy with the little girl?" he asked casually after the proffer of a cigar. "The one with the muscles bulging out all over him — who is he?"

"He comes by that tough mug honestly. That's Jerry Durand."

"The prize-fighter?"

"Yep. Used to be. He's a gang leader in New York now. On his way back from the big fight in 'Frisco."

"He was some scrapper," admitted the range-rider. "Almost won the championship once, did n't he?"

"Lost on a foul. He always was a dirty fighter. I saw him the time he knocked out Reddy Moran."

"What do you mean gang leader?"

"He's boss of his district, they say. Runs a gambling-house of his own, I've heard. You can't prove it by me."

When Lindsay returned to his place he settled himself with a magazine in a seat where he could see Kitty and her new friend. The very vitality of the girl's young life was no doubt a temptation to this man. The soft, rounded throat line, the oval cheek's rich coloring so easily moved to ebb and flow, the carmine of the full red lips: every detail helped to confirm the impression of a sensuous young creature, innocent as a wild thing of the forests and as yet almost as unspiritual. She was a child of the senses, and the man sitting beside her was weigh-ing and appraising her with a keen and hungry avidity.

Durand took the girl in to dinner with him and they sat not far from Lindsay. Kitty was lost to any memory of those about her. She was flirting joyously with a sense of newly awakened powers. The man from Graham County, Arizona, felt uneasy in his mind. The girl was flushed with life. In a way she was celebrating her escape from the narrow horizon in which she had lived. It was in the horoscope of her temperament to run forward gayly to meet adventure, but when the man opposite her ordered wine and she sipped it reluctantly with a little grimace, the cowpuncher was of opinion that she was likely to get more of this adventure than was good for her. In her unsophistication danger lay. For she was plainly easily influenced, and in the beat of her healthy young blood probably there was latent passion.

They left the diner before Clay. He passed them later in the vestibule of the sleeper. They were looking out together on the moonlit plain through which the train was rushing. The arm of the man was stretched behind her to the railing and with the motion of the car the girl swayed back slightly against him.

Again Clay sought the smoking compartment and was led into talk by the officer. It was well past eleven when he rose, yawned, and announced, "I'm goin' to hit the hay."

Most of the berths were made up and it was with a little shock of surprise that his eyes fell on Kitty Mason and her new friend, the sleek black head of the man close to her fair curls, his steady eyes holding her like a charmed bird while his caressing voice wove the fairy tale of New York to which she yielded herself in strange delight.

"Don't you-all want yo' berth made up, lady?"

It was the impatient porter who interrupted them. The girl sprang up tremulously to accept.

"Oh, please. Is it late?" Her glance swept down the car and took in the fact that her section alone was not made up. "I did n't know — why, what time is it?"

"Most twelve, ma'am," replied the aggrieved porter severely.

She flashed a look of reproach at her companion and blushed again as she fled with her bag to the ladies' dressing-room. As for the man, Lindsay presently came on him in the smoking-room where he sat with an unlit cigar between his teeth and his feet on a chair. Behind half-shuttered lids his opaque eyes glittered with excitement. Clearly he was reviewing in his mind the progression of his triumph. Clay restrained a good, healthy impulse to pick a row with him and go to the mat with the ex-prize-fighter. But after all it was none of his business.

The train was rolling through the cornfields of the Middle West when the Arizonan awoke. He was up early, but not long before Kitty Mason, who was joined at once by Durand.

"Shucks! Nothin' to it a-tall," the range-rider assured himself. "That li'l' girl sure must have the number of this guy. She's flirtin' with him to beat three of a kind, but I'll bet a dogie she knows right where she's at."

Clay did not in the least believe his own argument. If he had come from a city he would have dismissed the matter as none of his business. But he came from the clean Southwest where every straight girl is under the protection of every decent man. If she was in danger because of her innocence it was up to him to look after her. There was no more competent man in Graham County than Clay Lindsay, but he recognized that this was a delicate affair in which he must move warily.

On his way to the diner at noon the range-rider passed her again. She was alone for the moment and as she leaned back her soft round throat showed a beating pulse. Her cheeks were burning and her starry eyes were looking into the future with a happy smile.

"You pore little maverick," the man commented silently.

The two had the table opposite him. As the wheels raced over a culvert to the comparative quiet of the ballasted track beyond, the words of the man reached Clay.

". . . and we'll have all day to see the city, kid."

Kitty shook her head. There was hesitation in her manner, and the man was quick to make the most of it. She wanted to stay, wanted to skip a train and let this competent guide show her Chicago. But somewhere, deep in her consciousness, a bell of warning was beginning to ring. Some uneasy prescience of trouble was sifting into her light heart. She was not so sure of her fairy tale, a good deal less sure of her prince.

A second time the song of the rails lifted from a heavy, rumbling bass to a lighter note, and again a snatch of words drifted across the diner.

". . . the time of your young life, honey."

The girl was crumbling a bread ball with her fingers as a vent to her restless excitement. The heavy hand of the man moved across the table and rested on hers. "And it won't cost you a cent, girlie," the New Yorker added.

But the long lashes of the girl lifted and her baby-blue eyes met his with shy reproach. "I don't think I ought," she breathed, color sweeping her face in a vivid flame.

"You should worry," he scoffed.

The chant of the wheels rose again, increased to a dull roar, and deadened the sound of all talk. But Lindsay knew the girl was weakening. She was no match for this big, dominant, two-fisted man.

The jaw of the cowpuncher set. This child was not fair game for a man like Durand. When Clay rose to leave the diner he knew that he meant to sit in and take a hand.

Either the Limited was ahead of its time schedule or the engineer had orders to run into the city very slowly. The train was creeping through the thickly settled quarter where the poorer people are herded when Clay touched Durand on the shoulder.

"Like to see you a moment in the vestibule," he said in his gentle voice.

The eyes of the two men met and the gambler knew at once that this man and he were destined to be enemies. Some sixth sense of safety, cultivated by a lifetime of battle, flashed him sure warning of this. The fellow meant to make trouble of some kind. The former near-champion of the ring had not the least idea what about or in what way. Nor did he greatly care. He had supreme confidence in his ability to look after himself. It was one factor of the stock in trade that had made him a dominant figure in the underworld of New York. He was vain enough to think that if it came to the worst there were few men living who could best him in a rough-and-tumble fight. Certainly no hill-billy from Arizona could do it.

No man had ever said that Jerry Durand was not game. He rose promptly and followed the Westerner from the car, swinging along with the light, catlike tread acquired by many pugilists.

The floor of the vestibule had been raised and the outer door of the car opened. Durand found time to wonder why.

The cowpuncher turned on him with an abrupt question. "Can you swim?"

The eyes of the ward boss narrowed. "What's that to you?" he demanded truculently.

"Nothin' to me, but a good deal to you. I'm aimin' to drop you in the river when we cross."

"Is that so?" snarled Durand. "You're quite a joker, ain't you? Well, you can't start somethin' too soon to suit me. But let's get this clear so we'll know where we're at. What's ailin' you, rube?"

"I don't like the color of yore hair or the cut of yore clothes," drawled Lindsay. "You've got a sure-enough bad eye, and I'm tired of travelin' in yore company. Let's get off, me or you one."

In the slitted eyes of the Bowery graduate there was no heat at all. They were bleak as a heavy winter morn. "Suits me fine. You'll not travel with me much farther. Here's where you beat the place."

The professional lashed out suddenly with his left. But Clay was not at the receiving end of the blow. Always quick as chain lightning, he had ducked and clinched. His steel-muscled arms tightened about the waist of the other. A short-arm jolt to the cheek he disregarded.

Before Durand had set himself to meet the plunge he found himself flying through space. The gambler caught at the rail, missed it, landed on the cinders beside the roadbed, was flung instantly from his feet, and rolled over and over down an incline to a muddy gully.

Clay, hanging to the brass railing, leaned out and looked back. Durand had staggered to his feet, plastered with mud from head to knees, and was shaking furiously a fist at him. The face of the man was venomous with rage.

The cowpuncher waved a debonair hand and mounted the steps again. The porter was standing in the vestibule looking at him with amazement.

"You throwed a man off'n this train, mistah," he charged.

"So I did," admitted Clay, and to save his life he could not keep from smiling.

The porter sputtered. This beat anything in his previous experience. "But — but — it ain't allowed to open up the cah. Was you-all havin' trouble?"

"No trouble a-tall. He bet me a cigar I could n't put him off."

Clay palmed a dollar and handed it to the porter as he passed into the car. The eyes of that outraged official rolled after him. The book of rules did not say anything about wrestling-matches in the vestibule. Besides, it happened that Durand had called him down sharply not an hour before. He decided to brush off his passengers and forget what he had seen.

Clay stopped in front of Kitty and said he hoped she would have no trouble making her transfer in the city. The girl was no fool. She had sensed the antagonism that had flared up between them in that moment when they had faced each other five minutes before.

"Where's Mr. Durand?" she asked.

"He got off."

"But the train has n't stopped."

"It's just crawlin' along, and he was in a hurry."

Her gaze rested upon an angry bruise on his cheek. It had not been there when last she saw him. She started to speak, then changed her mind.

Clay seated himself beside her. "Chicago is a right big town, 1 reckon. If I can help you any, Miss Kitty, I'd be glad to do what I can."

The girl did not answer. She was trying to work out this puzzle of why a man should get off before the train reached the station.

"I'm a stranger myself, but I expect I can worry along somehow," he went on cheerfully.

"Mr. Durand did n't say anything to me about getting off," she persisted.

"He made up his mind in a hurry. Just took a sudden notion to go."

"Without saying anything about his suitcases?"

"Never mentioned 'em."

"You did n't have — any trouble with him?" she faltered.

"Not a bit," he told her genially. "Sorry our tickets take us by different roads to New York. Maybe we'll meet up with each other there, Miss Kitty."

"I don't understand it," she murmured, half to herself. "Why would he get off before we reach the depot?"

She was full of suspicions, and the bruise on the Westerner's cheek did not tend to allay them. They were still unsatisfied when the porter took her to the end of the car to brush her clothes.

The discretion of that young man had its limits. While he brushed the girl he told her rapidly what he had seen in the vestibule.

"Was he hurt?" she asked breathlessly.

"No 'm. I looked out and seen him standin' beside the track jes' a-cussin' a blue streak. He's a sho-'nough bad actor, that Jerry Durand."

Kitty marched straight to her section. The eyes of the girl flashed anger.

"Please leave my seat, sir," she told Clay.

The Arizonan rose at once. He knew that she knew. "I was intendin' to help you off with yore grips," he said.

She flamed into passionate resentment of his interference. "I'll attend to them. I can look out for myself, sir."

With that she turned her back on him.

CHAPTER III

THE BIG TOWN

WHEN Clay stepped from the express into the Pennsylvania Station he wondered for a moment if there was a circus or a frontier-day show in town. The shouts of the porters, the rush of men and women toward the gates, the whirl and eddy of a vast life all about him, took him back to the few hours he had spent in Chicago.

As he emerged at the Thirty-Fourth Street entrance New York burst upon him with what seemed almost a threat. He could hear the roar of it like a river rushing down a cañon. Clay had faced a cattle stampede. He had ridden out a blizzard hunched up with the drifting herd. He had lived rough all his young and joyous life. But for a moment he felt a chill drench at his heart that was almost dread. He did not know a soul in this vast populace. He was alone among seven or eight million crazy human beings.

He had checked his suitcase to be free to look about. He had no destination and was in no hurry. All the day was before him, all of many days. He drifted down the street and across to Sixth Avenue. He clung to the safety of one of the L posts as the traffic surged past. The clang of surface cars and the throb of motors filled the air constantly. He wondered at the daring of a pink-cheeked slip of a girl driving an automobile with sure touch through all this tangle of traffic. While he waited

to plunge across the street there came a roar overhead
that reminded him again of a wall of water he had once
heard tearing down a cañon in his home land.

Instinctively one arm clutched at the post. A monster
went flying through the air with a horrible, grinding
menace. It was only the Elevated on its way uptown.
Clay looked around in whimsical admiration of the
hurrying people about him. None of them seemed aware
either of the noise or the crush of vehicles. They went on
their preoccupied way swiftly and surely.

"I never did see such a town, and me just hittin' the
fringes of it yet," Clay moaned aloud in comic despair,
unaware that even New York has no noisier street than
Sixth Avenue.

Chance swept him up Sixth to Herald Square. He was
caught in the river of humanity that races up Broadway.
His high-heeled boots clicked on the pavement of one of
the world's great thoroughfares as far as Forty-Second
Street. Under the shadow of the Times Building he
stopped to look about him. Motor-cars, street-cars, and
trucks rolled past in endless confusion. Every instant
the panorama shifted, yet it was always the same. He
wondered where all this rush of people was going. What
crazy impulses sent them surging to and fro? And the
girls -- Clay surrendered to them at discretion. He had
not supposed there were so many pretty, well-dressed
girls in the world.

"I reckon money grows on trees in New York," he
told himself aloud with a grin.

Broadway fascinated him. He followed it uptown
toward Longacre Circle. The street was as usual in a

state of chronic excavation. His foot slipped and he fell into a trench while trying to cross. When he emerged it was with a pound or two of Manhattan mud on his corduroy suit. He looked at himself again with a sense that his garb did not quite measure up to New York standards.

"First off I'm goin' to get me a real city suit of clothes," he promised himself. "This here wrinkled outfit is some too woolly for the big town. It's a good suit yet — 'most as good as when I bought it at the Boston Store in Tucson three years ago. But I reckon I'll save it to go home in."

To a policeman directing traffic at a crossing he applied for information.

"Can you tell me where there's a dry-goods store in this man's town?" he asked. "I fell into this here Broadway and got kinda messed up."

"Watcha want?"

"Suit o' clothes."

The traffic cop sized him up in one swift glance. "Siventh Avenue," he said, and pointed in that direction.

Clay took his advice. He stopped in front of a store above which was the legend "I. Bernstein, Men's Garments." A small man with sharp little eyes and well-defined nose was standing in the doorway.

"Might you would want a good suit of qvality clothes, my friendt," he suggested.

"You've pegged me right," agreed the Westerner with his ready smile. "Lead me to it."

Mr. Bernstein personally conducted his customer to

the suit department. "I wait on you myself on account you was a stranger to the city," he explained.

The little man took a suit from a rack and held it at arm's length to admire it. His fingers caressed the woof of it lovingly. He evidently could bring himself to part with it only after a struggle.

"Worsted. Fine goods." He leaned toward the range-rider and whispered a secret. "Imported."

Clay shook his head. "Not what I want." His eyes ranged the racks. "This is more my notion of the sort of thing I like." He pointed to a blue serge with a little stripe in the pattern.

The eyes of Mr. Bernstein marveled at the discrimination of his customer. "If you had taken an advice from me, it would have been to buy that suit. A man gets a chance at a superior garment like that, understan' me, only once in a while occasionally."

"How much?" asked Lindsay.

The dealer was too busy to hear this crass question. That suit, Clay gathered, had been the pride of his heart ever since he had seen it first. He detached the coat lovingly from the hanger and helped his customer into it. Then he fell back, eyes lit with enthusiastic amazement. Only fate could have brought together this man and this suit, so manifestly destined for each other since the hour when Eve began to patch up fig leaves for Adam.

"Like a coat of paint," he murmured aloud.

The cowpuncher grinned. He understood the business that went with selling a suit in some stores. But it happened that he liked this suit himself. "How much?" he repeated.

The owner of the store dwelt on the merits of the suit, its style, its durability, the perfect fit. He covered his subject with artistic thoroughness. Then, reluctantly, he confided in a whisper the price at which he was going to sacrifice this suit among suits.

"To you, my friendt, I make this garment for only sixty-five dollars." He added another secret detail. "Below wholesale cost."

A little devil of mirth lit in Lindsay's eye. "I'd hate to have you rob yoreself like that. And me a perfect stranger to you too."

"Qvality, y' understan' me. Which a man must got to live garments like I done to appreciate such a suit. All wool. Every thread of it. Unshrinkable. This is a qvality town. If you want the best it costs a little more, but you got anyhow a suit which a man might be married in without shame, understan' me."

The Arizonan backed off in apparent alarm. "Say, is this a weddin' garment you're onloadin' on me? Do I have to sashay down a church aisle and promise I do?"

Mr. Bernstein explained that this was not obligatory. All he meant was that the suit was good enough to be married in, or for that matter to be buried in.

"Or to be born anew in when Billy Sunday comes to town and I hit the sawdust trail," suggested the purchaser.

Mr. Bernstein caressed it again. "One swell piece of goods," he told himself softly, almost with tears in his eyes.

"All wool, you say?" asked Clay, feeling the texture.

He had made up his mind to buy it, though he thought the price a bit stiff.

Mr. Bernstein protested on his honor that there was not a thread of cotton in it. "Which you could take it from me that when I sell a suit of clothes it is like I am dealing with my own brother," he added. "Every garment out of this store takes my personal guarantee."

Clay tried on the trousers and looked at himself in the glass. So far as he could tell he looked just like any other New Yorker.

The dealer leaned forward and spoke in a whisper. Apparently he was ashamed of his softness of heart. "Fifty-five dollars — to you."

"I'll take it," the Westerner said.

The clothier called his tailor from the rear of the store to make an adjustment in the trousers. Meanwhile he deftly removed the tags which told him in cipher that the suit had cost him just eleven dollars and seventy-five cents.

Half an hour later Clay sat on top of a Fifth-Avenue bus which was jerking its way uptown. His shoes were shined to mirror brightness. He was garbed in a blue serge suit with a little stripe running through the pattern. That suit just now was the apple of his eye. It proved him a New Yorker and not a wild man from the Arizona desert.

CHAPTER IV

A NEW USE FOR A WATER HOSE

THE motor-bus ran up Fifth Avenue, cut across to Broadway, passed Columbus Circle, and swept into the Drive. It was a day divinely young and fair. The fragrance of a lingering spring was wafted to the nostrils. Only the evening before the trees had been given a bath of rain and the refreshment of it showed in every quivering leaf. From its little waves the Hudson reflected a million sparkles of light. Glimpses of the Park tempted Clay. Its winding paths! The children playing on the grass while their maids in neat caps and aprons gossiped together on the benches near! This was the most human spot the man from Arizona had seen in the metropolis.

Somewnere in the early three-figure streets he descended from the top of the bus and let his footsteps follow his inclinations into the Park. A little shaver in a sailor suit ran across the path and fell sprawling at the feet of Clay. He picked up and began to comfort the howling four-year-old.

"That sure was a right hard fall, sonny, but you're not goin' to make any fuss about it. You're Daddy's little man and —"

A sharp, high voice cut into his consolation.

"Cedric, come here!"

The little boy went, bawling lustily to win sympathy. The nursemaid shook him impatiently. "How many times have I told you to look where you're going? Serves you just right. Now be still."

There was a deep instinct in Clay to stand by those in trouble when they were weak. A child or a woman in distress always had a claim on him.

"I reckon the li'l' fellow was in a hurry, Miss," he said, smiling. "I 'most always was at his age. But he ain't hurt much."

The maid looked Clay up and down scornfully before she turned her back on him and began to talk with another nurse.

Beneath the tan of the range-rider's cheeks the color flamed. This young woman had not mistaken the friendliness of the West for the impudence of a street masher. The impulse of snobbery had expressed itself in her action.

The cowpuncher followed a path that took him back to the street. He grinned, but there was no smile in his heart. He was ashamed of this young woman who could meet good-will with scorn, and he wanted to get away from her without any unnecessary delay. What were the folks like in this part of the country that you could n't speak to them without getting insulted?

He struck across the Drive into a side street. An apartment house occupied the corner, but from the other side a row of handsome private dwellings faced him.

The janitor of the apartment house was watering the parking beyond the sidewalk. The edge of the stream from the nozzle of the hose sprayed the path in front of Clay. He hesitated for a moment to give the man time to turn aside the hose.

But the janitor on this particular morning had been fed up with trouble. One of the tenants had complained of him to the agent of the place. Another had moved away without tipping him for an hour's help in packing he had given her. He was sulkily of the opinion that the whole world was in a conspiracy to annoy him. Just now the approaching rube typified the world.

A little flirt of the hose deluged Clay's newly shined boots and the lower six inches of his trousers.

"Look out what you're doing!" protested the man from Arizona.

"I tank you better look where you're going," retorted the one from Sweden. He was a heavy-set, muscular man with a sullen, obstinate face.

"My shoes and trousers are sopping wet."

"Yust you bate it oop street. I ant look for no trouble with no rubes."

"I believe you did it on purpose."

"Tank so? Val, yust one teng I lak to tell you. I got no time for damn fule talk."

The Westerner started on his way. There was no use having a row with a sulky janitor.

But the Swede misunderstood his purpose. At Clay's first step forward he jerked round the nozzle and let the range-rider have it with full force.

Clay was swept back to the wall by the heavy pressure of water that played over him. The stream moved swiftly up and down him from head to foot till it had drenched every inch of the perfect fifty-five-dollar suit. He drowned fathoms deep in a water spout. He was swept over Niagara Falls. He came to life again to find

himself the choking center of a world flood. He sputtered
furiously while his arms flailed like windmills to keep
back the river of water that engulfed him.

The thought that brought him back to action was one
that had to do with the blue serge. The best fifty-five-
dollar suit in New York was ruined in this submarine
disaster.

He gave a strangled whoop and charged straight at
the man behind the hose. The two clinched. While they
struggled, the writhing hose slapped back and forth
between them like an agitated snake. Clay had one
advantage. He was wet through anyhow. It did not
matter how much of the deluge struck him. The janitor
fought to keep dry and he had not a chance on earth to
succeed.

For one hundred and seventy-five pounds of Arizona
bone and muscle, toughened by years of hard work in
sun and wind, had clamped itself upon him. The nozzle
twisted toward the janitor. He ducked, went down, and
was instantly submerged. When he tried to rise, the
stream beat him back. He struggled halfway up, slipped,
got again to his feet, and came down sitting with a hard
bump when his legs skated from under him.

A smothered "Vat t'ell!" rose out of the waters. It
was both a yelp of rage and a wail of puzzled chagrin.
The janitor could not understand what was happening
to him. He did not know that he was being treated to a
new form of the water cure.

Before his dull brain had functioned to action an iron
grip had him by the back of the neck. He was jerked to
his feet and propelled forward to the curb. Every inch of

the way the heavy stream from the nozzle broke on his face and neck. It paralyzed his resistance, jarred him so that he could not gather himself to fight. He was still sputtering "By damn," when Clay bumped him up against a hitching-post, garroted him, and swung the hose around the post in such a way as to encircle the feet of the man.

The cowpuncher drew the hose tight, slipped the nozzle through the iron ring, and caught the flapping arms of the man to his body. With the deft skill of a trained roper Clay swung the rubber pipe round the body of the man again and again, drawing it close to the post and knotting it securely behind. The Swede struggled, but his furious rage availed him nothing. He was in the hands of the champion roper of Graham County, a man who had hogtied a wild hill steer in thirty-three seconds by the watch.

It took longer than this to rope up the husky janitor with a squirming hose, but when Clay stepped back to inspect his job he knew he was looking at one that had been done thoroughly.

"I keel you, by damn, ef you don't turn me loose!" roared the big man in a rage.

The range-rider grinned gayly at him. He was having the time of his young life. He did not even regret his fifty-five-dollar suit. Already he could see that Arizona had nothing on New York when it came to getting action for your money.

"Life's just loaded to the hocks with disappointment, Olie," he explained, and his voice was full of genial sympathy. "I'll bet a dollar Mex you'd sure like to beat me on the haid with a two by four. But I don't reckon you'll ever get that fond wish gratified. We're not liable to meet up with each other again *pronto*. To-day we're here and to-morrow we're at Yuma, Arizona, say, for life is short and darned fleetin', as the poet fellow says."

He waved a hand jauntily and turned to go. But he changed his mind. His eye had fallen on a young woman standing at a French window of the house opposite. She was beckoning to him imperiously.

The young woman disappeared as he crossed the street, but in a few moments the door opened and she stood there waiting for him. Clay stared. He had never before seen a girl dressed like this. She was in riding-boots, breeches, and coat. Her eyes dilated while she looked at him.

"Wyoming?" she asked at last in a low voice.

"Arizona," he answered.

"All one. Knew it the moment I saw you tie him. Come in." She stood aside to let him pass.

That hall, with its tapestried walls, its polished floors, and Oriental rugs, was reminiscent of "the movies" to Clay. Nowhere else had he seen a home so stamped with the mark of ample means.

"Come in," she ordered again, a little sharply.

He came in and she closed the door.

"I'm sopping wet. I'll drip all over the floor."

"What are you going to do? You'll be arrested, you know." She stood straight and slim as a boy, and the frank directness of her gaze had a boy's sexless unconsciousness.

"Thought I'd give myself up to the marshal."

She laughed outright at this. "Not in this town. A stranger like you would have no chance. Listen." There came to them from outside the tap-tap-tap-tap of a policeman's night stick rattling on the curbstone. "He's calling help."

"I can explain how it happened."

"No. He would n't understand. They'd find you guilty."

He moved from the rug where he was standing to let the water drip on the hardwood floor.

"Sho! Folks are mostly reasonable. I'd tell the judge how it come about."

"No."

"Well, I can't stay here."

"Yes — till they've gone."

Her imperative warmed his heart, but he tried to explain gently why he could not. "I can't drag you into this. Like as not the Swede saw me come in."

To a manservant standing in the background the young woman spoke. "Jenkins, have Nora clean up the floor and the steps outside. And remember — I don't want the police to know this gentleman is here."

"Yes, Miss."

"Come!" said the girl to her guest. She led Clay to the massive stairway, but stopped at the first tread to call back an order over her shoulder. "Refer the officers to me if they insist on coming into the house."

"I'll see to it, Miss."

Clay followed his hostess to the stairs and went up them with her, but he went protesting, though with a chuckle of mirth. "He sure ruined my clothes a heap. I ain't fit to be seen."

The suit he had been so proud of was shrinking so that his arms and legs stuck out like signposts. The color had run and left the goods a peculiar bilious-looking overall blue.

She lit a gas-log in a small library den.

"Just a minute, please."

She stepped briskly from the room. In her manner was a crisp decision, in her poise a trim gallantry that won him instantly.

"I'll bet she'd do to ride with," he told himself in a current Western idiom.

When she came back it was to take him to a dressing-room. A complete change of clothing was laid out for him on a couch. A man whom Clay recognized as a valet — he had seen his duplicate in the moving-picture theaters at Tucson — was there to supply his needs and attend to the temperature of his bath.

"Stevens will look after you," she said; "when you are ready come back to Dad's den."

His eyes followed to the door her resilient step. Once, when he was a boy, he had seen Ada Rehan play in "As You Like It." Her acting had entranced him. This girl carried him back to that hour. She was boyish as Rosalind, woman in every motion of her slim and lissom body.

At the head of the stairway she paused. Jenkins was moving hurriedly up to meet her.

"It's a policeman, Miss. 'E's come about the — the person that came in, and 'e's talkin' to Nora on the steps. She's a-jollyin' 'im, as you might say, Miss."

His young mistress nodded. She swept the hall with the eye of a general. Swiftly she changed the position of a Turkish rug so as to hide a spot on the polished floor that had been recently scrubbed and was still moist. It seemed best to discover Nora's plan of campaign before taking over the charge of affairs.

"Many's the time I've met yuh goin' down the Avenoo with your heels clickin' an' your head high," came the rich brogue of Nora O'Flannigan. "An' I've said to myself, sez I, who's the handsome officer that sets off his uniform so gr-rand?"

The girl leaned on her mop and gave the policeman a slant glance out of eyes of Irish brown. It was not Nora's fault that she was as pretty a colleen as ever came out of Limerick, but there was no law that made her send such a roguish come-hither look at the man in blue.

He beamed. He was as pleased as a cat that has been stroked and fed cream.

"Well, an' yuh're not the only wan that notices, Miss Nora. I'm a noticin' lad mesilf. An' it's the truth that I'd be glad enough to meet yuh some fine evenin' when I'm off duty. But about this strong-arm guy that tied up the janitor. The Swede says he went into wan av these houses. Now here's the wet color from his suit that ran over the steps. He musta come up here."

"Before he ran down the street. Sure, an' that's just what he done. Yuh're a janious, officer."

"Maybe he got into the house somehow."

"Now, how could he do that? With all av us upstairs and down."

"I don't say he did. But if I was to just take a look inside so as to report that I'd searched —"

"Och! Yuh 'd be wastin' your time, officer."

"Sure, I know that. But for the report —"

The young woman in the riding costume chose this moment to open the door and saunter out.

"Does the officer want something, Nora?" she asked innocently, switching the end of a crop against her riding-boots.

"Yes, Miss. There's been a ruffian batin' up Swedes an' tyin' 'em to posts. This officer thinks he came here," explained Nora.

"Does he want to look in the house?"

"Yes, Miss."

"Then let him come in." The young mistress took the responsibility on her own shoulders. She led the policeman into the hall. "I don't really see how he could have got in here without some of us seeing him, officer."

"No, ma'am. I don't see how he could." The patrolman scratched his red head. "The janitor's a Swede, anyhow. He jist guessed it. I came to make sure av it. I'll be sorry for troubling yuh, Miss."

The smile she gave him was warm and friendly. "Oh, that's all right. If you'd care to look around. . . . But there really is no use."

"No." The forehead under the red thatch wrinkled in thought. "He *said* he seen him come in here or next door, an' he came up the steps. But nobody could have got in without some of youse seein' him. That's a lead pipe." The officer pushed any doubt that remained from his mind. "Only a muddle-headed Swede."

"It was good of you to come. It makes us feel safer to have officers like you. If you'll give me your name I'll call up the precinct captain and tell him so."

The man in uniform turned beet red. "McGuffey, Miss, and it's a pleasure to serve the likes of yuh," he said, pleased and embarrassed.

He bowed himself out backward, skidded on the polished floor, and saved himself from going down by a frantic fling of arms and some fancy skating. When he recovered, his foot caught in a rug and wadded it to a knot.

Nora giggled behind her fingers, but her mistress did not even smile at the awkwardness of Patrolman McGuffey.

"Thank you *so* much," she said sweetly.

CHAPTER V

A CONTRIBUTION TO THE SALVATION ARMY

WHILE Beatrice Whitford waited in the little library for the Arizonan to join her, she sat in a deep chair, chin in hand, eyes fixed on the jetting flames of the gas-log. A little flush had crept into the oval face. In her blood there tingled the stimulus of excitement. For into her life an adventure had come from faraway Cattleland.

A crisp, strong footstep sounded in the hall. Her fingers flew to pat into place the soft golden hair coiled low at the nape of the neck. At times she had a boylike unconcern of sex; again, a spirit wholly feminine.

The clothes of her father fitted Lindsay loosely, for Colin Whitford had begun to take on the flesh of middle age and Clay was lean and clean of build as an elk. But the Westerner was one of those to whom clothes are unimportant. The splendid youth of him would have shone through the rags of a beggar.

"My name is Clay Lindsay," he told her by way of introduction.

"Mine is Beatrice Whitford," she answered.

They shook hands.

"I'm to wait here till my clothes dry, yore man says."

"Then you'd better sit down," she suggested.

Within five minutes she knew that he had been in New York less than three hours. His impressions of the city amused and entertained her. He was quite simple. She could look into his mind as though it were a deep, clear well. There was something inextinguishably boyish **and** buoyant about him. But in his bronzed face and steady, humorous eyes were strength and shrewdness. He was the last man in the world a bunco-steerer could play for a sucker. She felt that. Yet he made no pretenses of a worldly wisdom he did not have.

A voice reached them from the top of the stairs.

"Do you know where Miss Whitford is, Jenkins?"

"Hin the Red Room, sir." The answer was in the even, colorless voice of a servant.

The girl rose at once. "If you'll excuse me," she said, and stepped out of the room.

"Hello, Bee. What do you think? I never saw such idiots as the police of this town are. They're watching this house for a desperado who assaulted some one outside. I met a sergeant on our steps. Says he doesn't think the man's here, but there's just a chance he slipped into the basement. It's absurd."

"Of course it is." There was a ripple of mirth in the girl's voice. "He didn't come in by the basement at all, but walked in at the front door."

"Who are you talking about?"

"The desperado, Dad."

"The front door!" exploded her father. "What do you mean? Who let him in?"

"I did. He came as my guest, at my invitation."

"What?"

"Don't shout, Dad," she advised. "I thought I had brought you up better."

"But — but — but — what do you mean?" he sputtered. "Is this ruffian in the house now?"

"Oh, yes. He's in the Red Room here — and unless he's very deaf he hears everything we are saying," the girl answered calmly, much amused at the amazement of her father. "Won't you come in and see him? He does n't seem very desperate."

Clay rose, pinpoints of laughter dancing in his eyes. He liked the gay audacity of this young woman, just as he liked the unconventional pluck with which she had intruded herself into his affairs as a rescuer and the businesslike efficiency that had got him out of his wet rags into comfortable clothes.

A moment later he was offering a brown hand to Colin Whitford, who took it reluctantly, with the same wariness a boxer does that of his opponent in the ring. His eyes said plainly, "What the deuce are you doing here, sitting in my favorite chair, smoking one of my imported cigars, wearing my clothes, and talking to my daughter?"

"Glad to meet you, Mr. Whitford. Yore daughter has just saved my life from the police," the Westerner said, and his friendly smile was very much in evidence.

"You make yourself at home," answered the owner of a large per cent of the stock of the famous Bird Cage mine.

"My guests do, Dad. It's the proof that I'm a perfect hostess," retorted Beatrice, her dainty, provocative face flashing to mirth.

"Hmp!" grunted her father dryly. "I'd like to know, young man, why the police are shadowing this house?"

"I expect they're lookin' for me."

"I expect they are, and I'm not sure I won't help them find you. You'll have to show cause if I don't."

"His bark is much worse than his bite," the girl explained to Clay, just as though her father were not present.

"Hmp!" exploded the mining magnate a second time. "Get busy, young fellow."

Clay told the story of the fifty-five-dollar suit that I. Bernstein had wished on him with near-tears of regret at parting from it. The cowpuncher dramatized the situation with some native talent for mimicry. His arms gestured like the lifted wings of a startled cockerel. "A man gets a chance at a garment like that only once in a while occasionally. Which you can take it from me that when I. Bernstein sells a suit of clothes it is shust like he is dealing with his own brother. Qvality, my friendts, qvality! Why, I got anyhow a suit which I might be married in without shame, un'erstan' me."

Colin Whitford was of the West himself. He had lived its rough-and-tumble life for years before he made his lucky strike in the Bird Cage. He had moved from Colorado to New York only ten years before. The sound of Clay's drawling voice was like a message from home. He began to grin in spite of himself. This man was too good to be true. It wasn't possible that anybody could come to the big town and import into it so naïvely such a genuine touch of the outdoor West. It was not possible, but it had happened just the same. Of course Manhattan would soon take the color out of him. It always did out of everybody. The city was so big, so overpowering, so individual itself, that it tolerated no individuality in its

citizens. Whitford had long since become a conformist.
He was willing to bet a hat that this big brown Arizonan
would eat out of the city's hand within a week. In the
meantime he wanted to be among those present while
the process of taming the wild man took place. Long
before the cowpuncher had finished his story of hog-
tying the Swede to a hitching-post with his own hose,
the mining man was sealed of the large tribe of Clay
Lindsay's admirers. He was ready to hide him from all
the police in New York.

Whitford told Stevens to bring in the fifty-five-dollar
suit so that he could gloat over it. He let out a whoop
of delight at sight of its still sodden appearance. He
examined its sickly hue with chuckles of mirth.

"Guaranteed not to fade or shrink," murmured Clay
sadly.

He managed to get the coat on with difficulty. The
sleeves reached just below his elbows.

"You look like a lifer from Sing Sing," pronounced
Whitford joyously. "Get a hair-cut, and you won't have
a chance on earth to fool the police."

"The color did run and fade some," admitted Clay.

"Worth every cent of nine ninety-eight at a bargain
sale before the Swede got busy with it — and he let you
have it at a sacrifice for fifty-five dollars!" The millionaire wept happy tears as a climax of his rapture. He
swallowed his cigar smoke and had to be pounded on the
back by his daughter.

"Would you mind getting yore man to wrop it up
for me? I'm goin' to have a few pleasant words with
I. Bernstein," said Clay with mock mournfulness.

"When?" asked Whitford promptly.

"Never you mind when, sah. I'm not issuin' any tickets of admission. It's goin' to be a strictly private entertainment."

"Are you going to take a water hose along?"

"That's right," reproached Clay. "Make fun of me because I'm a stranger and come right from the alfalfa country." He turned to Beatrice cheerfully. "O' course he bit me good and proper. I'm green. But I'll bet he loses that smile awful quick when he sees me again."

"You're not going to —"

"Me, I'm the gentlest citizen in Arizona. Never in trouble. Always peaceable and quiet. Don't you get to thinkin' me a bad-man, for I ain't."

Jenkins came to the door and announced "Mr. Bromfield."

Almost on his heels a young man in immaculate riding-clothes sauntered into the room. He had the assured ease of one who has the run of the house. Miss Whitford introduced the two young men and Bromfield looked the Westerner over with a suave insolence in his dark, handsome eyes.

Clay recognized him immediately. He had shaken hands once before with this well-satisfied young man, and on that occasion a fifty-dollar bill had passed from one to the other. The New Yorker evidently did not know him.

It became apparent at once that Bromfield had called to go riding in the Park with Miss Whitford. That young woman came up to say good-bye to her new acquaintance.

"Will you be here when I get back?"

"Not if our friends outside give me a chance for a getaway," he told her.

Her bright, unflinching eyes looked into his. "You'll come again and let us know how you escaped," she invited.

"I'll ce'tainly do that, Miss Whitford."

"Then we'll look for you Thursday afternoon, say."

"I'll be here."

"If the police don't get you."

"They won't," he promised serenely.

"When you're quite ready, Bee," suggested Bromfield in a bored voice.

She nodded casually and walked out of the room like a young Diana, straight as a dart in her trim slenderness.

Clay slipped out of the house by the back way, cut across to the subway, and took a downtown train. He got out at Forty-Second Street and made his way back to the clothing establishment of I. Bernstein.

That gentleman was in his office in the rear of the store. Lindsay walked back to it, opened and closed the door, locked it, and put the key in his pocket.

The owner of the place rose in alarm from the stool where he was sitting. "What right do you got to lock that door?" he demanded.

"I don't want to be interrupted while I'm sellin' you this suit, Mr. Bernstein," the cowpuncher told him easily, and he proceeded to unwrap the damp package under his arm. "It's a pippin of a suit. The color won't run or fade, and it's absolutely unshrinkable. You won't often get a chance at a suit like this. Notice the style, the cut, the quality of the goods. And it's only goin' to cost you fifty-five dollars."

The clothing man looked at the misshapen thing with eyes that bulged. "Where is it you been with this suit — in the East River, my friendt?" he wanted to know.

"I took a walk along Riverside Drive. That's all. I got a strong guarantee with this suit when I bought it. I'm goin' to give you the same one I got. It won't shrink or fade and it will wear to beat a 'Pache pup. Oh, you won't make any mistake buyin' this suit."

"You take from me an advice. Unlock that door and get out."

"I can give you better advice than that. Buy this suit right away. You'll find it's a bargain."

The steady eyes of the Westerner daunted the merchant, but he did not intend to give up fifty-five dollars without a murmur.

"If you don't right avay soon open that door I call the police. Then you go to jail, ain't it?"

"How's yore heart, Mr. Bernstein?" asked Clay tenderly.

"What?"

"I'm askin' about yore heart. I don't know as you're hardly strong enough to stand what I'll do to you if you let a single yelp out of you. I kinda hate to hurry yore funeral," he added regretfully, still in his accustomed soft drawl.

The man beside the stool attempted one shout. Instantly Clay filled his mouth with a bunch of suit samples that had been lying on the desk. With one arm he held the struggling little man close to his body. With his foot and the other hand he broke in two a yardstick and fitted the two parts together.

"Here's the programme," he said by way of explanation. "I'm goin' to put you over my knee and paddle you real thorough. When you make up yore mind that you want to buy that suit for fifty-five dollars, it will be up to you to let me know. Take yore own time about it. Don't let me hurry you."

Before the programme had more than well started, the victim of it signified his willingness to treat with the foe. To part with fifty-five dollars was a painful business, but not to part with it was going to hurt a good deal more. He chose the lesser of two evils.

While he was counting out the bills Clay bragged up the suit. He praised its merits fluently and cheerfully. When he left he locked the door of the office behind him and handed the key to one of the clerks.

"I've got a kinda notion Mr. Bernstein wants to get out of his office. He's actin' sort o' restless, seems like."

Restless was hardly the word. He was banging on the door like a wild man. "Police! Murder! Help!" he shouted in a high falsetto.

Clay wasted no time. He and the fifty-five dollars vanished into the street. In his haste he bumped into a Salvation Army lassie with a tambourine.

She held it out to him for a donation, and was given the shock of her life. For into that tambourine the big brown man crammed a fistful of bills. He waited for no thanks, but cut round the corner toward Broadway in a hurry.

When the girl reached headquarters and counted the contribution she found it amounted to just fifty-five dollars.

CHAPTER VI

CLAY TAKES A TRANSFER

FROM the top of a bus Clay Lindsay looked down a cañon which angled across the great city like a river of light.

He had come from one land of gorges to another. In the walls of this one, thousands and tens of thousands of cliff-dwellers hid themselves during the day like animals of some queer breed and poured out into the cañon at sunset.

Now the river in its bed was alive with a throbbing tide. Cross-currents of humanity flowed into it from side streets and ebbed out of it into others. Streams of people were swept down, caught here and there in swirling eddies. Taxis, private motors, and trolley-cars struggled in the raceway.

Electric sky-signs flashed and changed. From the foyer of theaters and moving-picture palaces thousands of bulbs flung their glow to the gorge. A mist of light hung like an atmosphere above the Great White Way.

All this Clay saw in a flash while his bus crossed Broadway on its way to the Avenue. His eyes had become accustomed to this brilliance in the weeks that had passed since his descent upon New York, but familiarity had not yet dulled the wonder of it.

The Avenue offered a more subdued picture. This facet showed a glimpse of the city lovelier and more leisurely, though not one so feverishly gay. It carried his mind to Beatrice Whitford. Some touch of the quality of Fifth Avenue was in her soul. It expressed itself in the simple elegance of her dress and in the fineness of the graceful, vital body. Her gayety was not at all the high spirits of Broadway, but there were times when her kinship to Fifth Avenue knifed the foolish hopes in his heart.

He had become a fast friend of Miss Whitford. Together they had tramped through Central Park and motored up the Hudson in one of her father's cars. They had explored each other's minds along with the country and each had known the surprise and delight of discoveries, of finding in the other a quality of freshness and candor.

Clay sensed in this young woman a spirit that had a way of sweeping up on gay young wings to sudden joys stirred by the simplest causes. Her outlook on life was as gallant as that of a fine-tempered schoolboy. A gallop in the Park could whip the flag of happiness into her cheeks. A wild flower nestling in a bed of moss could bring the quick light to her eyes. Her responsiveness was a continual delight to him just as her culture was his despair. Of books, pictures, and music she knew much more than he.

The bus jerked down Fifth Avenue like a boat in heavy seas, pausing here and there at the curb to take on a passenger. While it was getting under way after one such stop, another downtown bus rolled past.

Clay came to a sudden alert attention. His eyes focused on a girl sitting on a back seat. In the pretty, childish face he read a wistful helplessness, a pathetic hint of misery that called for sympathy.

Arizona takes short cuts to its ends. Clay rose instantly, put his foot on the railing, and leaped across to the top of the bus rolling parallel with the one he was on. In another second he had dropped into the seat beside the girl.

"Glad to meet you again, Miss Kitty," he said cheerfully. "How's the big town been using you?"

The girl looked at him with a little gasp of surprise. "Mr. Lindsay!" Sudden tears filmed her eyes. She forgot that she had left him with the promise never again to speak to him. She was in a far country, and he was a friend from home.

The conductor bustled down the aisle. "Say, where do you get this movie-stunt stuff? You can't jump from the top of one bus to another."

Clay smiled genially. "I can't, but I did."

"That ain't the system of transfers we use in this town. You might 'a' got killed."

"Oh, well, let's not worry about that now."

"I'd ought to have you pulled. Three years I've been on this run and —"

"Nice run. Wages good?"

"Don't get gay, young fellow. I can tell you one thing. You've got to pay another fare."

Clay paid it.

The conductor retired to his post. He grinned in spite of his official dignity. There was something about this young fellow he liked. After he had been in New York awhile he would be properly tamed.

"What about that movie job? Is it pannin' out pay gold?" Lindsay asked Kitty.

Bit by bit her story came out. It was a common enough one. She had been flim-flammed out of her money by the alleged school of moving-picture actors, and the sharpers had decamped with it.

As she looked at her recovered friend, Kitty gradually realized an outward transformation in his appearance. He was dressed quietly in clothes of perfect fit made for him by Colin Whitford's tailor. From shoes to hat he was a New Yorker got up regardless of expense. But the warm smile, the strong, tanned face, the grip of the big brown hand that buried her small one — all these were from her own West. So too had been the nonchalance with which he had stepped from the rail of one moving bus to that of the other, just as though this were his usual method of transfer.

"I've got a job at last," she explained to him. "I could n't hardly find one. They say I'm not trained to do anything."

"What sort of a job have you?"

"I'm working downtown in Greenwich Village, selling cigarettes. I'm Sylvia the Cigarette Girl. At least that's what they call me. I carry a tray of them evenings into the cafés."

"Greenwich Village?" asked Clay.

Kitty was not able to explain that the Village is a state of mind which is the habitat of long-haired men and short-haired women, the brains of whom functioned in a way totally alien to all her methods of thought. The meaning of Bohemianism was quite lost on her simple soul.

"They're just queer," she told him. "The women bob

their hair and wear smocks and sandals. The men are long-haired softies. They all talk kinda foolish." Kitty despaired of making the situation clear to him and resorted to the personal. "Can't you come down to-night to The Purple Pup or The Sea Siren and see for yourself?" she proposed, and gave him directions for finding the classic resorts.

"I reckon they must be medicine fakirs," decided Clay. "I've met up with these long-haired guys before. Sure I'll come."

"To-night?"

"You betcha, little pardner, I'll be there."

"I'm dressed silly — in bare feet and sandals and what they call a smock. You won't mind that, will you?"

"You'll look good to me, no matter what you wear, little Miss Colorado," he told her with his warm, big brother's smile.

"You're good," the girl said simply. "I knew that on the train even when I — when I was mean to you." There came into her voice a small tremor of apprehension. "I'm afraid of this town. It's so — so kinda cruel. I've got no friends here."

He offered instant reassurance with a strong grip of his brown hand. "You've got one, little pardner. I'll promise that one big husky will be on the job when you need him. Don't you worry."

She gave him her shy eyes gratefully. There was a mist of tears in them.

"You're good," she said again naïvely.

CHAPTER VII

ARIZONA FOLLOWS ITS LAWLESS IMPULSE

WHEN Clay two hours later took the Sixth Avenue L for a plunge into Bohemianism he knew no more about Greenwich Village than a six-months-old pup does about Virgil. But it was characteristic of him that on his way downtown he proceeded to find out from his chance seat-mate something about this unknown terrain he was about to visit.

The man he sat beside was a patrolman off duty, and to this engaging Westerner he was quite ready to impart any information he might have.

"Fakirs," he pronounced promptly. "They're a bunch of long-haired nuts, most of 'em — queer guys who can't sell their junk and kid themselves into thinking they're artists and writers. They pull a lot of stuff about socialism and anarchy and high art."

"Just harmless cranks — gone loco, mebbe?"

"Some of 'em. Others are there for the mazuma. Uptown the Village is supposed to be one hell of a place. The people who own the dumps down there have worked up that rep to draw the night trade. They make a living outa the wickedness of Greenwich. Nothin' to it — all fake stuff. They advertise September Morn balls with posters something fierce, and when you go they are just like any other dances. Bum drawings of naked women on the walls done by artist yaps, decorations of purple cows, pirates' dens — that's the kind of dope they have."

The Sea Siren was already beginning to fill up when Clay descended three steps to a cellar and was warily admitted. A near-Hawaiian orchestra was strumming out a dance tune and a few couples were on the floor. Waitresses, got up as Loreleis, were moving about among the guests delivering orders for refreshments.

The Westerner sat down in a corner and looked about him. The walls were decorated with crude purple crayons of underfed sirens. A statue of a nude woman distressed Clay. He did not mind the missing clothes, but she was so dreadfully emaciated that he thought it wise for her to cling to the yellow-and-red draped barber pole that rose from the pedestal. On the base was the legend, "The Weeping Lady." After he had tasted the Sea Siren fare the man from Arizona suspected that both her grief and her anæmia arose from the fact that she had been fed on it.

A man in artist's velveteens, minus a haircut, with a large, fat, pasty face, sat at an adjoining table and discoursed to his friends. Presently, during an intermission of the music, he rose and took the rest of those present into his confidence. With rapt eyes on the faraway space of distant planets he chanted his apologia.

"I believe in the Cosmic Urge, in the Sublimity of my Ego. I follow my Lawless Impulse where the Gods of Desire shall drive. I am what I Am, Son of the Stars, Lord of my Life. With Unleashed Love I answer the psychic beat of Pulse to Pulse, Laughter, Tears and Woe, the keen edge of Passion, the Languor of Satiety: all these are life. Open-armed, I embrace them. I drink and assuage my thirst. For Youth is here to-day. To-

morrow, alas, it has gone. Now I am. In the Then I
shall not be. Kismet!"

The poet's fine frenzy faded. He sank back into his
chair, apparently worn out by his vast mental effort.

Clay gave a deep chuckle of delight. This was good.

"Heap much oration," he murmured. "Go to it, old-
timer. Steam off again. Git down in yore collar to it."

To miss none of the fun he hitched a little closer on
the bench. But the man without the haircut was through
effervescing. He began to talk in a lower voice on world
politics to admiring friends who were basking in his reflected glory.

"Bourgeois to the core," he announced with finality,
speaking of the United States, in answer to a question.
"What are the idols we worship? Law, the chain which
binds an enslaved people; thrift, born of childish fear;
love of country, which is another name for crass pro-
vincialism. I — I am a Cosmopolite, not an American.
Bohemia is my land, and all free souls are my brothers.
Why should I get wrinkles because Germany sunk the
Lusitania a month or two ago? That's her business, not
mine."

Clay leaned forward on a search for information.
"Excuse me for buttin' in, and me a stranger. But is n't
it yore business when she murders American women and
children?"

The pasty-faced man looked at him with thinly dis-
guised contempt. "You would n't understand if I explained."

"Mebbeso I would n't, but you take a whirl at it and
I'll listen high, wide, and handsome."

The man in velveteens unexpectedly found himself doing as he was told. There was a suggestion of compulsion about the gray-blue eyes fastened on his, something in the clamp of the strong jaw that brought him up for a moment against stark reality.

"The *intelligentsia* of a country knows that there can be no freedom until there is no law. Every man's duty is to disregard duty. So, by faring far on the wings of desire, he helps break down the slavery that binds us. Obey the Cosmic Urge of your soul regardless of where it leads you, young man."

It was unfortunate for the poet of Bohemia that at this precise moment Kitty Mason, dressed in sandals and a lilac-patterned smock, stood before him with a tray of cigarettes asking for his trade. The naïve appeal in her soft eyes had its weight with the poet. What is the use of living in Bohemia if one cannot be free to follow impulse? He slipped an arm about the girl and kissed the crimson lips upturned to him.

Kitty started back with a little cry of distress.

The freedom taken by the near-poet was instantly avenged.

A Cosmic Urge beat in the veins of the savage from Arizona. He took the poet's advice and followed his Lawless Impulse where it led. Across the table a long arm reached. Sinewy fingers closed upon the flowing neckwear of the fat-faced orator and dragged him forward, leaving overturned glasses in the wake of his course.

The man in velveteens met the eyes of the energetic manhandler and quailed. This brown-faced barbarian looked very much like business.

"Don't you touch me! Don't you dare touch me!" the apostle of anarchy shrilled as the table crashed down. "I'll turn you over to the police!"

Clay jerked him to his feet. Hard knuckles pressed cruelly into the soft throat of the Villager. "Git down on yore ham bones and beg the lady's pardon, Son of the Stars, or I'll sure make you see a whole colony of yore ancestors. Tell her you're a yellow pup, but you don't reckon you'll ever pull a bone like that again. Speak right out in meetin' *pronto* before you bump into the tears and woe you was makin' heap much oration about."

The proprietor of the café seized the cowpuncher by the arm hurriedly. "Here, stop that! You get out of the place! I'll not stand for any rough-house." And he murmured something about getting in bad with the police.

Clay tried to explain. "Me, I'm not rough-housing. I'm tellin' this here Lord of Life to apologize to the little lady and let her know that he's sorry he was fresh. If he don't I'll most ce'tainly muss up the Sublimity of his Ego."

The companions of the poet rushed forward to protest at the manhandling of their leader. Those in the rear jammed the front ones close to Clay and his captive. The cowpuncher gently but strongly pushed them back.

"Don't get on the prod," he advised in his genial drawl. "The poet he's got an important engagement right now."

A kind of scuffle developed. The proprietor increased it by his hysterical efforts to prevent any trouble. Men joined themselves to the noisy group of which Clay was the smiling center. The excitement increased. Distant

corners of the room became the refuge of the women.
Some one struck at the cowpuncher over the heads of
those about him. The mass of closely packed human
beings showed a convulsive activity. It became suddenly
the most popular indoor sport at the Sea Siren to slay
this barbarian from the desert who had interfered with
the amusements of Bohemia.

But Clay took a lot of slaying. In the rough-and-
tumble life of the outdoor West he had learned how to
look out for his own hand. The copper hair of his strong
lean head rose above the tangle of the *mêlée* like the
bromidic Helmet of Navarre. A reckless light of mirth
bubbled in his dare-devil eyes. The very number of the
opponents who interfered with each other trying to get
at him was a guarantee of safety. The blows showered at
him lacked steam and were badly timed as to distance.

The pack rolled across the room, tipped over a table,
and deluged an artist and his affinity with hot chocolate
before they could escape from the avalanche. Chairs
went over like ninepins. Stands collapsed. Men grunted
and shouted advice. Girls screamed. The Sea Siren was
being wrecked by a cyclone from the bad lands.

Against the wall the struggling mob brought up with
a crash. The velveteen poet caught at "The Weeping
Lady" to save himself from going down. She descended
from her pedestal into his arms and henceforth waltzed
with him as a part of the subsequent proceedings.

The writhing mass caromed from the wall and re-
volved toward the musicians. A colored gentleman
jumped up in alarm and brandished his instrument as a
weapon.

"Keep away from this heah niggah!" he warned, and simultaneously he aimed the drum of the mandolin at the red head which was the core of the tangle. His aim was deflected and the wood crashed down upon the crown of "The Weeping Lady." For the rest of the two-step it hung like a large ruff around her neck.

Arms threshed wildly to and fro. The focal point of their destination was the figure at the center of the disturbance. Most of the blows found other marks. Four or five men could have demolished Clay. Fifteen or twenty found it a tough job because they interfered with each other at every turn. They were packed too close for hard hitting. Clay was not fighting but wrestling. He used his arms to push with rather than to strike blows that counted.

The Arizonan could not afterward remember at exactly what stage of the proceedings the face of Jerry Durand impinged itself on his consciousness. Once, when the swirl of the crowd flung him close to the door, he caught a glimpse of it, tight-lipped and wolf-eyed, turned to him with relentless malice. The gang leader was taking no part in the fight.

The crowd parted. Out of the pack a pair of strong arms and lean broad shoulders ploughed a way for a somewhat damaged face that still carried a debonair smile. With pantherish litheness the Arizonan ducked a swinging blow. The rippling muscles of the plunging shoulders tossed aside a little man in evening dress clawing at him. Yet a moment, and he was outside taking the three steps that led to the street.

Into his laboring lungs he drew deliciously the soft

breath of the night. It cooled the fever of his hammered
face, was like an icy bath to his hot body. A little dizzy
from the blows that had been rained on him, he stood
for a moment uncertain which way to go. From his
throat there rippled a low peal of joyous mirth. The
youth in him delighted in the free-for-all from which he
had just emerged.

Then again he became aware of Durand. The man was
not alone. He had with him a hulking ruffian whose
heavy, hunched shoulders told of strength. There was a
hint of the gorilla in the way the long arms hung straight
from the shoulders as he leaned forward. Both of the
men were watching the cowpuncher as steadily as alley
cats do a housefinch.

"Hell's going to pop in about three seconds," announced Clay to himself.

Silently, without lifting their eyes from their victim
for an instant, the two men moved apart to take him on
both sides. He clung to the wall, forcing a frontal attack.
The laughter had gone out of his eyes now. They had
hardened to pinpoints. This time it was no amateur
horseplay. He was fighting for his life. No need to tell
Clay Lindsay that the New York gangster meant to
leave him as good as dead.

The men rushed him. He fought them back with clean
hard blows. Jerry bored in like a wild bull. Clay caught
him off his balance, using a short arm jolt which had
back of it all that twenty-three years of clean outdoors
Arizona could give. The gangster hit the pavement
hard.

He got up furious and charged again. The Arizonan,

busy with the other man, tried to sidestep. An uppercut jarred him to the heel. In that instant of time before his knees began to sag beneath him his brain flashed the news that Durand had struck him on the chin with brass knucks. He crumpled up and went down, still alive to what was going on, but unable to move in his own defense. Weakly he tried to protect his face and sides from the kicks of a heavy boot. Then he floated balloon-like in space and vanished into unconsciousness.

CHAPTER VIII

"THE BEST SINGLE-BARRELED SPORT IVER I MET"

CLAY drifted back to a world in which the machinery of his body creaked. He turned his head, and a racking pain shot down his neck. He moved a leg, and every muscle in it ached. From head to foot he was sore.

Voices somewhere in space, detached from any personal ownership, floated vaguely to him. Presently these resolved themselves into words and sentences.

"We're not to make a pinch, Tim. That's the word he gave me before he left. This is wan av Jerry's private little wars and he don't want a judge askin' a lot of unnicessary questions, y' understand."

"Mother av Moses, if this he-man from Hell's Hinges had n't the luck av the Irish, there'd be questions a-plenty asked. He'd be ready for the morgue this blissed minute. Jerry's a murderin' divvle. When I breeze in I find him croakin' this lad proper and he acts like a crazy man when I stand him and Gorilla Dave off till yuh come a-runnin'. At that they may have given the bye more than he can carry. Maybe it'll be roses and a nice black carriage for him yet."

The other policeman, a sergeant — by this time the voices had localized themselves in persons — laughed with reluctant admiration.

"Him! He's got siven lives like a cat. Take a look at the Sea Siren, Tim. 'T is kindling the lad has made of the place. The man that runs the dump put up a poor mouth, but I told him and the nuts that crowded round squawkin' for an arrest that if they hollered the police would close the place and pull the whole bunch for disorderly conduct. They melted away, believe me." He added, with an access of interest, "Yuh've heard the byes tell the story of the rube that tied up the Swede janitor on the Drive into a knot with his own hose. This'll be the same lad, I'm thinkin'."

The other nodded. He was bending over Clay and sprinkling water on his face. "He'll be black and blue ivery inch of him, but his eyelids are flickering. Jerry's an ill man to cross, I've heard teli. Yuh'd think this lad had had enough. But Jerry's still red-eyed about him and swears they can't both live in the same town. You'll remember likely how Durand did for Paddy Kelly? It was before my time."

"Yuh're a chump copper, Tim Muldoon, else yuh'd know we don't talk about that in the open street. Jerry has long ears," the older man warned, lowering his voice.

Clay opened his eyes, flexed his arm muscles, and groaned. He caressed tenderly his aching ribs.

"Some wreck," he gasped weakly. "They did n't do a thing to me — outside of beatin' me up — and stompin' on me — and runnin' a steam roller — over the dear departed."

"Whose fault will that be? Don't yuh know better than to start a fight with a rigiment?" demanded the sergeant of police severely.

"That was n't a fight. It was a waltz." The faint, unconquered smile of brown Arizona broke through the blood and bruises of the face. "The fight began when Jerry Durand and his friend rushed me — and it ended when Jerry landed on me with brass knucks. After that I was a football." The words came in gasps. Every breath was drawn in pain.

"We'd ought to pinch yuh," the sergeant said by way of reprimand. "Think yuh can come to New York and pull your small-town stuff on us? We'll show youse. If yuh was n't alfalfa green I'd give yuh a ride."

"You mean if Durand had n't whispered in yore ear. I'll call that bluff, sheriff. Take me to yore calaboose. I've got one or two things to tell the judge about this guy Durand."

The officer dropped his grumbling complaint to a whisper. "Whisht, bye. Take a straight tip from a man that knows. Beat it out of town. Get where the long arm of — of a friend of ours — can't reach yuh. Yuh may be a straight guy, but that won't help yuh. Yuh'll be framed the same as if yuh was a greengoods man or a gopher or a porch-climber. He's a revingeful inemy if ever there was wan."

"You mean that Durand —"

"I'm not namin' names," the officer interrupted doggedly. "I'm tellin' yuh somethin' for your good. Take it or leave it."

"Thanks, I'll leave it. This is a free country, and no man livin' can drive me away," answered Clay promptly. "Ouch, I'm sore. Give me a lift, sergeant."

They helped the cowpuncher to his feet. He took a limping step or two. Every move was torture to his outraged flesh.

"Can you get me a taxi? That is, if you're sure you don't want me in yore calaboose," the range-rider said, leaning against the wall.

"We'll let yuh go this time."

"Much obliged — to Mr. Jerry Durand. Tell him for me that maybe I'll meet up with him again sometime — and hand him my thanks personal for this first-class wallopin'." From the bruised, bleeding face there beamed again the smile indomitable, the grin still gay and winning. Physically he had been badly beaten, but in spirit he was still the man on horseback.

Presently he eased himself into a taxi as comfortably as he could. "Home, James," he said jauntily.

"Where?" asked the driver.

"The nearest hospital," explained Clay. "I'm goin' to let the doctors worry over me for a while. Much obliged to both of you gentlemen. I always did like the Irish. Friend Jerry is an exception."

The officers watched the cab disappear. The sergeant spoke the comment that was in the mind of them both.

"He's the best single-barreled sport that iver I met in this man's town. Not a whimper out of the guy and him mauled to a pulp. Game as they come. Did youse see that spark o' the divvle in his eye, and him not fit to crawl into the cab?"

"Did I see it? I did that. If iver they meet man to man, him and Jerry, it'll be wan grand little fight."

"Jerry's the best rough-and-tumble fighter on the island."

"Wan av the best. I would n't put him first till after

him and this guy had met alone in a locked room. S'long,
Mike."

"S'long, Tim. No report on this rough-house, mind
yuh."

"Sure, Mike."

CHAPTER IX

BEATRICE UP STAGE

IF you vision Clay as a man of battles and violent death, you don't see him as he saw himself. He was a peaceful citizen from the law-abiding West. It was not until he had been flung into the whir'pool of New York that violent and melodramatic mishaps befell this innocent. The Wild East had trapped him into weird adventure foreign to his nature.

This was the version of himself that he conceived to be true and the one he tried to interpret to Bee Whitford when he emerged from the hospital after two days of seclusion and presented himself before her.

It was characteristic of Beatrice that when she looked at his battered face she asked no questions and made no exclamations. After the first startled glance one might have thought from her expression that he habitually wore one black eye, one swollen lip, one cauliflower ear, and a strip of gauze across his cheek.

The dark-lashed eyes lifted from him to take on a business-like directness. She rang for the man.

"Have the runabout brought round at once, Stevens. I'll drive myself," she gave orders.

With the light ease that looked silken strong she swept the car into the Park. Neither she nor Clay talked. Both of them knew that an explanation of his appearance was due her and in the meantime neither cared to fence with small talk. He watched without appearing to do so the slender girl in white at the wheel. Her motions delighted him. There was a very winning charm in the softly curving contours of her face, in that flowerlike and precious quality in her personality which lay back of her boyish comradeship.

She drew up to look at some pond lilies, and they talked about them for a moment, after which her direct eyes questioned him frankly.

He painted with a light brush the picture of his adventure into Bohemia. The details he filled in whimsically, in the picturesque phraseology of the West. Up stage on his canvas was the figure of the poet in velveteens. That Son of the Stars he did full justice. Jerry Durand and Kitty Mason were accessories sketched casually.

Even while her face bubbled with mirth at his story of the improvised tango that had wrecked the Sea Siren, the quick young eyes of the girl were taking in the compelling devil-may-care charm of Lindsay. Battered though he was, the splendid vigor of the man still showed in a certain tigerish litheness that sore, stiff muscles could not conceal. No young Greek god's head could have risen more superbly from the brick-tanned column of his neck than did this bronzed one.

"I gather that Mr. Lindsay of Arizona was among those present," Beatrice said, smiling.

"I was givin' the dance," he agreed, and his gay eyes met hers.

Since she was a woman, one phase of his story needed expansion for Miss Whitford. She made her comment carelessly while she adjusted the mileage on the speedometer.

"Queer you happened to meet some one you knew down there. You *did* say you knew the girl, did n't you?"

"We were on the same train out of Denver. I got acquainted with her."

Miss Whitford asked no more questions. But Clay could not quite let the matter stand so. He wanted her to justify him in her mind for what he had done. Before he knew it he had told her the story of Kitty Mason and Durand.

Nor did this draw any criticism of approval or the reverse.

"I could n't let him hypnotize that little girl from the country, could I?" he asked.

"I suppose not." Her whole face began to bubble with laughter in the way he liked so well. "But you'll be a busy knight errant if you undertake to right the wrongs of every girl you meet in New York." A dimple flashed near the corner of her mouth. "Of course she's pretty."

"Well, yes. She *is* right pretty."

"Describe her to me."

He made a lame attempt. Out of his tangled sentences she picked on some fragments. ". . . blooms like a cherokee rose . . . soft like a kitten."

"I'm glad she's so charming. That excuses any indiscretion," the girl said with a gleam of friendly malice. "There's no fun in rescuing the plain ones, is there?"

"They don't most usually need so much rescuin'," Clay admitted.

"Don't you think it possible that you rescued her out of a job?"

The young man nodded his head ruefully. "That's exactly what I did. After all her trouble gettin' one I've thrown her out again. I'm a sure-enough fathead."

"You've been down to find out?" she asked with a sidelong tilt of her quick eyes.

"Yes. I went down this mawnin' with Tim Muldoon. He's a policeman I met down there. Miss Kitty has n't been seen since that night. We went out to the Pirate's Den, the Purple Pup, Grace Godwin's Garret, and all the places where she used to sell cigarettes. None of them have seen anything of her."

"So that really your championship has n't been so great a help to her after all, has it?"

"No."

"And I suppose it ruined the business of the man that owns the Sea Siren."

"I don't reckon so. I've settled for the furniture. And Muldoon says when it gets goin' again the Sea Siren will do a big business on account of the fracas. It's Kitty I'm worried about."

"She's a kind of cuddly little girl who needs the protection of some nice man, you say?"

"That's right."

The eyes of Miss Whitford were unfathomable. "Fluffy and — kind of helpless."

"Yes."

"I would n't worry about her if I were you. She'll land on her feet," the girl said lightly.

Her voice had not lost its sweet cadences, but Clay sensed in it something that was almost a touch of cool contempt. He felt vaguely that he must have blundered in describing Kitty. Evidently Miss Whitford did not see her quite as she was.

The young woman pressed the starter button. "We must be going home. I have an engagement to go riding with Mr. Bromfield."

The man beside the girl kept his smile working and concealed the little stab of jealousy that dirked him. Colin Whitford had confided to Lindsay that his daughter was practically engaged to Clarendon Bromfield and that he did not like the man. The range-rider did not like him either, but he tried loyally to kill his distrust of the clubman. If Beatrice loved him there must be good in the fellow. Clay meant to be a good loser anyhow.

There had been moments when the range-rider's heart had quickened with a wild, insurgent hope. One of these had been on a morning when they were riding in the Park, knee to knee, in the dawn of a new clean world. It had come to him with a sudden clamor of the blood that in the eternal rightness of things such mornings ought to be theirs till the youth in them was quenched in sober age. He had looked into the eyes of this slim young Diana, and he had throbbed to the certainty that she too in that moment of tangled glances knew a sweet confusion of the blood. In her cheeks there had been a quick flame of flying color. Their talk had fallen from them, and they had ridden in a shy, exquisite silence from which she had escaped by putting her horse to a canter.

But in the sober sense of sanity Clay knew that this wonderful thing was not going to happen to him. He was not going to be given her happiness to hold in the hollow of his hand. Bee Whitford was a modern young woman, practical-minded, with a proper sense of the values that the world esteems. Clarendon Bromfield was a catch even in New York. He was rich, of a good family, assured social position, good-looking, and manifestly in love with her. Like gravitates to like the land over. Miracles no longer happen in this workaday world. She would marry the man a hundred other girls would have given all they had to win, and perhaps in the long years ahead she might look back with a little sigh for the wild colt of the desert who had shared some perfect moments with her once upon a time.

Bromfield, too, had no doubt that Bee meant to marry him. He was in love with her as far as he could be with anybody except himself. His heart was crusted with selfishness. He had lived for himself only and he meant to continue so to live. But he had burned out his first youth. He was coming to the years when dissipation was beginning to take its toll of him. And as he looked into the future it seemed to him an eminently desirable thing that the fresh, eager beauty of this girl should belong to him, that her devotion should stand as a shield between him and that middle age with which he was already skirmishing. He wanted her — the youth, the buoyant life, the gay, glad comradeship of her — and he had always been lucky in getting what he desired. That was the use of having been born with a silver spoon in his mouth.

But though Clarendon Bromfield had no doubt of the issue of his suit, the friendship of Beatrice for this fellow from Arizona stabbed his vanity. It hurt his class pride and his personal self-esteem that she should take pleasure in the man's society. Bee never had been well broken to harness. He set his thin lips tight and resolved that he would stand no nonsense of this sort after they were married. If she wanted to flirt it would have to be with some one in their own set.

The clubman was too wise to voice his objections now except by an occasional slur. But he found it necessary sometimes to put a curb on his temper. The thing was outrageous — damnably bad form. Sometimes it seemed to him that the girl was gratuitously irritating him by flaunting this bounder in his face. He could not understand it in her. She ought to know that this man did not belong to her world — could not by any chance be a part of it.

Beatrice could not understand herself. She knew that she was behaving rather indiscreetly, though she did not fathom the cause of the restlessness that drove her to Clay Lindsay. The truth is that she was longing for an escape from the empty life she was leading, had been seeking one for years without knowing it. Her existence was losing its savor, and she was still so young and eager and keen to live. Surely this round of social frivolities, the chatter of these silly women and smug tailor-made men, could not be all there was to life. She must have been made for something better than that.

And when she was with Clay she knew she had been. He gave her a vision of life through eyes that had known open, wide spaces, clean, wholesome, and sun-kissed. He stood on his own feet and did his own thinking. Simply, with both hands, he took hold of problems and examined them stripped of all trimmings. The man was elemental, but he was keen and broad-gauged. He knew the value of the things he had missed. She was increasingly surprised to discover how wide his information was. It amazed her one day to learn that he had read William James and understood his philosophy much better than she did.

There was in her mind no intention whatever of letting herself do anything so foolish as to marry him. But there were moments when the thought of it had a dreadful fascination for her. She did not invite such thoughts to remain with her.

For she meant to accept Clarendon Bromfield in her own good time and make her social position in New York absolutely secure. She had been in the fringes too long not to appreciate a chance to get into the social Holy of Holies.

CHAPTER X

JOHNNIE SEES THE POSTMASTER

A BOW-LEGGED little man in a cheap, wrinkled suit with a silk kerchief knotted loosely round his neck stopped in front of a window where a girl was selling stamps.

"I wantta see the postmaster."

"Corrid'y'right. Takel'vatorthir'doorleft," she said, just as though it were two words.

The freckle-faced little fellow opened wider his skim-milk eyes and his weak mouth. "Come again, ma'am, please."

"Corrid'y'right. Takel'vatorthir'doorleft," she repeated. "Next."

The inquirer knew as much as he did before, but he lacked the courage to ask for an English translation. A woman behind was prodding him between the shoulder-blades with the sharp edge of a package wrapped for mailing. He shuffled away from the window and wandered helplessly, swept up by the tide of hurrying people that flowed continuously into the building and ebbed out of it. From this he was tossed into a backwater that brought him to another window.

"I wantta see the postmaster of this burg," he announced again with a plaintive whine.

"What about?" asked the man back of the grating.

"Important business, *amigo*. Where's he at?"

The man directed him to a door upon which was

printed the legend, "Superintendent of Complaints." Inside, a man was dictating a letter to a stenographer The bow-legged man in the wrinkled suit waited awkwardly until the letter was finished, twirling in his hands a white, broad-rimmed hat with pinched-in crown. He was chewing tobacco. He wondered whether it would be "etiquette" to squirt the juice into a waste-paper basket standing conveniently near.

"Well, sir! What can I do for you?" the man behind the big desk snapped.

"I wantta see the postmaster."

"What about?"

"I got important business with him."

"Who are you?"

"Me, I'm Johnnie Green of the B-in-a-Box Ranch. I just drapped in from Arizona and I wantta see the postmaster."

"Suppose you tell your troubles to me."

Johnnie changed his weight to the other foot. "No, suh, I allow to see the postmaster himself personal."

"He's busy," explained the official. "He can't possibly see anybody without knowing his business."

"Tha's all right. I've lost my pal. I wantta see —"

The Superintendent of Complaints cut into his parrotlike repetition. "Yes, you mentioned that. But the postmaster does n't know where he is, does he?"

"He might tell me where his mail goes, as the old sayin' is."

"When did you lose your friend?"

"I ain't heard from him since he come to New York. So bein' as I got a chanct to go from Tucson with a

jackpot trainload of cows to Denver, I kinda made up
my mind to come on here the rest of the way and look
him up. I'm afraid some one's done him dirt."

"Do you know where he's staying?"

"No, suh, I don't."

The Superintendent of Complaints tapped with his
fingers on the desk. Then he smiled. The postmaster was
fond of a joke. Why not let this odd little freak from the
West have an interview with him?

Twenty minutes later Johnnie was telling his story to
the postmaster of the City of New York. He had written
three times to Clay Lindsay and had received no answer. So he had come to look for him.

"And seein' as I was here, thinks I to myself thinks I
it costs nothin' Mex to go to the postmaster and ask
where Clay's at," explained Johnnie with his wistful,
ingratiating, give-me-a-bone smile. "Thinks I, it cayn't
be but a little ways down to the office."

"Is your friend like you?" asked the postmaster, interested in spite of himself.

"No, suh." Johnnie, *alias* the Runt, began to beam.
"He's a sure-enough go-getter, Clay is, every jump of
the road. I'd follow his dust any day of the week. You
don't never need to think he's any shorthorn cattleman,
for he ain't. He's the livest proposition that ever come
out of Graham County. You can ce'tainly gamble on
that."

The postmaster touched a button. A clerk appeared,
received orders, and disappeared.

Johnnie, now on the subject of his hero, continued to
harp on his points. "You're damn whistlin' Clay ain't

like me. He's the best hawss-buster in Arizona. The
bronco never was built that can pile him, nor the man
that can lick him. Clay's no bad *hombre*, you understand, but there can't nobody run it over him. That's
whatever. All I'm afraid of is some one's gave him a raw
deal. He's the best blamed old son-of-a-gun I ever did
meet up with."

The clerk presently returned with three letters addressed to Clay Lindsay, General Delivery, New York.
The postmaster handed them to the little cowpuncher.

"Evidently he never called for them," he said.

Johnnie's chin fell. He looked a picture of helpless
woe. "They're the letters I set down an' wrote him my
own se'f. Something has sure happened to that boy,
looks like," he bemoaned.

"We'll try Police Headquarters. Maybe we can get a
line on your friend," the postmaster said, reaching for
the telephone. "But you must remember New York is a
big place. It's not like your Arizona ranch. The city has
nearly eight million inhabitants."

"I sure found that out already, Mr. Postmaster. Met
every last one of 'em this mo'nin', I'll bet. Never did see
so many humans millin' around. I'll say they're thick
as cattle at a round-up."

"Then you'll understand that when one man gets lost
it isn't always possible to find him."

"Why not? We got some steers down in my country
— about as many as you got men in this here town of
yourn. Tha's what we ride the range for, so's not to
lose 'em. We've traced a B-in-a-Box steer clear from
Tucson to Denver, done it more'n onct or twice too. I

notice you got a big bunch of man-punchers in uniform here. Ain't it their business to rustle up strays?"

"The police," said the postmaster, amused. "That is part of their business. We'll pass the buck to them anyhow."

After some delay and repeated explanations of who he was, the postmaster got at the other end of the wire his friend the commissioner. Their conversation was brief. When the postmaster hung up he rang for a stenographer and dictated a letter of introduction. This he handed to Johnnie, with explicit instructions.

"Go to Police Headquarters, Center Street, and take this note to Captain Luke Byrne. He'll see that the matter is investigated for you."

Johnnie was profuse, but somewhat incoherent in his thanks. "Much obliged to meet you, Mr. Postmaster. An' — an' if you ever hit the trail for God's Country I'll sure — I'll sure — Us boys at the B-in-a-Box we'd be right glad to — to meet up with you. Tha's right, as the old sayin' is. We sure would. Any ol' time."

The cowpuncher's hat was traveling in a circle propelled by red, freckled hands. The official cut short Johnnie's embarrassment.

"Do you know the way to Police Headquarters?"

"I reckon I can find it. Is it fur?" The man from Arizona looked down at the high-heeled boots in which his tortured feet had clumped over the pavements of the metropolis all morning.

"I'll send you in a taxi." The postmaster was thinking that this babe in the woods of civilization never would be able to find his way alone.

As the driver swept the car in and out among the traffic of the narrow streets Johnnie clung to the top of the door fearfully. Every moment he expected a smash. His heart was in his throat. The tumult, the rush of business, the intersecting cross-town traffic, the hub-bub of the great city, dazed his slow brain. The hurricane deck of a bronco had no terrors for him, but this wild charge through the humming trenches shook his nerve.

"I come mighty nigh askin' you would you just as lief drive slower," he said with a grin to the chauffeur as he descended to the safety of the sidewalk. "I ain't awful hardy, an' I sure was plumb scared."

A sergeant took Johnnie in tow and delivered him at length to the office waiting-room of Captain Anderson, head of the Bureau of Missing Persons. The Runt, surveying the numbers in the waiting-room and those passing in and out, was ready to revise his opinion about the possible difficulty of the job. He judged that half the population of New York must be missing.

After a time the captain's secretary notified Johnnie that it was his turn. As soon as he was admitted the puncher began his little piece without waiting for any preliminaries.

"Say, Captain, I want you to find my friend Clay Lindsay. He —"

"Just a moment," interrupted the captain. "Who are you? Don't think I got your name."

Johnnie remembered the note of introduction and his name at the same time. He gave both to the big man who spent his busy days and often part of the nights looking for the lost, strayed, and stolen among New York's millions.

The captain's eyes swept over the note. "Sit down, Mr. Green, and let's get at your trouble."

As soon as it permeated Johnnie's consciousness that he was Mr. Green he occupied precariously the front three inches of a chair. His ever-ready friend the cowboy hat began to revolve.

"This note says that you're looking for a man named Clay Lindsay who came to New York several months ago. Have you or has anybody else heard from him in that time?"

"We got a letter right after he got here. He ain't writ since."

"Perhaps he's dead. We'd better look up the morgue records."

"Morgue!" The Runt grew excited instantly. "That place where you keep folks that get drowned or bumped off? Say, Captain, I'm here to tell you Clay was the livest man in Arizona, which is the same as sayin' anywheres. Cowpunchers don't take naturally to morgues. No, sir. Clay ain't in no morgue. Like as not he's helped fill this yere morgue if any crooks tried their rough stuff on him. Don't get me wrong, Cap. Clay is the squarest he-man ever God made. All I'm sayin' is —"

The captain interrupted. He asked sharp, incisive questions and got busy. Presently he reached for a 'phone, got in touch with a sergeant at the police desk in the upper corridor, and sent an attendant with Johnnie to the Police Department.

The Irish sympathies of the sergeant were aroused by

the naïve honesty of the little man. He sent for another sergeant, had card records brought, consulted a couple of patrolmen, and then turned to Johnnie.

"We've met your friend all right," he said with a grin. "He's wan heluva lad. Fits the description to a T. There can't be but one like him here." And he went on to tell the story of the adventure of the janitor and the hose and that of its sequel, the resale of the fifty-five-dollar suit to I. Bernstein, who had reported his troubles to the police.

The washed-out eyes of the puncher lit up. "That's him. That's sure him. If the' was two of him they'd ce'tainly be a hell-poppin' team. Clay he's the best-natured fellow you ever did see, but there can't nobody run a whizzer on him, y' betcha. Tell me where he's at?"

"We don't know. We can show you the place where he tied the janitor, but that's the best we can do." The captain hesitated. "If you find him, give him a straight tip from me. Tell him to buy a ticket for Arizona and take the train for home. This town is no healthy place for him."

"Because he hogtied a Swede," snorted Johnnie indignantly.

"No. He's got into more serious trouble than that. Your friend has made an enemy — a powerful one. He'll understand if you tell him."

"Who is this here enemy?"

"Never mind. He hit up too fast a pace."

"You can't tell me a thing against Clay — not a thing," protested Johnnie hotly. "He'll sure do to take

along, Clay will. There can't any guy knock him to me
if he does wear a uniform."

"I'm not saying a thing against him," replied the
officer impatiently. "I'm giving him a friendly tip to
beat it, if you see him. Now I'm going to send you uptown with a plain-clothes man. He'll show you where
your friend made his New York *début*. That's all we can
do for you."

An hour later the little cowpuncher was gazing wistfully at the hitching-post. His face was twisted pathet-
ically to a question mark. It was as though he thought
he could conjure from the post the secret of Clay's
disappearance. Where had he gone from here? And
where was he now?

In the course of the next two days the Runt came
back to that post many times as a starting-point for
weary, high-heeled tramps through streets within a
circuit of a mile. He could not have explained why he
did so. Perhaps it was because this was the only spot in
the city that held for him any tangible relationship to
Clay. Some one claimed to have seen him vanish into
one of these houses. Perhaps he might come back again.
It was a very tenuous hope, but it was the only one
Johnnie had. He clumped over the pavements till his
feet ached in protest.

His patience was rewarded. On the second day, while
he was gazing blankly at the post a groom brought two
horses to the curb in front of the house opposite. One of
the horses had a real cowboy's saddle. Johnnie's eyes
gleamed. This was like a breath of honest-to-God
Arizona. The door opened, and out of it came a man and

a slim young woman. Both of them were dressed for riding, she in the latest togs of the town, he in a well-cut sack suit and high tan boots.

Johnnie threw up his hat and gave a yell. "You blamed old horn-toad! Might 'a' knowed you was all right! Might 'a' knowed you would n't bite off more 'n you could chew! Oh, you Arizona!"

Clay gave one surprised look — and met him in the middle of the street. The little cowpuncher did a war dance of joy while he clung to his friend's hand. Tears brimmed into his faded eyes.

"Hi yi yi, doggone yore old hide, if it ain't you big as coffee, Clay. Thinks I to myse'f, who is that pilgrim? And, by gum, it's old hell-a-mile jes' a-hittin' his heels. Where you been at, you old skeezicks?"

"How are you, Johnnie? And what are you doin' here?"

The Runt was the kind of person who tells how he is when any one asks him. He had no imagination, so he stuck to the middle of the road for fear he might get lost.

"I'm jes' tol'able, Clay. I got a kinda misery in my laigs from trompin' these hyer streets. My feet are plumb burnin' up. You did n't answer my letters, so I come to see if you was all right."

"You old scalawag. You came to paint the town red."

Johnnie, highly delighted at this charge, protested. "Honest I did n't, Clay. I was n't feelin' so tur'ble peart. Seemed like the boys picked on me after you left. So I jes' up and come."

If Clay was not delighted to have his little Fidus

Achates on his hands he gave no sign of it. He led him across the road and introduced him to Miss Whitford.

Clay blessed her for her kindness to this squat, snub-nosed adherent of his whose lonely heart had driven him two thousand miles to find his friend. It would have been very easy to slight him, but Beatrice had no thought of this. The loyalty of the little man touched her greatly. Her hand went out instantly. A smile softened her eyes and dimpled her cheeks.

"I'm very glad to meet any friend of Mr. Lindsay. Father and I will want to hear all about Arizona after you two have had your visit out. We'll postpone the ride till this afternoon. That will be better, I think."

Clay agreed. He grudged the loss of his hour with her, but under the circumstances it had to be. For a moment he and Beatrice stood arranging the time for their proposed ride. Then, with a cool little nod that included them both, she turned and ran lightly up the steps into the house.

"Some sure-enough queen," murmured Johnnie in naïve admiration, staring after her with open mouth.

Clay smiled. He had an opinion of his own on that point.

CHAPTER XI

JOHNNIE GREEN — MATCH-MAKER

JOHNNIE GREEN gave an upward jerk to the frying-pan and caught the flapjack deftly as it descended.

"Fust and last call for breakfast in the dining-cyar. Come and get it, old-timer," he sang out to Clay.

That young man emerged from his bedroom glowing. He was one or two shades of tan lighter than when he had reached the city, but the paint of Arizona's untempered sun still distinguished him from the native-born, if there are any such among the inhabitants of upper New York.

"You're one sure-enough cook," he drawled to his satellite. "Some girl will ce'tainly have a good wife when she gets you. I expect I'd better set one of these suffragette ladies on yore trail."

"Don't you, Clay," blushed Johnnie. "I ain't no ladies' man. They make me take to the tall timber when I see 'em comin'."

"That ain't hardly fair to them, and you the best flapjack artist in Graham County."

"Sho! I don't make no claims, old sock. Mebbe I'm handy with a fry-pan, mebbe I ain't. Likely you're jest partial to my flapjacks," the little man said in order to have his modest suggestion refuted.

"They suit me, Johnnie." And Clay reached for the maple syrup. "Best flapjacks ever made in this town."

The Runt beamed all over. If he had really been a

puppy he would have wagged his tail. Since he could n't do that he took it out in grinning. Any word of praise from Clay made the world a sunshiny one for him.

"This here place ain't Arizona, but o' course we got to make the best of it. You *know* I can cook when I got the fixin's," he agreed.

The two men were batching it. They had a little apartment in the Bronx and Johnnie looked after it for his friend. One of Johnnie's vices — according to the standard of the B-in-a-Box boys — was that he was as neat as an old maid. He liked to hang around a mess-wagon and cook doughnuts and pies. His talent came in handy now, for Clay was no housekeeper.

After the breakfast things were cleared away Johnnie fared forth to a certain house adjoining Riverside Drive, where he earned ten dollars a week as outdoors man. His business was to do odd jobs about the place. He cut and watered the lawn. He made small repairs. Beatrice had a rose garden, and under her direction he dug, watered, and fertilized.

Incidentally, the snub-nosed little puncher with the unfinished features adored his young mistress in the dumb, uncritical fashion a schoolboy does a Ty Cobb or an Eddie Collins. For him the queen could do no wrong. He spent hours mornings and evenings at their rooms telling Clay about her. She was certainly the finest little lady he ever had seen. In his heart he had hopes that Clay would fall in love with and marry her. She was the only girl in the world that deserved his paragon. But her actions worried him. Sometimes he wondered if she really understood what a catch Clay was.

He tried to tell her his notions on the subject the morning Clay praised his flapjacks.

She was among the rose-bushes, gloved and hatted, clipping American Beauties for the dining-room, a dainty but very self-reliant little personality.

"Miss Beatrice, I been thinkin' about you and Clay," he told her, leaning on his spade.

"What have you been thinking about us?" the girl asked, snipping off a big rose.

She liked Johnnie and listened often with amusement to his point of view. It was so different from that of anybody else she had ever met. Perhaps this was why she encouraged him to talk. There may have been another reason. The favorite theme of his conversation interested her.

"How you're the best-lookin' couple that a man would see anywheres."

Into her clear cheeks the color flowed. "If I thought nonsense like that I would n't say it," she said quietly. "We're not a couple. He's a man. I'm a woman. I like him and want to stay friends with him if you'll let me."

"Sure. I know tha', but —" Johnnie groped helplessly to try to explain what he had meant. "Clay he likes you a heap," he finished inadequately.

The eyes of the girl began to dance. There was no use taking offense at this simple soul. After all he was not a servant, but a loyal follower whose brain was not quite up to the job of coping with the knotty problem of bringing two of his friends together in matrimony. "Does he? I'm sure I'm gratified," she murmured, busy with her scissors among the roses.

"Yep. I never knowed Clay to look at a girl before. He sure thinks a heap of you."

She gave a queer little bubbling laugh. "You're flattering me."

"Honest, I ain't." Johnnie whispered a secret across the rose-bushes. "Say, if you work it right I believe you can get him."

The girl sparkled. Here was a new slant on matrimonial desirability. Clearly the view of the little cowpuncher was that Clay had only to crook his fingers to summon any girl in the world that he desired.

"Do you think so — with so many attractive girls in New York?" she pleaded.

"He don't pay no 'tention to them. Honest, I believe you can if you don't spill the beans."

"What would you advise me to do?" she dimpled.

"Sho! I dunno." He shyly unburdened himself of the warning he had been leading up to. "But I'd tie a can to that dude fellow that hangs around — the Bromfield guy. O' course I know he ain't one two three with you while Clay 's on earth, but I don't reckon I'd take any chances, as the old sayin' is. No, ma'am, I'd ce'tainly lose him *pronto*. Clay might get sore. Better get shet of the dude."

Miss Whitford bit her lip to keep from exploding in a sudden gale of mirth. But the sight of her self-appointed chaperon set her off into peals of laughter in spite of herself. Every time she looked at Johnnie she went off into renewed chirrups. He was so homely and so deadly earnest. The little waif was staring at her in perplexed surprise, mouth open and chin fallen. He could see no occasion for gayety at his suggestion. There was nothing subtle about the Runt. In his social code wealth did not figure. A forty-dollar-a-month bronco buster was free to offer advice to the daughter of a millionaire about her matrimonial prospects if it seemed best.

And just now it seemed to Johnnie decidedly best. He scratched his tow head, for he had mulled the whole thing over and decided reluctantly to do his duty by the girl. So far as he could make out, Beatrice Whitford played no favorites in her little court of admirers. Clay Lindsay and Clarendon Bromfield were with her more than any of the others. If she inclined to either of the two, Johnnie could see no evidence of it. She was gay and frank with both, a jolly comrade for a ride, a dinner dance, or a theater party.

This was what troubled Johnnie. Of course she must be in love with Clay and want to marry him, since she was a normal human being. But if she continued to play with Bromfield the Westerner might punish her by sheering off. That was the reason why the Runt was doing his conscientious duty this fine morning.

"Clay ain't one o' the common run of cowpunchers, ma'am. You bet you, by jollies, he ain't. Clay he owns a half-interest in the B-in-a-Box. O' course it ain't what he's got, but what he is that counts. He's the best darned pilgrim ever I did see."

"He's all right, Johnnie," the girl admitted with an odd little smile. "Do you want me to tell him that I'll be glad to drop our family friends to meet his approval? I don't suppose he asked you to speak to me about it, did he?"

The little range-rider missed the irony of this. "No, ma'am, I jest butted in. Mebbe I had n't ought to of spoke."

The frank eyes of the girl met his fairly. A patch of heightened color glowed in her soft cheeks. "That would have been better, Johnnie. But since you have introduced the subject, I'll tell you that Mr. Lindsay and I are friends. Neither of us has the slightest intention of being anything more. You may not understand such things."

"No'm," he admitted humbly. "I reckon I'm a plumb idjit."

His attitude was so dejected that she relented.

"You need n't feel badly, Johnnie. There's no harm done — if you don't say anything about it to Mr. Lindsay. But I don't think you were intended for a match-maker. That takes quite a little finesse, does n't it?"

The word "finesse" was not in Johnnie's dictionary, but he acquiesced in her verdict.

"I reckon, ma'am, you're right."

CHAPTER XII

CLAY READS AN AD AND ANSWERS IT

CLAY was waiting for lunch at a *rôtisserie* on Sixth Avenue, and in order to lose no time — of which he had more just now than he knew what to do with — was meanwhile reading a newspaper propped against a water-bottle. From the personal column there popped out at him three lines that caught his attention:

> If this meets the eye of C. L. of Arizona
> please write me, Box M-21, The Herald.
> Am in trouble.   KITTY M.

He read it again. There could be no doubt in the world. It was addressed to him, and from Kitty. While he ate his one half spring chicken Clay milled the situation over in his mind. She had been on the lookout for him, just as he had been searching for her. By good luck her shot at a venture had reached him. He remembered now that on the bus he had casually mentioned to her that he usually read the "Herald."

After he had eaten, Clay walked down Broadway and left a note at the office of the "Herald" for Kitty.

The thought of her was in his mind all day. He had worried a good deal over her disappearance. It was not alone that he felt responsible for the loss of her place as cigarette girl. One disturbing phase of the situation was that Jerry Durand must have seen her. What more likely than that he had arranged to have her spirited away? Lindsay had read that hundreds of girls disappeared every year in the city. If they ever came to the surface again it was as dwellers in that underworld in the current of which they had been caught.

Jerry was a known man in New York. It had been easy for Clay to find out the location of his saloon and the hotel where he lived. The cattleman had done some quiet sleuthing, but he had found no trace of Kitty. Now he knew that she had turned to him in her need and cried for help.

That she was in trouble did not surprise him. The girl was born for it as naturally as the sparks fly upward. She was a provocation to those who prey. In her face there was a disturbing quality quite apart from her prettiness. Back of the innocence lay some hint of slumberous passion. Kitty was one of those girls who have the misfortune to stir the imaginations of men without the ability to keep them at arm's length. Just what her present difficulty was Clay did not know, but he was quite sure it had to do with a man. Already he had decided to rescue her. He had promised to be her friend. It never occurred to him to stand back when she called.

He had an engagement that afternoon to walk with Beatrice Whitford. She was almost the only girl in her set who knew how to walk and had the energy for it. In her movement there was the fluent, untamed grace that expressed a soul not yet stunted by the claims of convention. The golden little head was carried buoyantly. In her step was the rhythm of perfect ease. The supple resilience of her was another expression of the spiritual quality that spoke in the vivid face.

Clay, watching her as she moved, thought of a paragraph from Mark Twain's "Eve's Diary":

She is all interest, eagerness, vivacity, the world is to her a charm, a wonder, a mystery, a joy; she can't speak for delight when she finds a new flower, she must pet it and caress it and smell it and talk to it, and pour out endearing names upon it. And she is color mad: brown rocks, yellow sand, gray moss, green foliage, blue sky; the pearl of the dawn, the purple shadow on the mountains, the golden islands floating in crimson seas at sunset, the pallid moon sailing through the shredded cloud-rack, the star-jewels glittering in the waste of space. . . .

But the thing that tantalized him about her and filled him with despair was that, though one moment she might be the first woman in the birthday of the world filled with the primitive emotions of the explorer, the next she was a cool, Paris-gowned-and-shod young modern, about as competent to meet emergencies as anything yet devised by heaven and a battling race.

They crossed to Morningside Park and moved through it to the northern end where the remains of Fort Laight, built to protect the approach to the city during the War of 1812, can still be seen and traced.

Beatrice had read the story of the earthworks. In the midst of the telling of it she stopped to turn upon him with swift accusation, "You're not listening."

"That's right, I was n't," he admitted.

"Have you heard something about your cigarette girl?"

Clay was amazed at the accuracy of her center shot.

"Yes." He showed her the newspaper.

She read. The golden head nodded triumphantly. "I told you she could look out for herself. You see when she had lost you she knew enough to advertise."

Was there or was there not a faint note of malice in the girl's voice? Clay did not know. But it would have neither surprised nor displeased him. He had long since discovered that his imperious little friend was far from an angel.

At his rooms he found a note awaiting him.

Come to-night after eleven. I am locked in the west rear room of the second story. Climb up over the back porch. Don't make any noise. The window will be unbolted. A friend is mailing this. For God's sake, don't fail me.

The note was signed "Kitty." Below were given the house and street number. Clay studied the letter a long time — the wording of it, the formation of the letters, the spirit that had actuated the writer. It was written upon a sheet of cheap lined paper torn from a pad. The envelope was one of those sold at the post-office already stamped.

Was the note genuine? Or did it lead to a trap? He could not tell. It might be a plant or it might be a wail of real distress. There was only one way to find out unless he went to the police. That way was to go through with the adventure. The police! Clay went back to the thought of them several times. The truth was that he had put himself out of court there. He was in bad with the blue-coats and would probably be arrested if he showed up at headquarters.

He decided to play a lone hand except for such help as Johnnie could give him.

Clay took a downtown car and rode to the cross-street mentioned in the letter for a preliminary tour of investigation. The street designated was one of plain brownstone fronts with iron-grilled doors. The blank faces of the houses invited no confidence. It struck him that there was something sinister about the neighborhood, but perhaps the thought was born of the fear. Number 121 had windows barred with ornamental grilles. This might be to keep burglars out. It would serve equally well to keep prisoners in.

At the nearest grocery store Clay made inquiries. He was looking, he said, for James K. Sanger. He did not know the exact address. Could the grocery man help him run down his party? How about the folks living at Number 121?

"Don't know 'em. They've been in only for a few days. They don't trade here."

Clay tried the telephone, but Information could tell him only that there was no 'phone at 121.

On the whole Clay inclined to think that the letter was not a forgery. In his frank, outdoor code there was no reason why Durand should hate him enough to go to such trouble to trap him. The fellow had more than squared accounts when he had beaten him up outside the Sea Siren. Why should he want to do anything more to him? But he had had two warnings that the ex-prize-fighter was not through with him — both of them from members of the police force, one direct from the sergeant who had helped rescue him, the other by way of the Runt

from headquarters. When he recalled the savage hatred
of that flat, pallid face he did not feel so sure of immu-
nity. Clay had known men in the West, wolf-hearted
killers steeped in a horrible lust for revenge, who never
forgot or forgave an injury — until their enemy had
paid the price in full. Jerry Durand might be one of this
stamp. He was a man of a bad reputation, one about
whom evil murmurs passed in secret. Not many years
ago he had been tried for the murder of one Paddy
Kelly, a rival gangsman in his neighborhood, and had
been acquitted on the ground of self-defense. But there
had been a good deal of talk about evidence framed in
his behalf. Later he had been arrested for graft, but the
case somehow had never been acted upon by the district attorney's office. The whisper was that his pull had
saved him from trial.

The cattleman did not linger in that street lined with
houses of sinister faces. He did not care to call attention
to his presence by staying too long. Besides, he had some
arrangements to make for the night at his rooms.

These were simple and few. He oiled and loaded his
revolver carefully, leaving the hammer on the one
chamber left empty to prevent accidents after the
custom of all careful gunmen. He changed into the
wrinkled suit he had worn when he reached the city, and
substituted for his shoes a pair of felt-soled gymnasium
ones.

The bow-legged little puncher watched his friend, just
as a faithful dog does his master. He asked no questions.
In good time he knew he would be told all it was necessary for him to know.

As they rode from the Bronx, Clay outlined the situation and told his plans so far as he had any.

"So I'm goin' to take a whirl at it, Johnnie. Mebbe they're lyin' low up in that house to get me. Mebbe the note's the real thing. You can search me which it is. The only way to find out is to go through with the thing. Yore job is to stick around in front of the *hacienda* and wait for me. If I don't show up inside of thirty minutes, get the police busy right away breakin' into the place. Do you get me, Johnnie?"

"Lemme go with you into the house, Clay," the little man pleaded.

"No, this is a one-man job. If the note is straight goods I've got to work on the Q.T. Do exactly as I say. That's how you can help me best."

"What's the matter with me goin' into the house instead o' you? It don't make no difference much if they do gun me. I'm jest the common run of the pen. But you — you're graded stock," argued the Runt.

"Nothin' doin', old-timer. This is my job, and I don't reckon I'll let anybody else tackle it. Much obliged, just the same. You're one sure-enough white man, Johnnie."

The little fellow knew that the matter was settled. Clay had decided and what he said was final. But Johnnie worried about it all the way. At the last moment, when they separated at the street corner, he added one last word.

"Don't you be too venturesome, son. If them guys got you it sure would break me all up."

Clay smiled cheerfully. "They're not goin' to get me,

Johnnie. Don't forget to remember not to forget yore part. Keep under cover for thirty minutes; then if **I** have n't shown up, holler yore head off for the cops."

They were passing an alley as Clay finished speaking. He slipped into its friendly darkness and was presently lost to sight. It ran into an inner court which was the center of tortuous passages. The cattleman stopped to get his bearings, selected the likeliest exit, and brought up in the shelter of a small porch. This, he felt sure, must be the rear of the house he wanted.

A strip of lattice-work ran up the side of the entrance. Very carefully, testing every slat with his weight before trusting himself to it, he climbed up and edged forward noiselessly upon the roof. On hands and knees he crawled to the window and tried to peer in.

The blind was down, but he could see that the room was dark. What danger lurked behind the drawn blind he could not guess, but after a moment, to make sure that the revolver beneath his belt was ready for instant use, he put his hand gently on the sash.

His motions were soundless as the fall of snowflakes. The window moved slowly, almost imperceptibly, under the pressure of his hands. It gave not the faintest creak of warning. His fingers found the old-fashioned roller blind and traveled down it to the bottom. With the faintest of clicks he released the spring and guided the blind upward.

Warily he lifted one leg into the room. His head followed, then the rest of his body. He waited, every nerve tensed.

There came to him a sound that sent cold finger-tips

playing a tattoo up and down his spine. It was the in-
take of some one's cautious breathing.

His hand crept to the butt of the revolver. He
crouched, poised for either attack or retreat.

A bath of light flooded the room and swallowed the
darkness. Instantly Clay's revolver leaped to the air.

CHAPTER XIII

A LATE EVENING CALL

A YOUNG woman in an open-neck nightgown sat up in bed, a cascade of black hair fallen over her white shoulders. Eyes like jet beads were fastened on him. In them he read indignation struggling with fear.

"Say, what are you anyhow — a moll buzzer? If you're a porch-climber out for the props you've sure come to the wrong dump. I got nothin' but bum rocks."

This was Greek to Clay. He did not know that she had asked him if he were a man who robs women, and that she had told him he could get no diamonds there since hers were false.

The Arizonan guessed at once that he was not in the room mentioned in the letter. He slipped his revolver back into its place between shirt and trousers.

"Is this house number 121?" he asked.

"No, it's 123. What of it?"

"It's the wrong house. I'm ce'tainly one chump."

The black eyes lit with sardonic mockery. The young woman knew already that she had nothing to fear from this brown-faced man. His face was not that of a thug. It carried its own letter of recommendation written on it. Instinctively she felt that he had not come to rob. A lively curiosity began to move in her.

"Say, do I look like one of them born-every-minute kind?" she asked easily. "Go ahead and spring that old one on me about how you got tanked at the club and come in at the window on account o' your wife havin' a temper somethin' fierce."

"No, I — I was lookin' for some one else. I'm awful sorry I scared you. I'd eat dirt if it would do any good, but it won't. I'm just a plumb idiot. I reckon I'll be pushin' on my reins." He turned toward the window.

"Stop right there where you're at," she ordered sharply. "Take a step to that window and I'll holler for a harness bull like a Bowery bride gettin' a wallopin' from friend husband. I gotta have an explanation. And who told you I was scared? Forget that stuff. Take it from Annie that she ain't the kind that scares."

The girl sat up in bed, fingers laced around the knees beneath the blanket. There was an *insouciance* about her he did not understand. She did not impress him in the least as a wanton, but if he read that pert little face aright she was a good deal less embarrassed than he.

"I came to see some one else, but I got in the wrong house," he explained again lamely.

"That's twice I heard both them interestin' facts. Who is this goil you was comin' through a window to see in the middle o' the night. And what's that gat for if it ain't to croak some other guy? You oughtta be a shamed of yourself for not pullin' a better wheeze than that on me."

Clay blushed. In spite of the slangy impudence that dropped from the pretty red lips the girl was slim and looked virginal.

"You're 'way off. I wasn't callin' on her to —" He stuck hopelessly.

"Whadya know about that?" she came back with

obvious sarcasm. "You soitainly give me a pain. I'll say you were n't callin' to arrange no Sunday School picnic. Listen. Look at that wall a minute, will you?"

When he turned again at her order she was sitting on the side of the bed wrapped in a kimono, her feet in bedroom slippers. He saw now that she was a slender-limbed slip of a girl. The lean forearm, which showed bare to the elbow when she raised it to draw the kimono closer round her, told Clay that she was none too well nourished.

"I'll listen now to your fairy tale, Mr. Gumshoe Guy, but I wantta wise you that I'm hep to men. Doncha try to string me," she advised.

Clay did not. It had occurred to him that she might give him information of value. There was something friendly and kindly about the humorous little mouth which parroted worldly wisdom so sagely and the jargon of criminals so readily. He told her the story of Kitty Mason. He could see by the girl's eyes that she had jumped to the conclusion that he was in love with Kitty. He did not attempt to disturb that conviction. It might enlist her sympathy.

"Honest, Annie, I believe this guy's on the level," the young woman said aloud as though to herself. "If he ain't, he's sure a swell mouthpiece. He don't look to me like no flat-worker — not with that mug of his. But you never can tell."

"I'm not, Miss. My story's true." Eyes clear as the Arizona sky in a face brown as the Arizona desert looked straight at her.

. Annie Millikan had never seen a man like this before,

so clean and straight and good to look at. From childhood she had been brought up on the fringe of that
underworld the atmosphere of which is miasmic. She
was impressed in spite of herself.

"Say, why don't you go into the movies and be one of
these here screen ideals? You'd knock 'em dead," she
advised flippantly, crossing her bare ankles.

Clay laughed. He liked the insolent little twist to her
mouth. She made one strong appeal to him. This bit of a
girl, so slim that he could break her in his hands, was
game to the core. He recognized it as a quality of kinship.

"This is my busy night. When I've got more time I'll
think of it. Right now —"

She took the subject out of his mouth. "Listen, how
do you know the girl ain't a badger-worker?"

"You'll have to set 'em up on the other alley, Miss,"
the Westerner said. "I don't get yore meanin'."

"Could n't she 'a' made this date to shake you down?
Blackmail stuff."

"No chance. She's not that kind."

"Mebbe you're right. I meet so many hop-nuts and
dips and con guys and gun-molls that I get to thinkin'
there's no decent folks left," she said with a touch of
weariness.

"Why don't you pull yore picket-pin and travel to a
new range?" he asked. "They're no kind of people for
you to be knowin'. Get out to God's country where men
are white and poor folks get half a chance."

The girl shrugged her shoulders. "Little old New
York is my beat. It's the biggest puddle in the world

and I'll do my kickin' here." Abruptly she switched the talk back to his affairs. "You wantta go slow when you tackle Jerry Durand. I can tell you one thing. He's in this business up to the neck. I seen his shadow Gorilla Dave comin' outa the house next door twice to-day."

"Seen anything of the girl?"

"Nope. But she may be there. Honest, you're up against a tough game. There's no use rappin' to the bulls. They'd tip Jerry off and the girl would n't be there when they pulled the house."

"Then I must work this alone."

"Why don't you lay down on it?" she asked, her frank eyes searching his. "You soitainly will if you've got good sense."

"I'm goin' through."

Her black eyes warmed. "Say, I'll bet you're some guy when you get started. Hop to it and I hope you get Jerry good."

"I don't want Jerry. He's too tough for me. Once I had so much of him I took sick and went to the hospital. It's the girl I want."

"Say, listen! I got a hunch mebbe it's a bum steer, but you can't be sure till you try it. Why don't you get in through the roof instead o' the window?"

"Can I get in that way?"

"Surest thing you know — if the trapdoor ain't latched. Say, stick around outside my room half a sec, will you?"

The cattleman waited in the darkness of the passage. If his enemies were trying to ambush him in the house next door the girl's plan might save him. He would have a chance at least to get them unexpectedly in the rear.

It could have been scarcely more than two minutes later that the young woman joined him.

Her small hand slipped into his to guide him. They padded softly along the corridor till they came to a flight of stairs running up. The girl led the way, taking the treads without noise in her stockinged feet. Clay followed with the utmost caution.

Again her hand found his in the darkness of the landing. She took him toward the rear to a ladder which ended at a dormer half-door leading to the roof. Clay fumbled with his fingers, found a hook, unfastened it, and pushed open the trap. He looked up into a starlit night and a moment later stepped out upon the roof. Presently the slim figure of the girl stood beside him.

They moved across to a low wall, climbed it and came to the dormer door of the next house. Clay knelt and lifted it an inch or two very slowly. He lowered it again and rose.

"I'm a heap obliged to you, Miss," he said in a low voice. "You're a game little gentleman."

She nodded. "My name is Annie Millikan."

"Mine is Clay Lindsay. I want to come and thank you proper some day."

"I take tickets at Heath's Palace of Wonders two blocks down," she whispered.

"You'll sure sell me a ticket one of these days," Clay promised.

"Look out for yourself. Don't let 'em get you. Give 'em a chance, and that gang would croak you sure."

"I'll be around to buy that ticket. Good-night, Miss Annie. Don't you worry about me."

"You *will* be careful, won't you?"

"I never threw down on myself yet."

The girl's flippancy broke out again. "Say, lemme know when the weddin' is and I'll send you a salad bowl," she flashed at him saucily as he turned to go.

Clay was already busy with the door.

CHAPTER XIV

STARRING AS A SECOND-STORY MAN

DARKNESS engulfed Clay as he closed the trapdoor overhead. His exploring feet found each tread of the ladder with the utmost caution. Near the foot of it he stopped to listen for any sound that might serve to guide him. None came. The passage was as noiseless as it was dark.

Again he had that sense of cold finger-tips making a keyboard of his spine. An impulse rose in him to clamber up the ladder to the safety of the open-skyed roof. He was a son of the wide outdoors. It went against his gorge to be blotted out of life in this trap like some foul rodent.

But he trod down the panic and set his will to carry on. He crept forward along the passage. Every step or two he stopped to listen, nerves keyed to an acute tension.

A flight of stairs brought him to what he knew must be the second floor. To him there floated a murmur of sounds. They came vague and indistinct through a closed door. The room of the voices was on the left-hand side of the corridor.

He soft-footed it closer, reached the door, and dropped noiselessly to a knee. A key was in the lock on the outside. With infinite precaution against rattling he turned it, slid it out, and dropped it in his coat pocket. His eye fastened to the opening.

Three men were sitting round a table. They were making a bluff at playing cards, but their attention was focused on a door that evidently led into another room.

Two automatic revolvers were on the table close to the hands of their owners. A blackjack lay in front of the third man. Clay recognized him as Gorilla Dave. The other two were strangers to him.

They were waiting. Sometimes they talked in low voices. For the most part they were silent, their eyes on the door of the trap that had been baited for a man Clay knew and was much interested in. Something evil in the watchfulness of the three chilled momentarily his veins. These fellows were the gunmen of New York he had read about — paid assassins whose business it was to frame innocent men for the penitentiary or kill them in cold blood. They were of the underworld, without conscience and without honor. As he looked at them through the keyhole, the watcher was reminded by their restless patience of mountain wolves lying in wait for their kill. Gorilla Dave sat stolidly in his chair, but the other two got up from time to time and paced the room silently, always with an eye to the door of the other room.

Then things began to happen. A soft step sounded in the corridor behind the man at the keyhole. He had not time to crawl away nor even to rise before a man stumbled against him.

Clay had one big advantage over his opponent. He had been given an instant of warning. His right arm went up around the neck of his foe and tightened there. His left hand turned the doorknob. Next moment the two men crashed into the room together, the Westerner rising to his feet as they came, with the body of the other lying across his back from hip to shoulder.

Gorilla Dave leaped to his feet. The other two gun-men, caught at disadvantage a few feet from the table, dived for their automatics. They were too late. Clay swung his body downward from the waist with a quick, strong jerk. The man on his back shot heels over head as though he had been hurled from a catapult, crashed face up on the table, and dragged it over with him in his forward plunge to the wall.

Before any one else could move or speak, Lindsay's gun was out.

"Easy now." His voice was a gentle drawl that carried a menace. "Lemme be boss of the *rodeo* a while. No, Gorilla, I would n't play with that club if I was you. I'm sure hell-a-mile on this gun stuff. Drop it!" The last two words came sharp and crisp, for the big thug had telegraphed an unintentional warning of his purpose to dive at the man behind the thirty-eight.

Gorilla Dave was thick-headed, but he was open to persuasion. Eyes hard as diamonds bored into his, searched him, dominated him. The barrel of the revolver did not waver a hair-breadth. His fingers opened and the blackjack dropped from his hand to the floor.

"For the love o' Mike, who is this guy?" demanded one of the other men.

"I'm the fifth member of our little party," explained Clay.

"Wot t'ell do youse mean? And what's the big idea in most killin' the chief?"

The man who had been flung across the table turned over and groaned. Clay would have known that face among a thousand. It belonged to Jerry Durand.

"I came in at the wrong door and without announcin'
myself," said the cattleman, almost lazily, the unhurried
indolence of his manner not shaken. "You see I wanted
to be on time so as not to keep you waitin'. I'm Clay
Lindsay."

The more talkative of the gunmen from the East Side
flashed one look at the two automatics lying on the
floor beside the overturned table. They might as well
have been in Brazil for all the good they were to him.

"For the love o' Mike," he repeated again helplessly.
"You're the — the —"

"— the hick that was to have been framed for house-
breaking. Yes, I'm him," admitted Clay idiomatically.
"How long had you figured I was to get on the Island?
Or was it yore intention to stop my clock for good?"

"Say, how did youse get into de house?" demanded
big Dave.

"Move over to the other side of the room, Gorilla,
and join yore two friends," suggested the master of
ceremonies. "And don't make any mistake. If you do
you won't have time to be sorry for it. I'll ce'tainly
shoot to kill."

The big-shouldered thug shuffled over. Clay stepped
sideways, watching the three gunmen every foot of the
way, kicked the automatics into the open, and took
possession of them. He felt safer with the revolvers in his
coat pocket, for they had been within reach of Durand,
and that member of the party was showing signs of a
return to active interest in the proceedings.

"When I get you right I'll croak you. By God, I will,"
swore the gang leader savagely, nursing his battered

head. "No big stiff from the bushes can run anything over on me."

"I believe you," retorted Clay easily. "That is, I believe you're tellin' me yore intentions straight. There's no news in that to write home about. But you'd better make that *if* instead of *when*. This is three cracks you've had at me and I'm still a right healthy rube."

"Don't bank on fool luck any more. I'll get you sure," cried Durand sourly.

The gorge of the Arizonan rose. "Mebbeso. You're a dirty dog, Jerry Durand. From the beginning you were a rotten fighter — in the ring and out of it. You and yore strong-arm men! Do you think I'm afraid of you because you surround yoreself with dips and yeggmen and hop-nuts, all scum of the gutter and filth of the earth? Where I come from men fight clean and out in the open. They'd stomp you out like a rattlesnake."

Clay moved back to the door and looked around from one to another, a scorching contempt in his eyes. "Rats — that's what you are, vermin that feed on offal. You have n't got an honest fight in you. All you can do is skulk behind cover to take a man when he ain't lookin'."

He whipped open the door, stepped out, closed it, and took the key from his pocket. A moment, and he had turned the lock.

From within there came a rush that shook the panels. Clay was already busy searching for Kitty. He tore open door after door, calling her loudly by name. Even in the darkness he could see that the rooms were empty of furniture.

There was a crash of splintering panels, the sound of a

bursting lock. Almost as though it were an echo of it came a heavy pounding upon the street door. Clay guessed that the thirty minutes were up and that the Runt was bringing the police. He dived back into one of the empty rooms just in time to miss a rush of men pouring along the passage to the stairs.

Cut off from the street, Clay took to the roof again. It would not do for him to be caught in the house by the police. He climbed the ladder, pushed his way through the trapdoor opening, and breathed deeply of the night air.

But he had no time to lose. Already he could hear the trampling of feet up the stairs to the second story.

Lightly he vaulted the wall and came to the roof door leading down to number 123. He found it latched.

The caves of the roof projected so far that he could not from there get a hold on the window casings below. He made a vain circuit of the roof, then passed to the next house.

Again he was out of luck. The tenants had made safe the entrance against prowlers of the night. He knew that at any moment now the police might appear in pursuit of him. There was no time to lose.

He crossed to the last house in the block — and found himself barred out. As he rose from his knees he heard the voices of men clambering through the scuttle to the roof. At the same time he saw that which brought him to instant action. It was a rope clothes-line which ran from post to post, angling from one corner of the building to another and back to the opposite one.

No man in Manhattan's millions knew the value of a

rope or could handle one more expertly than this cattle-man. His knife was open before he had reached the nearest post. One strong slash of the blade severed it. In six long strides he was at the second post unwinding the line. He used his knife a second time at the third post.

Through the darkness he could see the dim forms of men stopping to examine the scuttle. Then voices came clear to him in the still night.

"If he reached the roof we've got him."

"Unless he found an open trap," a second answered.

With deft motions Clay worked swiftly. He was fastening the rope to the chimney of the house. Every instant he expected to hear a voice raised in excited discovery of him crouched in the shadows. But his fingers were as sure and as steady as though he had minutes before him instead of seconds.

"There's the guy — over by the chimney."

Clay threw the slack of the line from the roof. He had no time to test the strength of the rope nor its length. As the police rushed him he slid over the edge and began to lower himself hand under hand.

Would they cut the rope? Or would they take pot shots at him. He would know soon enough.

The wide eaves protected him. A man would have to hang out from the wall above the ledge to see him.

Clay's eyes were on the gutter above while he jerked his way down a foot at a time. A face and part of a body swung out into sight.

"We've got yuh. Come back or I'll shoot," a voice called down.

A revolver showed against the black sky.

The man from Arizona did not answer and did not stop. He knew that shooting from above is an art that few men have acquired.

A bullet sang past his ear just as he swung in and crouched on the window-sill. Another one hit the bricks close to his head.

The firing stopped. A pair of uniformed legs appeared dangling from the eaves. A body and a head followed these. They began to descend jerkily.

Clay took a turn at the gun-play. He fired his revolver into the air. The spasmodic jerking of the blue legs abruptly ceased.

"He's got a gun!" the man in the air called up to those above.

The fact was obvious. It could not be denied.

"Yuh'd better give up quietly. We're bound to get yuh," an officer shouted from the roof by way of parley.

The cattleman did not answer except by the smashing of glass. He had forced his way into two houses within the past hour. He was now busy breaking into a third. The window had not yielded to pressure. Therefore he was knocking out the glass with the butt of his revolver.

He crawled through the opening just as some one sat up in bed with a frightened exclamation.

"Who — is — s — s — s it?" a masculine voice asked, teeth chattering.

Clay had no time to gratify idle curiosity. He ran through the room, reached the head of the stairs, and went down on the banister to the first floor. He fled back to the rear of the house and stole out by the kitchen door.

The darkness of the alley swallowed him, but he could still hear the shouts of the men on the roof and answering ones from new arrivals below.

Five minutes later he was on board a street car. He was not at all particular as to its destination. He wanted to be anywhere but here. This neighborhood was getting entirely too active for him.

CHAPTER XV

THE GANGMAN SEES RED

EXACTLY thirty minutes after Clay had left him to break into the house, Johnnie lifted his voice in a loud wail for the police. He had read somewhere that one can never find an officer when he is wanted, but the Bull-of-Bashan roar of the cowpuncher brought them running from all directions.

Out of the confused explanations of the range-rider the first policeman to reach him got two lucid statements.

"They're white-slavin' a straight girl. This busher says his pal went in to rescue her half an hour ago and has n't showed up since," he told his mates.

With Johnnie bringing up the rear they made a noisy attack on the front door of Number 121. Almost immediately it was opened from the inside. Four men had come down the stairs in a headlong rush to cut off the escape of one who had outwitted and taunted them.

Those who wanted to get in and those who wanted to get out all tried to talk at once, but as soon as the police recognized Jerry Durand they gave him the floor.

"We're after a flat-worker," explained the ex-pugilist. "He must be tryin' for a roof getaway." He turned and led the joint forces back up the stairs.

Thugs and officers surged up after him, carrying with them in their rush the Runt. He presently found himself on the roof with those engaged in a man-hunt for his

friend. When Clay shattered the window and disappeared
inside after his escape from the roof, Johnnie gave a
deep sigh of relief. This gun-play got on his nerves, since
Lindsay was the target of it.

The bandy-legged range-rider was still trailing along
with the party ten minutes later when its scattered members drew together in tacit admission that the hunted
man had escaped.

"Did youse get a look at his mug, Mr. Durand?"
asked one of the officers. "It's likely we've got it down
at headquarters in the gall'ry."

Durand had already made up his mind on that point.

"We did n't see his face in the light, Pete. No, I
would n't know him again."

His plug-uglies took their cue from him. So did the
officers. If Durand did not want a pinch there would, of
course, not be one.

The gang leader was in a vile temper. If this story
reached the newspapers all New York would be laughing
at him. He could appeal to the police, have Clay Lindsay
arrested, and get him sent up for a term on the charge of
burglary. But he could not do it without the whole tale
coming out. One thing Jerry Durand could not stand
was ridicule. His vanity was one of his outstanding quali-
ties, and he did not want it widely known that the book
he had intended to trap had turned the tables on him,
manhandled him, jeered at him, and locked him in a
room with his three henchmen.

Johnnie Green chose this malapropos moment for
reminding the officers of the reason for the coming to the
house.

"What about the young lady?" he asked solicitously.

Durand wheeled on him, looked him over with an insolent, malevolent eye, and jerked a thumb in his direction. "Who is this guy?"

"He's the fellow tipped us off his pal was inside," answered one of the patrolmen. He spoke in a whisper close to the ear of Jerry. "Likely he knows more than he lets on. Shall I make a pinch?"

The eyes of the gang leader narrowed. "So he's a friend of this second-story bird, is he?"

"Y'betcha!" chirped up Johnnie, "and I'm plumb tickled to take his dust too. Now about this yere young lady —"

Jerry caught him hard on the side of the jaw with a short arm jolt. The range-rider hit the pavement hard. Slowly he got to his feet nursing his cheek.

"What yuh do that for, doggone it?" he demanded resentfully. "Me, I wasn't lookin' for no trouble. Me, I —"

Durand leaped at him across the sidewalk. His strong fingers closed on the throat of the bow-legged puncher. He shook him as a lion does his kill. The rage of the pugilist found a vent in punishing the friend of the man he hated. Johnnie grew black in the face. His knees sagged and his lips foamed.

The officers pried Jerry loose from his victim with the greatest difficulty. He tried furiously to get at him, lunging from the men who were holding his arms.

The puncher sank helplessly against the wall.

"He's got all he can carry, Mr. Durand," one of the

bluecoats said soothingly. "You don't wantta croak the little guy."

The ex-prize-fighter returned to sanity. "Says I'm white-slavin' a girl, does he? I'll learn him to lie about me," he growled.

Johnnie strangled and sputtered, fighting for breath to relieve his tortured lungs.

"Gimme the word, an' I'll run him in for a drunk," the policeman suggested out of the corner of a whispering mouth.

Jerry shook his head. "Nope. Let him go, Pete."

The policeman walked up to the Runt and caught him roughly by the arm. "Move along outa here. I'd ought to pinch you, but I'm not gonna do it this time. See? You beat it!"

Durand turned to one of his followers. "Tail that fellow. Find out where he's stayin' and report."

Helplessly Johnnie went staggering down the street. He did not understand why he had been treated so. His outraged soul protested at such injustice, but the instinct of self-preservation carried him out of the danger zone without argument about it. Even as he wobbled away he was looking with unwavering faith to his friend to right his wrongs. Clay would fix this fellow Durand for what he had done to him. Before Clay got through with him the bully would wish he had never lifted a hand to him.

CHAPTER XVI

A FACE IN THE NIGHT

CLAY did his best under the handicap of a lack of *entente* between him and the authorities to search New York for Kitty. He used the personal columns of the newspapers. He got in touch with taxicab drivers, ticket-sellers, postmen, and station guards. So far as possible he even employed the police through the medium of Johnnie. The East Side water-front and the cheap lodging-houses of that part of the city he combed with especial care. All the time he knew that in such a maze as Manhattan it would be a miracle if he found her.

But miracles are made possible by miracle-workers. The Westerner was a sixty-horse-power dynamo of energy. He felt responsible for Kitty and he gave himself with single-minded devotion to the job of discovering her.

His rides and walks with Beatrice were rare events now because he was so keen on the business of looking for his Colorado protégée. He gave them up reluctantly. Every time they went out together into the open Miss Whitford became more discontented with the hothouse existence she was living. He felt there was just a chance that if he were constant enough, he might sweep her off her feet into that deeper current of life that lay beyond the social shallows. But he had to sacrifice this chance. He was not going to let Kitty's young soul be shipwrecked if he could help it, and he had an intuition that she was not wise enough nor strong enough to keep off the rocks alone.

A part of his distress lay in the coolness of his imperious young friend who lived on the Drive. Beatrice resented his divided allegiance, though her own was very much in that condition. Clay and she had from the first been good comrades. No man had ever so deeply responded to her need of friendship. All sorts of things he understood without explanations. A day with him was one that brought the deep content of happiness. That, no doubt, she explained to herself, was because he was such a contrast to the men of cramped lives she knew. He was a splendid tonic, but of course one did not take tonics except occasionally.

Yet though Beatrice intended to remain heart-whole, she wanted to be the one woman in Clay's life until she released him. It hurt her vanity, and perhaps something deeper than her vanity, that such a girl as she conceived Kitty Mason to be should have first claim on the time she had come to consider her own. She made it plain to him, in the wordless way expert young women have at command, that she did not mean to share with him such odd hours as he chose to ask for. He had to come when she wanted him or not at all. Without the name of Kitty having been mentioned, he was given to understand that if he wished to remain in the good graces of Beatrice Whitford he must put the cigarette girl out of his mind.

For all his good nature Clay was the last man in the world to accept dictation of this sort. He would go through with anything he started, and especially where it was a plain call of duty. Beatrice might like it or not as

she pleased. He would make his own decisions as to his
conduct.

He did.

Bee was furious at him. She told herself that there was
either a weak streak in him or a low one, else he would
not be so obsessed by the disappearance of this flirta-
tious little fool who had tried to entrap him. But she did
not believe it. A glance at this brown-faced man was
sufficient evidence that he trod with dynamic force the
way of the strong. A look into his clear eyes was certifi-
cate enough of his decency.

When Clay met Kitty at last it was quite by chance.
As it happened Beatrice was present at the time.

He had been giving a box party at the Empire. The
gay little group was gathered under the awning outside
the foyer while the limousine that was to take them to
Shanley's for supper was being called. Colin Whitford,
looking out into the rain that pelted down, uttered an
exclamatory "By Jove!"

Clay turned to him inquiringly.

"A woman was looking out of that doorway at us,"
he said. "If she's not in deep water I'm a bad guesser. I
thought for a moment she knew me or some one of us.
She started to reach out her hands and then shrank
back."

"Young or old?" asked the cattleman.

"Young — a girl."

"Which door?"

"The third."

"Excuse me." The host was off in an instant, almost
on the run.

But the woman had gone, swallowed in the semi-darkness of a side street. Clay followed.

Beatrice turned to her father, eyebrows lifted. There was a moment's awkward silence.

"Mr. Lindsay will be back presently," Whitford said. "We'll get in and wait for him out of the way a little farther up the street."

When Clay rejoined them he was without his overcoat. He stood in the heavy rain beside the car, a figure of supple grace even in his evening clothes, and talked in a low voice with Beatrice's father. The mining man nodded agreement and Lindsay turned to the others.

"I'm called away," he explained aloud. "Mr. Whitford has kindly promised to play host in my place. I'm right sorry to leave, but it's urgent."

His grave smile asked Beatrice to be charitable in her findings. The eyes she gave him were coldly hostile. She, too, had caught a glimpse of the haggard face in the shadows and she hardened her will against him. The bottom of his heart went out as he turned away. He knew Beatrice did not and would not understand.

The girl was waiting where Clay had left her, crouched against a basement milliner's door under the shelter of the steps. She was wearing the overcoat he had flung around her. In its pallid despair her face was pitiable.

A waterproofed policeman glanced suspiciously at them as he sloshed along the sidewalk in the splashing rain.

"I — I've looked for you everywhere," moaned the girl. "It's been — awful."

"I know, but it's goin' to be all right now, Kitty," he

comforted. "You're goin' home with me to-night. To-morrow we'll talk it all over."

He tucked an arm under hers and led her along the wet, shining street to a taxicab. She crouched in a corner of the cab, her body shaken with sobs.

The young man moved closer and put a strong arm around her shoulders. "Don't you worry, Kitty. Yore big brother is on the job now."

"I — I wanted to — to kill myself," she faltered. "I tried to — in the river — and — it was so black — I could n't." The girl shivered with cold. She had been exposed to the night rain for hours without a coat.

He knew her story now in its essentials as well as he did later when she wept it out to him in confession. And because she was who she was, born to lean on a stronger will, he acquitted her of blame.

They swung into Broadway and passed taxis and limousines filled with gay parties just out of the theaters. Young women in rich furs, wrapped from the cruelty of life by the caste system in which wealth had encased them, exchanged badinage with sleek, well-dressed men. A ripple of care-free laughter floated to him across the gulf that separated this girl from them. By the cluster lights of Broadway he could see how cruelly life had mauled her soft youth. The bloom of her was gone, all the brave pride and joy of girlhood. It would probably never wholly return.

He saw as in a vision the infinite procession of her hopeless sisters who had traveled the road from which he was rescuing her, saw them first as sweet and merry children bubbling with joy, and again, after the world had misused them for its pleasure, haggard and tawdry, with dragging steps trailing toward the oblivion that awaited them. He wondered if life must always be so terribly wasted, made a bruised and broken thing instead of the fine, brave adventure for which it was meant.

CHAPTER XVII

As Kitty stepped from the cab she was trembling violently.

"Don't you be frightened, li'l' pardner. You've come home. There won't anybody hurt you here."

The soft drawl of Clay's voice carried inexpressible comfort. So too did the pressure of his strong hand on her arm. She knew not only that he was a man to trust, but that so far as could be he would take her troubles on his broad shoulders. Tears brimmed over her soft eyes.

The Arizonan ran her up to his floor in the automatic elevator.

"I've got a friend from home stayin' with me. He's the best-hearted fellow you ever saw. You'll sure like him," he told her without stress as he fitted his key to the lock.

He felt her shrink beneath his coat, but it was too late to draw back now. In another moment Lindsay was introducing her casually to the embarrassed and astonished joint proprietor of the apartment.

The Runt was coatless and in his stockinged-feet. He had been playing a doleful ditty on a mouth-organ. Caught so unexpectedly, he blushed a beautiful brick red to his neck.

Johnnie ducked his head and scraped the carpet with his foot in an attempt at a bow. "Glad to meet up with you-all, Miss. Hope you're feelin' tol'able."

Clay slipped the coat from her shoulders and saw that the girl was wet to the skin.

"Heat some water, Johnnie, and make a good stiff toddy. Miss Kitty has been out in the rain."

He lit the gas-log and from his bedroom brought towels, a bathrobe, pajamas, a sweater, and woolen slippers. On a lounge before the fire he dumped the clothes he had gathered. He drew up the easiest arm-chair in the room.

"I'm goin' to the kitchen to jack up Johnnie so he won't lay down on his job," he told her cheerily. "You take yore time and get into these dry clothes. We'll not disturb you till you knock. After that we'll feed you some chuck. You want to brag on Johnnie's cookin'. He thinks he's it when it comes to monkeyin' 'round a stove."

When her timid knock came her host brought in a steaming cup. "You drink this. It'll warm you good."

"What is it?" she asked shyly.

"Medicine," he smiled. "Doctor's orders."

While she sipped the toddy Johnnie brought from the kitchen a tray upon which were tea, fried potatoes, ham, eggs, and buttered toast.

The girl ate ravenously. It was an easy guess that she had not before tasted food that day.

Clay kept up a flow of talk, mostly about Johnnie's culinary triumphs. Meanwhile he made up a bed on the couch.

Once she looked up at him, her throat swollen with emotion. "You're good."

"Sho! We been needin' a li'l' sister to brace up our

manners for us. It's lucky for us I found you. Now **I** expect you're tired and sleepy. We fixed up yore bed in here because it's warmer. You'll be able to make out with it all right. The springs are good." Clay left her with a cheerful smile. "Turn out the light before you go to bed, Miss Colorado. Sleep tight. And don't you worry. You're back with old home folks again now, you know."

They heard her moving about for a time. Presently came silence. Tired out from tramping the streets without food and drowsy from the toddy she had taken, Kitty fell into deep sleep undisturbed by troubled dreams.

The cattleman knew he had found her in the nick of time. She had told him that she had no money, no room in which to sleep, no prospect of work. Everything she had except the clothes on her back had been pawned to buy food and lodgings. But she was young and resilient. When she got back home to the country where she belonged, time would obliterate from her mind the experiences of which she had been the victim.

It was past midday when Kitty woke. She heard a tuneless voice in the kitchen lifted up in a doleful song:

"There's hard times on old Bitter Creek
    That never can be beat.
It was root hog or die
Under every wagon sheet.
We cleared up all the Indians,
Drank all the alkali,
    And it's whack the cattle on, boys —
Root hog or die."

Kitty found her clothes dry. After she dressed she

opened the door that led to the kitchen. Johnnie was near the end of another stanza of his sad song:

> "Oh, I'm goin' home
>   Bull-whackin' for to spurn;
> I ain't got a nickel,
> And I don't give a dern.
> 'T is when I meet a pretty girl,
> You bet I will or try,
>   I'll make her my little wife —
> Root hog — "

He broke off embarrassed. "Did I wake you-all, ma'am, with my fool singin'? I'm right sorry if I did."

"You did n't." Kitty, clinging shyly to the side of the doorway, tried to gain confidence from his unease. "I was already awake. Is it a range song you were singing?"

"Yes'm. Cattle range, not kitchen range."

A wan little smile greeted his joke. The effect on Johnnie himself was more pronounced. It gave him confidence in his ability to meet the situation. He had not known before that he was a wit and the discovery of it tickled his self-esteem.

"'Course we did n't really clean up no Indians nor drink all the alkali. Tha's jes' in the song, as you might say." He began to bustle about in preparation for her breakfast.

"Please don't trouble. I'll eat what you've got cooked," she begged.

"It's no trouble, ma'am. If the's a thing on earth I enjoy doin' it's sure cookin'. Do you like yore aigs sunny side up or turned?"

"Either way. Whichever you like, Mr. Green.'

"You're eatin' them," Johnnie reminded her with a grin.

"On one side, then, please. Mr. Lindsay says you're a fine cook."

"Sho! I'm no great shakes. Clay he jes' brags on me."

"Lemme eat here in the kitchen. Then you won't have to set the table in the other room," she said.

The puncher's instinct was to make a spread on the dining-table for her, but it came to him with a flash of insight that it would be wise to let her eat in the kitchen. She would feel more as though she belonged and was not a guest of an hour.

While she ate he waited on her solicitously. Inside, he was a river of tears for her, but with it went a good deal of awe. Even now, wan-eyed and hollow-cheeked, she was attractive. In Johnnie's lonesome life he had never before felt so close to a girl as he did to this one. Moreover, for the first time he felt master of the situation. It was his business to put their guest at her ease. That was what Clay had told him to do before he left.

"You're the doctor, ma'am. You'll eat where you say."

"I — I don't like to be so much bother to you," she said again. "Maybe I can go away this afternoon."

"No, ma'am, we won't have that a-tall," broke in the range-rider in alarm. "We're plumb tickled to have you here. Clay he feels thataway too."

"I could keep house for you while I stay," she suggested timidly. "I know how to cook — and the place does need cleaning."

"Sure it does. Say, wha's the matter with you bein' Clay's sister, jes' got in last night on the train? Tha's the story we'll put up to the landlord if you'll gimme the word."

"I never had a brother, but if I'd had one I'd 'a' wanted him to be like Mr. Lindsay," she told his friend.

"Say, ain't he a go-getter?" cried Johnnie eagerly. "Clay's sure one straight-up son-of-a-gun. You'd ought to 'a' seen how he busted New York open to find you."

"Did he?"

Johnnie told the story of the search with special emphasis on the night Clay broke into three houses in answer to her advertisement.

"I never wrote it. I never thought of that. It must have been —"

"It was that scalawag Durand, y'betcha. I ain't still wearin' my pinfeathers none. Tha's who it was. I'm not liable to forget him. He knocked me hell-west and silly whilst I was n't lookin'. He was sore because Clay had fixed his clock proper."

"So you've fought on account of me too. I'm sorry." There was a little break in her voice. "I s'pose you hate me for — for bein' the way I am. I know I hate myself." She choked on the food she was eating.

Johnnie, much distressed, put down the coffee-pot and fluttered near. "Don't you take on, ma'am. I wisht I could tell you how pleased we-all are to he'p you. I hope you'll stay with us right along. I sure do. You'd be right welcome," he concluded bashfully.

"I've got no place to go, except back home — and I've got no folks there but a second cousin. She does n't want me. I don't know what to do. If I had a woman friend — some one to tell me what was best —"

Johnnie slapped his hand on his knee, struck by a sudden inspiration. "Say! Y'betcha, by jollies, I've got 'er — the very one! You're damn — you're sure whistlin'. We got a lady friend, Clay and me, the finest little pilgrim in New York. She's sure there when the gong strikes. You'd love her. I'll fix it for you — right away. I got to go to her house this afternoon an' do some chores. I'll bet she comes right over to see you."

Kitty was doubtful. She did not want to take any strange young women into her confidence until she had seen them. More than one good Pharisee had burned her face with a look of scornful contempt in the past weeks.

"Maybe we better wait and speak to Mr. Lindsay about it," she said.

"No, ma'am, you don't know Miss Beatrice. She's the *best* friend." He passed her the eggs and a confidence at the same time. "Why, I should n't wonder but that she and Clay might get married one o' these days. He thinks a lot of her."

"Oh." Kitty knew just a little more of human nature than the puncher. "Then I would n't tell her about me if I was you. She would n't like my bein' here."

"Sho! You don't know Miss Beatrice. She grades 'way up. I'll bet she likes you fine."

When Johnnie left to go to work that afternoon he took with him a resolution to lay the whole case before Beatrice Whitford. She would fix things all right. No need for anybody to worry after she took a hand and began to run things. If there was one person on earth Johnnie could bank on without fail it was his little boss.

CHAPTER XVIII

BEATRICE GIVES AN OPTION

It was not until Johnnie had laid the case before **Miss** Whitford and restated it under the impression that she could not have understood that his confidence ebbed. Even then he felt that he must have bungled it in the telling and began to marshal his facts a third time. He had expected an eager interest, a quick enthusiasm. Instead, he found in his young mistress a spirit beyond his understanding. Her manner had a touch of cool disdain, almost of contempt, while she listened to his tale. This was not at all in the picture he had planned.

She asked no questions and made no comments. What he had to tell met with chill silence. Johnnie's guileless narrative had made clear to her that Clay had brought Kitty home about midnight, had mixed a drink for her, and had given her his own clothes to replace her wet ones. Somehow the cattleman's robe, pajamas, and bedroom slippers obtruded unduly from his friend's story. Even the Runt felt this. He began to perceive himself a helpless medium of wrong impressions. When he tried to explain he made matters worse.

"I suppose you know that when the manager of your apartment house finds out she's there he'll send her packing." So Beatrice summed up when she spoke at last.

"No, ma'am, I reckon not. You see we done told

him she is Clay's sister jes' got in from the West," the puncher explained.

"Oh, I see." The girl's lip curled and her clean-cut chin lifted a trifle. "You don't seem to have overlooked anything. No, I don't think I care to have anything to do with your arrangements."

"She's an awful pretty cute little thing," the puncher added, hoping to modify her judgment.

"Indeed!"

Beatrice turned and walked swiftly into the house. A pulse of anger was beating in her soft throat. She felt a sense of outrage. To Clay Lindsay she had given herself generously in spirit. She had risked something in introducing him to her friends. They might have laughed at him for his slight social lapses. They might have rejected him for his lack of background. They had done neither. He was so genuinely a man that he had won his way instantly. In this City of Bluff, as O. Henry dubs New York, his simplicity had rung true as steel. Still, she had taken a chance and felt she deserved some recognition of it on his part. This he had never given. He had based their friendship on equality simply. She liked it in him, though her vanity had resented it a little. But this was different. She was still young enough, still so little a woman of the world, that she set a rigid standard which she expected her friends to meet. She had believed in Clay, and now he was failing her.

Pacing up and down her room, little fists clenched, her soul in passionate turmoil, Beatrice went over it all again as she had done through a sleepless night. She had given him so much, and he had seemed to give her even

more. Hours filled with a keen-edged delight jumped to
her memory, hours that had carried her away from the
falseness of social fribble to clean, wind-swept, open
spaces of the mind. And after this — after he had tacitly
recognized her claim on him — he had insulted her before her friends by deserting his guests to go off with this
hussy he had been spending weeks to search for.

Now his little henchman had the imbecility to ask
her help while this girl was living at Clay Lindsay's
apartment, passing herself off as his sister, and proposing to stay there ostensibly as the housekeeper. She felt
degraded, humiliated, she told herself. Not for a moment did she admit, perhaps she did not know, that an
insane jealousy was flooding her being, that her indignation was based on personal as well as moral grounds.

Something primitive stirred in her — a flare of feminine ferocity. She felt hot to the touch, an active volcano
ready for eruption. If only she could get a chance to
strike back in a way that would hurt, to wound him as
deeply as he had her!

Pat to her desire came the opportunity. Clay's card
was brought in to her by Jenkins.

"Tell Mr. Lindsay I'll see him in a few minutes," she
told the man.

The few minutes stretched to a long quarter of an hour
before she descended. To the outward eye at least Miss
Whitford looked a woman of the world, sheathed in a
plate armor of conventionality. As soon as his eyes fell on
her Clay knew that this pale, slim girl in the close-fitting
gown was a stranger to him. Her eyes, star-bright and
burning like live coals, warned him that the friend whose

youth had run out so eagerly to meet his was hidden deep in her to-day.

"I reckon I owe you and Mr. Whitford an apology," he said. "No need to tell you how I happened to leave last night. I expect you know."

"I know why you left — yes."

"I'd like to explain it to you so you'll understand."

"Why take the trouble? I think I understand." She spoke in an even, schooled voice that set him at a distance.

"Still, I want you to know how I feel."

"Is that important? I see what you do. That is enough. Your friend Mr. Green has carefully brought me the details I did n't know."

Clay flushed. Her clear voice carried an edge of scorn. "You must n't judge by appearances. I know you would n't be unfair. I had to take her home and look after her."

"I don't quite see why — unless, of course, you wanted to," the girl answered, tapping the arm of her chair with impatient finger-tips, eyes on the clock. "But of course it is n't necessary I should see."

Her cavalier treatment of him did not affect the gentle imperturbability of the Westerner.

"Because I'm a white man, because she's a little girl who came from my country and can't hold her own here, because she was sick and chilled and starving. Do you see now?"

"No, but it does n't matter. I'm not the keeper of your conscience, Mr. Lindsay," she countered, with hard lightness.

"You're judging me just the same."

Her eyes attacked him. "Am I?"

"Yes." The level gaze of the man met hers calmly. "What have I done that you don't like?"

She lost some of her debonair insolence that expressed itself in indifference.

"I'd ask that if I were you," she cried scornfully. "Can you tell me that this — friend of yours — is a good girl?"

"I think so. She's been up against it. Whatever she may have done she's been forced to do."

"Excuses," she murmured.

"If you'd ever known what it was to be starving —"

Her smoldering anger broke into a flame. "Good of you to compare me with her! That's the last straw!"

"I'm not comparing you. I'm merely saying that you can't judge her. How could you, when your life has been so different?"

"Thank Heaven for that."

"If you'd let me bring her here to see you —"

"No, thanks."

"You're unjust."

"You think so?"

"And unkind. That's not like the little friend I've come to — like so much."

"You're kind enough for two, Mr. Lindsay. She really does n't need another friend so long as she has you," she retorted with a flash of contemptuous eyes. "In New York we're not used to being so kind to people of her sort."

Clay lifted a hand. "Stop right there, Miss Beatrice.

You don't want to say anything you'll be sorry for."

"I'll say this," she cut back. "The men I know would n't invite a woman to their rooms at midnight and pass her off as their sister — and then expect people to know her. They would be kinder to themselves — and to their own reputations."

She was striking out savagely, relentlessly, in spite of the better judgment that whispered restraint. She wanted desperately to hurt him, as he had hurt her, even though she had to behave badly to do it.

"Will you tell me what else there was to do? Where could I have taken her at that time of night? Are reputable hotels open at midnight to lone women, wet and ragged, who come without baggage either alone or escorted by a man?"

"I'm not telling you what you ought to have done, Mr. Lindsay," she answered with a touch of hauteur. "But since you ask me — why could n't you have given her money and let her find a place for herself?"

"Because that would n't have saved her."

"Oh, would n't it?" she retorted dryly.

He walked over to the fireplace and put an elbow on the corner of the mantel. The blood leaped in the veins of the girl as she looked at him, a man strong as tested steel, quiet and forceful, carrying his splendid body with the sinuous grace that comes only from perfectly synchronized muscles. At that moment she hated him because she could not put him in the wrong.

"Lemme tell you a story, Miss Beatrice," he said presently. "Mebbe it'll show you what I mean. I was runnin' cattle in the Galiuros five years ago and I got caught in a storm 'way up in the hills. When it rains in my part of Arizona, which ain't often, it sure does come down in sheets. The clay below the rubble on the slopes got slick as ice. My hawss, a young one, slipped and fel' on me, clawed back to its feet, and bolted. Well, there I was with my laig busted, forty miles from even a whistlin' post in the desert, gettin' wetter and colder every blessed minute. Heaps of times in my life I've felt more comfortable than I did right then. I was hogtied to that shale ledge with my broken ankle, as you might say. And the weather and my game laig and things generally kept gettin' no better right along hour after hour.

"There was n't a chance in a million that anybody would hear, but I kept firin' off my fohty-five on the off hope. And just before night a girl on a *pinto* came down the side of that uncurried hill round a bend and got me. She took me to a cabin hidden in the bottom of a cañon and looked after me four days. Her father, a prospector, had gone into Tucson for supplies and we were alone there. She fed me, nursed me, and waited on me. We divided a one-room twelve-by-sixteen cabin. Understand, we were four days alone together before her dad came back, and all the time the sky was lettin' down a terrible lot of water. When her father showed up he grinned and said, 'Lucky for you Myrtle heard that six-gun of yore's pop!' He never thought one evil thing about either of us. He just accepted the situation as necessary. Now the question is, what ought she to have done? Left me to die on that hillside?"

"Of course not. That's different," protested Beatrice indignantly.

"I don't see it. What she did was more embarrassing for her than what I did for Kitty. At least it would have been mightily so if she had n't used her good hawss sense and forgot that she was a lone young female and I was a man. That's what I did the other night. Just because there are seven or eight million human beings here the obligation to look out for Kitty was no less."

"New York is n't Arizona."

"You bet it ain't. We don't sit roostin' on a fence when folks need our help out there. We go to it."

"You can't do that sort of thing here. People talk."

"Sure, and hens cackle. Let 'em!"

"There are some things men don't understand," she told him with an acid little smile of superiority. "When a girl cries a little they think she's heartbroken. Very likely she's laughing at them up her sleeve. This girl's making a fool of you, if you want the straight truth."

"I don't think so."

His voice was so quietly confident it nettled her.

"I suppose, then, you think I'm ungenerous," she charged.

The deep-set gray-blue eyes looked at her steadily. There was a wise little smile in them.

"Is that what you think?" she charged.

"I think you'll be sorry when you think it over."

She was annoyed at her inability to shake him, at the steadfastness with which he held to his point of view.

"You're trying to put me in the wrong," she flamed. "Well, I won't have it. That's all. You may take your choice, Mr. Lindsay. Either send that girl away — **give her up** — have nothing to do with her, or —"

"Or —?"

"Or please don't come here to see me any more."

He waited, his eyes steadily on her. "Do you sure enough mean that, Miss Beatrice?"

Her heart sank. She knew she had gone too far, but she was too imperious to draw back now.

"Yes, that's just what I mean."

"I'm sorry. You're leavin' me no option. I'm not a yellow dog. Sometimes I'm 'most a man. I'm goin' to do what I think is right."

"Of course," she responded lightly. "If our ideas of what that is differ —"

"They do."

"It's because we've been brought up differently, I suppose." She achieved a stifled little yawn behind her hand.

"You've said it." He gave it to her straight from the shoulder. "All yore life you've been pampered. When you wanted a thing all you had to do was to reach out a hand for it. Folks were born to wait on you, by yore way of it. You're a spoiled kid. You keep these manicured lah-de-dah New York lads steppin'. Good enough. Be as high-heeled as you're a mind to. I'll step some too for you — when you smile at me right. But it's time to serve notice that in my country folks grow man-size. You ask me to climb up the side of a house to pick you a bit of ivy from under the eaves, and I reckon I'll take a whirl at it. But you ask me to turn my back on a friend, and I've got to say, 'Nothin' doin'.' And if you was just a few years younger I'd advise yore pa to put you in yore room and feed you bread and water for askin' it."

The angry color poured into her cheeks. She clenched her hands till the nails bit her palms. "I think you're the most hateful man I ever met," she cried passionately.

His easy smile taunted her. "Oh, no, you don't. You just think you think it. Now, I'm goin' to light a shuck. I'll be sayin' good-bye, Miss Beatrice, until you send for me."

"And that will be never," she flung at him.

He rose, bowed, and walked out of the room.

The street door closed behind him. Beatrice bit her lip to keep from breaking down before she reached her room.

CHAPTER XIX

A LADY WEARS A RING

CLARENDON BROMFIELD got the shock of his life that evening. Beatrice proposed to him. It was at the Roberson dinner-dance, in the Palm Room, within sight but not within hearing of a dozen other guests.

She camouflaged what she was doing with occasional smiles and ripples of laughter intended to deceive the others present, but her heart was pounding sixty miles an hour.

Bromfield was not easily disconcerted. He prided himself on his aplomb. It was hard to get behind his cynical, decorous smile, the mask of a suave and worldly-wise Pharisee of the twentieth century. But for once he was amazed. The orchestra was playing a lively fox trot and he thought that perhaps he had not caught her meaning.

"I beg your pardon."

Miss Whitford laced her fingers round her knee and repeated. It was as though rose leaves had brushed the ivory of her cheeks and left a lovely stain there. Her eyes were hard and brilliant as diamonds.

"I was wondering when you are going to ask me again to marry you."

Since she had given a good deal of feminine diplomacy to the task of keeping him at a reasonable distance, Bromfield was naturally surprised.

"That's certainly a leading question," he parried. "What are you up to, Bee? Are you spoofing me?"

"I'm proposing to you," she explained, with a flirt of her hand and an engaging smile toward a man and a girl who had just come into the Palm Room. "I don't suppose I do it very well because I haven't had your experience. But I'm doing the best I can."

The New Yorker was a supple diplomatist. If Beatrice had chosen this place and hour to become engaged to him, he had no objection in the world. The endearments that usually marked such an event could wait. But he was not quite sure of his ground.

His lids narrowed a trifle. "Do you mean that you've changed your mind?"

"Have *you?*" she asked quickly with a sidelong slant of eyes at him.

"Do I act as though I had?"

"You don't help a fellow out much, Clary," she complained with a laugh not born of mirth. "I'll never propose to you again."

"I'm still very much at your service, Bee."

"Does that mean you still think you want me?"

"I don't think. I know it."

"Quite sure?"

"Quite sure."

"Then you're on," she told him with a little nod. "Thank you, kind sir."

Bromfield drew a deep breath. "By Jove, you're a good little sport, Bee. I think I'll get up and give three ringing cheers."

"I'd like to see you do that," she mocked.

"Of course you know I'm the happiest man in the world," he said with well-ordered composure.

"You're not exactly what I'd call a rapturous lover, Clary. But I'm not either for that matter, so I dare say we'll hit it off very well."

"I'm a good deal harder hit than I've ever let on, dear girl. And I'm going to make you very happy. That's a promise."

Nevertheless he watched her warily behind a manner of graceful eagerness. There had been a suggestion almost of bitterness in her voice. A suspicious little thought was filtering through the back of his mind. "What the deuce has got into the girl? Has she been quarreling with that bounder from Arizona?"

"I'm glad of that. I'll try to make you a good wife, even if —" She let the sentence die out unfinished.

 Beneath her fan their hands met for a moment.

"May I tell everybody how happy I am?"

"If you like," she agreed.

"A short engagement," he ventured.

"Yes," she nodded. "And take me away for a while. I'm tired of New York, I think."

"I'll take you to a place where the paths are primrose-strewn and where nightingales sing," he promised rashly.

She smiled incredulously, a wise old little smile that had no right on her young face.

The report of the engagement spread at once. Bromfield took care of that. It ran like wildfire upstairs and down in the Whitford establishment. Naturally Johnnie, who was neither one of the servants nor a member of the family, was the last to hear of it. One day the word was

carried to him, and a few hours later he read the con-
firmation of it on the hand of his young mistress.

The Runt had the clairvoyance of love. He knew that
Clay was not now happy, though the cattleman gave no
visible sign of it except a certain quiet withdrawal into
himself. He ate as well as usual. His talk was cheerful.
He joked the puncher and made Kitty feel at home by
teasing her. In the evenings he shooed out the pair of
them to a moving-picture show and once or twice went
along. But he had a habit of falling into reflection, his
deep-set eyes fixed on some object he could not see.
Johnnie worried about him.

The evening of the day the Runt heard of the engagement he told his friend about it while Kitty was in the
kitchen.

"Miss Beatrice she's wearin' a new ring," he said by
way of breaking the news gently.

Clay turned his head slowly and looked at Johnnie.
He waited without speaking.

"I heerd it to-day from one of the help. Then I seen it
on her finger," the little man went on reluctantly.

"Bromfield?" asked Clay.

"Yep. That's the story."

"The ring was on the left hand?"

"Yep."

Clay made no comment. His friend knew enough to
say no more to him. Presently the cattleman went out.
It was in the small hours of the morning when he returned. He had been tramping the streets to get the fever
out of his blood.

But Johnnie discussed with Kitty at length this new

development, just as he had discussed with her the fact that Clay no longer went to see the Whitfords. Kitty made a shrewd guess at the cause of division. She had already long since drawn from the cowpuncher the story of how Miss Beatrice had rejected his proposal that she take an interest in her.

"They must 'a' quarreled — likely about me being here. I'm sorry you told her."

"I don't reckon that's it." Johnnie scratched his head to facilitate the process of thinking. He wanted to remain loyal to all of his three friends. "Miss Beatrice she's got too good judgment for that."

"I ought to go away. I'm only bringing Mr. Lindsay trouble. If he just could hear from his friends in Arizona about that place he's trying to get me, I'd go right off."

He looked at her wistfully. The bow-legged range-rider was in no hurry to have her go. She was the first girl who had ever looked twice at him, the first one he had ever taken out or talked nonsense with or been ordered about by in the possessive fashion used by the modern young woman. Hence he was head over heels in love.

Kitty had begun to bloom again. Her cheeks were taking on their old rounded contour and occasionally dimples of delight flashed into them. She was a young person who lived in the present. Already the marks of her six-weeks misery among the submerged derelicts of the city was beginning to be wiped from her mind like the memory of a bad dream from which she had awakened. Love was a craving of her happy, sensuous nature.

She wanted to live in the sun, among smiles and laughter. She was like a kitten in her desire to be petted, made much of, and admired. Almost anybody who liked her could win a place in her affection.

Johnnie's case was not so hopeless as he imagined it.

CHAPTER XX

THE CAUTIOUS GUY SLIPS UP

OVER their good-night smoke Clay gave a warning. "Keep yore eyes open, Johnnie. I was trailed to the house to-day by one of the fellows with Durand the night I called on him. It spells trouble. I reckon the 'Paches are going to leave the reservation again."

"Do you allow that skunk is aimin' to bushwhack you?"

"He's got some such notion. It's a cinch he ain't through with me yet."

"Say, Clay, ain't you gettin' homesick for the whinin' of a rawhide? Wha's the matter with us hittin' the dust for good old Tucson? I'd sure like to chase cowtails again."

"You can go, Johnnie. I'm not ready yet — quite. And when I go it won't be because of any rattlesnake in the grass."

"Whadyou mean I can go?" demanded his friend indignantly. "I don't aim to go and leave you here alone."

"Perhaps I'll be along, too, after a little. I'm about fed up on New York."

"Well, I'll stick around till you come. If this Jerry Durand's trying to get you I'll be right there followin' yore dust, old scout."

"There's more than one way to skin a cat. Mebbe the fellow means to strike at me through you or Kitty. I've a mind to put you both on a train for the B-in-a-Box Ranch."

"You can put the li'l' girl on a train. You can't put me on none less'n you go too," answered his shadow stoutly.

"Then see you don't get drawn into any quarrels while you and Kitty are away from the house. Stick to the lighted streets. I think I'll speak to her about not lettin' any strange man talk to her."

"She would n't talk to no strange man. She ain't that kind," snorted Johnnie.

"Keep yore shirt on," advised Clay, smiling. "What I mean is that she must n't let herself believe the first story some one pulls on her. I think she had better not go out unless one of us is with her."

"Suits me."

"I thought that might suit you. Well, stick to main-traveled roads and don't take any chances. If you get into trouble, yell bloody murder *poco pronto.*"

"And don't you take any, old-timer. That goes double. I'm the cautious guy in this outfit, not you."

Within twenty-four hours Clay heard some one pounding wildly on the outer door of the apartment and the voice of the cautious guy imploring haste.

"Lemme in, Clay. Hurry! Hurry!" he shouted.

Lindsay was at the door in four strides, but he did not need to see the stricken woe of his friend's face to guess what had occurred. For Johnnie and Kitty had started together to see a picture play two hours earlier.

"They done took Kitty — in an auto," he gasped. "Right before my eyes. Claimed a lady had fainted."

"Who took her?"

"I dunno. Some men. Turned the trick slick, me never liftin' a hand. Ain't I a heluva man?"

"Hold yore hawsses, son. Don't get excited. Begin at the beginnin' and tell me all about it," Clay told him quietly.

Already he was kicking off his house slippers and was reaching for his shoes.

"We was comin' home an' I took Kitty into that Red Star drug-store for to get her some ice cream. Well, right after that I heerd a man say how the lady had fainted —"

"What lady?"

"The lady in the machine."

"Were you in the drug-store?"

"No. We'd jes' come out when this here automobile drew up an' a man jumped out hollerin' the lady had fainted and would I bring a glass o' water from the drug-store. 'Course I got a jump on me and Kitty she moved up closeter to the car to he'p if she could. When I got back to the walk with the water the man was hoppin' into the car. It was already movin'. He slammed the door shut and it went up the street like greased lightnin'."

"Was it a closed car?"

"Uh-huh."

"Can you describe it?"

"Why, I dunno —"

"Was it black, brown, white?"

"Kinda roan-colored, looked like."

"Get the number?"

"No, I — I plumb forgot to look."

Clay realized that Johnnie's powers of observation were not to be trusted.

"Sure the car was n't tan-colored?" he asked to test him.

"It might 'a' been tan, come to think of it."

"You're right certain Kitty was in it?"

"I heerd her holler from inside. She called my name. I run after the car, but I could n't catch it."

Clay slipped a revolver under his belt. He slid into a street coat. Then he got police headquarters on the wire and notified the office of what had taken place. He knew that the word would be flashed in all directions and that a cordon would be stretched across the city to intercept any suspicious car. Over the telephone the desk man at headquarters fired questions at him, most of which he was unable to answer. He promised fuller particulars as soon as possible.

It had come on to rain and beneath the street lights the asphalt shone like a river. The storm had driven most people indoors, but as the Westerner drew near the drug-store Clay saw with relief a taxicab draw up outside. Its driver, crouched in his seat behind the waterproof apron as far back as possible from the rain, promptly accepted Lindsay as a fare.

"Back in a minute," Clay told him, and passed into the drug-store.

The abduction was still being discussed. There was a disagreement as to whether the girl had stepped voluntarily into the car or been lifted in by the man outside. This struck the cattleman as unimportant. He pushed home questions as to identification. One of the men in

the drug-store had caught a flash of the car number. He
was sure the first four figures were 3967. The fifth he did
not remember. The car was dark blue and it looked like
a taxi. This information Clay got the owner of the car to
forward to the police.

He did not wait to give it personally, but joined Johnnie in the cab. The address he gave to the driver with the
waterproof hat pulled down over his head was that of a
certain place of amusement known as Heath's Palace of
Wonders. A young woman he wanted to consult was
wont to sit behind a window there at the receipt of cus-
toms.

"It's worth a fiver extra if you make good time,"
Lindsay told the driver.

"You're on, boss," answered the man gruffly.

Johnnie, in a fever of anxiety, had trotted along beside his chief to the drug-store in silence. Now, as they
rushed across the city, he put a timid question with a
touch of bluff bravado he did not feel.

"We'll get her back sure, don't you reckon?"

"We'll do our best. Don't you worry. That won't buy
us anything."

"No — no, I ain't a-worryin' none, but — Clay, I'd
hate a heap for any harm to come to that li'l' girl." His
voice quavered.

"Sho! We're right on their heels, Johnnie. So are the
cops. We'll make a gather and get Kitty back all right."

Miss Annie Millikan's pert smile beamed through the
window at Clay when he stepped up.

"Hello, Mr. Flat-Worker," she sang out. "How
many?"

"I'm not going in to see the show to-night. I want to talk with you if you can get some one to take yore place here."

"Say, whatta you think I am — one o' these here Fift' Avenoo society dames? I'm earnin' my hot dogs and coffee right at this window. . . . Did you say two, lady?" She shoved two tickets through the window in exchange for dimes.

Clay explained that his business was serious. "I've got to see you alone — now," he added.

"If you gotta you gotta." The girl called an usher, who found a second usher to take her place.

Annie walked down the street a few steps beside Clay. The little puncher followed them dejectedly. His confidence had gone down to chill zero.

"What's the big idea in callin' me from me job in the rush hours?" asked Miss Millikan. "And who's this gumshoe guy from the bush league tailin' us? Breeze on and wise Annie if this here business is so important."

Clay told his story.

"Some of Jerry's strong-arm work," she commented.

"Must be. Can you help me?"

Annie looked straight at him, a humorous little quirk to her mouth. "Say, what're you askin' me to do — t'row down my steady?"

Which remark carries us back a few days to one sunny afternoon after Clay's midnight call when he had dropped round to see Miss Annie. They had walked over to Gramercy Park and sat down on a bench as they talked. Most men and all women trusted Clay. He had in him some quality of unspoken sympathy that drew

confidences. Before she knew it Annie found herself
telling him the story of her life.

Her father had been a riveter in a shipyard and had
been killed while she was a baby. Later her mother had
married unhappily a man who followed the night paths
of the criminal underworld. Afterward he had done time
at Sing Sing. Through him Annie had been brought for
years into contact with the miserable types that make
an illicit living by preying upon the unsuspecting in big
cities. Always in the little Irish girl there had been a
yearning for things clean and decent, but it is almost
impossible for the poor in a great city to escape from the
environment that presses upon them.

She was pretty, and inevitably she had lovers. One of
these was "Slim" Jim Collins, a confidential follower of
Jerry Durand. He was a crook, and she knew it. But some
quality in him — his good looks, perhaps, or his game-
ness — fascinated her in spite of herself. She avoided
him, even while she found herself pleased to go to Coney
with an escort so well dressed and so glibly confident.
Another of her admirers was a policeman, Tim Muldoon
by name, the same one that had rescued Clay from the
savagery of Durand outside the Sea Siren. Tim she
liked. But for all his Irish ardor he was wary. He had
never asked her to marry him. She thought she knew the
reason. He did not want for a wife a woman who had
been "Slim" Jim's girl. And Annie — because she was
Irish too and perverse — held her head high and went
with Collins openly before the eyes of the pained and
jealous patrolman.

Clay had come to Annie Millikan now because of

what she had told him about "Slim" Jim. This man was one of Durand's stand-bys. If there was any underground work to be done it was an odds-on chance that he would be in charge of it.

"I'm askin' you to stand by a poor girl that's in trouble," he said in answer to her question.

"You've soitainly got a nerve with you. I'll say you have. You want me to throw the hooks into Jim for a goil I never set me peepers on. I wisht I had your crust."

"You wouldn't let Durand spoil her life if you could stop it."

"Wouldn't I? Hmp! Soft-soap stuff. Well, what's my cue? Where do I come in on this rescue-the-be-eutiful heroine act?"

"When did you see 'Slim' Jim last?"

"I might 'a' seen him this afternoon an' I might not," she said cautiously, looking at him from under a broad hat-brim.

"When?"

"I didn't see him after I got behind that 'How Many?' sign. If I seen him must 'a' been before two."

"Did he give you any hint of what was in the air?"

"Say, what's the lay-out? Are you framin' Jim for up the river?"

"I'm tryin' to save Kitty."

"Because she's your goil. Where do I come in at? What's there in it for me to go rappin' me friend?" demanded Annie sharply.

"She's not my girl," explained Clay. Then, with that sure instinct that sometimes guided him, he added, "The young lady I — I'm in love with has just become engaged to another man."

Miss Millikan looked at him, frankly incredulous. "For the love o' Mike, where's her eyes? Don't she know a real man when she sees one? I'll say she don't."

"I'm standin' by Kitty because she's shy of friends. Any man would do that, would n't he? I came to you for help because — oh, because I know you're white clear through."

A flush beat into Annie's cheeks. She went off swiftly at a tangent. "Would n't it give a fellow a jar? This guy Jim Collins slips it to me confidential that he's off the crooked stuff. Nothin' doin' a-tall in gorilla work. He kids me that he's quit goin' out on the spud and porch-climbin' don't look good to him no more. A four-room flat, a little wifie, an' the straight road for 'Slim' Jim. I fall for it, though I'd orta be hep to men. An' he dates me up to-night for the chauffeurs' ball."

"But you did n't go?"

"No; he sidesteps it this aft with a fairy tale about drivin' a rich old dame out to Yonkers. All the time he was figurin' on pinchin' this goil for Jerry. He's a rotten crook."

"Why don't you break with him, Annie? You're too good for that sort of thing. He'll spoil your life if you don't."

"Listens fine," the girl retorted bitterly. "I take Jim like some folks do booze or dope. He's a habit."

"Tim's worth a dozen of him."

"Sure he is, but Tim's got a notion I'm not on the level. I dunno as he needs to pull that stuff on me. I'm not strong for a harness bull anyhow." She laughed, a little off the key.

"What color is 'Slim' Jim's car?"

"A dirty blue. Why?"

"That was the car."

Annie lifted her hands in a little gesture of despair. "I'm dead sick of this game. What's there in it? I live straight and eat in a beanery. No lobster palaces in mine. Look at me cheap duds. And Tim gives me the over like I was a street cat. What sort of a chance did I ever have, with toughs and gunmen for me friends?"

"You've got yore chance now, Annie. Tim will hop off that fence he's on and light a-runnin' straight for you if he thinks you've ditched 'Slim' Jim."

She shook her head slowly. "No, I'll not t'row Jim down. I'm through with him. He lied to me right while he knew this was all framed up. But I wouldn't snitch on him, even if he'd told me anything. And he didn't peep about what he was up to."

"Forget Jim while you're thinkin' about this. You don't owe Jerry Durand anything, anyhow. Where would he have Kitty taken? You can give a guess."

She had made her decision before she spoke. "Gimme paper and a pencil."

On Clay's notebook she scrawled hurriedly an address.

"Jim'd croak me if he knew I'd given this," she said, looking straight at the cattleman.

"He'll never know — and I'll never forget it, Annie."

Clay left her and turned to the driver. From the slip of paper in his hand he read aloud an address. "Another five if you break the speed limit," he said.

As Clay slammed the door shut and the car moved forward he had an impression of something gone wrong, of a cog in his plans slipped somewhere. For Annie, standing in the rain under a sputtering misty street light, showed a face stricken with fear.

Her dilated eyes were fixed on the driver of the taxicab.

CHAPTER XXI

AT THE HEAD OF THE STAIRS

THE cab whirled round the corner and speeded down a side street that stretched as far as they could see silent and deserted in the storm.

The rain, falling faster now, beat gustily in a slant against the left window of the cab. It was pouring in rivulets along the gutter beside the curb. Some sixth sense of safety — one that comes to many men who live in the outdoors on the untamed frontier — warned Clay that all was not well. He had felt that bell of instinct ring in him once at Juarez when he had taken a place at a table to play poker with a bad-man who had a grudge at him. Again it had sounded when he was about to sit down on a rock close to a crevice where a rattler lay coiled.

The machine had swung to the right and was facing from the wind instead of into it. Clay was not very well acquainted with New York, but he did know this was not the direction in which he wanted to go.

He beat with his knuckles on the front of the cab to attract the attention of the driver. In the swishing rain, and close to the throb of the engine, the chauffeur either did not or would not hear.

Lindsay opened the door and swung out on the running-board. "We're goin' wrong. Stop the car!" he ordered.

The man at the wheel did not turn. He speeded up.

His fare wasted no time in remonstrances. A moment, and the chauffeur threw on the brake sharply. His reason was a good one. The blue nose of a revolver was jammed hard against his ribs. He had looked round once to find out what it was prodding him. That was enough to convince him he had better stop.

Under the brake the back wheels skidded and brought up against the curb. Clay, hanging on by one hand, was flung hard to the sidewalk. The cab teetered, regained its equilibrium, gathered impetus with a snort, and leaped forward again.

As the cattleman clambered to his feet he caught one full view of the chauffeur's triumphant, vindictive face. He had seen it before, at a reception especially arranged for him by Jerry Durand one memorable night. It belonged to the more talkative of the two gunmen he had surprised at the pretended poker game. He knew, too, without being told that this man and "Slim" Jim Collins were one and the same. The memory of Annie's stricken face carried this conviction home to him.

The Arizonan picked up his revolver in time to see the car sweep around the next corner and laughed ruefully at his own discomfiture. He pushed a hand through the crisp, reddish waves of his hair.

"I don't reckon I'll ride in that taxi any farther. Johnnie will have to settle the bill. Hope he plays his hand better than I did," he said aloud.

The rain pelted down as he moved toward the brighter lighted street that intersected the one where he had been dropped. The lights of a saloon caught his eye at the corner. He went in, got police headquarters on the wire, and learned that a car answering the description of the one used by his abductor had been headed into Central Park by officers and that the downtown exits were being watched.

He drew what comfort he could from that fact.

Presently he picked up another taxi. He hesitated whether to go to the address Annie had given him or to join the chase uptown. Reluctantly, he decided to visit the house. His personal inclination was for the hunt rather than for inactive waiting, but he sacrificed any immediate chance of adventure for the sake of covering the possible rendezvous of the gang.

Clay paid his driver and looked at the house numbers as he moved up the street he wanted. He was in that part of the city from which business years ago marched uptown. Sometime in decades past people of means had lived behind these brownstone fronts. Many of the residences were used to keep lodgers in. Others were employed for less reputable purposes.

His overcoat buttoned to his neck, Clay walked without hesitation up the steps of the one numbered 243. He rang the bell and waited, his right hand on the pocket of his overcoat.

The door opened cautiously a few inches and a pair of close-set eyes in a wrinkled face gimleted Clay.

"Whadya want?"

"The old man sent me with a message," answered the Arizonan promptly.

"Spill it."

"Are you alone?"

"You *know* it."

"Got everything ready for the girl?"

"Say, who the hell are youse?"

"One of Slim's friends. Listen, we got the kid — picked her up at a drug-store."

"I don' know watcher fairy tale's about. If you gotta message come through with it."

Clay put his foot against the door to prevent it from being closed and drew his hand from the overcoat pocket. In the hand nestled a blue-nosed persuader.

Unless the eyes peering into the night were bad barometers of their owner's inner state, he was in a panic of fear.

"Love o' Gawd, d-don't shoot!" he chattered. "I ain't nobody but the caretaker."

He backed slowly away, followed by Lindsay. The barrel of the thirty-eight held his eyes fascinated. By the light of his flash Clay discovered the man to be a chalk-faced little inconsequent.

"Say, don't point that at me," the old fellow implored.

"Are you alone?"

"I told you I was."

"Is Jerry comin' himself with the others?"

"They don't none of them tell me nothin'. I'm nobody. I'm only Joey."

"Unload what you know. Quick. I'm in a hurry."

The man began a rambling, whining tale.

The Arizonan interrupted with questions, crisp and incisive. He learned that a room had been prepared on the second floor for a woman. Slim had made the arrangements. Joe had heard Durand's name mentioned, but knew nothing of the plans.

"I'll look the house over. Move along in front of me and don't make any mistakes. This six-gun is liable to permeate yore anatomy with lead."

The cattleman examined the first floor with an especial view to the exits. He might have to leave in a hurry. If so, he wanted to know where he was going. The plan of the second story was another point he featured as he passed swiftly from room to room. From the laundry in the basement he had brought up a coil of clothes-line. With this he tied Joe hand and foot. After gagging him, he left the man locked in a small rear room and took the key with him.

Clay knew that he was in a precarious situation. If Durand returned with Kitty and captured him here he was lost. The man would make no more mistakes. Certainly he would leave no evidence against him except that of his own tools. The intruder would probably not be killed openly. He would either simply disappear or he would be murdered with witnesses framed to show self-defense. The cattleman was as much outside the law as the criminals were. He had no legal business in this house. But one thing was fixed in his mind. He would be no inactive victim. If they got him at all it would be only after a fighting finish.

To Clay, standing at the head of the stairs, came a sound that stiffened him to a tense wariness. A key was being turned in the lock of the street door below. He moved back into the deeper shadows as the door swung open.

Two men entered. One of them cursed softly as he stumbled against a chair in the dark hall.

"Where's that rat Joe?" he demanded in a subdued voice.

Then came a click of the lock. The sound of the street rain ceased. Clay knew that the door had been closed and that he was shut in with two desperate criminals.

What have they done with Kitty? Why was she not with them? He asked himself that question even as he slipped back into a room that opened to the left.

He groped his way through the darkness, for he dared not flash his light to guide him. His fingers found the edge of a desk. Round that he circled toward a closet he remembered having noted. Already the men were tramping up the stairs. They were, he could tell, in a vile humor. From this he later augured hopefully that their plans had not worked out smoothly, but just now more imperative business called him.

His arm brushed the closet door. Next moment he was inside and had closed it softly behind him.

And none too soon. For into the room came the gunmen almost on his heels.

CHAPTER XXII

TWO MEN IN A LOCKED ROOM

"Jerry'll raise hell," a heavy voice was saying as they entered the room. "And that ain't all. We'll land in stir if we don't look out. We just ducked a bad fall. The bulls pretty near had us that time we poked our nose out from the Park at Seventy-Second Street."

Some one pressed a button and the room leaped to light. Through the open crack of the closed door Clay recognized Gorilla Dave. The second of the gunmen was out of range of his vision.

From the sound of creaking furniture Clay judged that the unseen man had sat down heavily. "It was that blowout queered us. And say — how came the bulls so hot on our trail? Who rapped to 'em?"

"Must 'a' been that boob wit' the goil. He got busy quick. Well, Jerry won't have to salve the cops this time. We made our getaway all right," said Dave.

"Say, where's Joey?"

"Pulled a sneak likely. Wha's it matter? Listen! What's that?"

Some one was coming up the stairs.

The men in the room moved cautiously to the door. The hall light was switched on.

"'Lo, Jerry," Gorilla Dave called softly.

He closed the room door and the sound of the voices was shut off instantly.

The uninvited guest dared not step out of the closet

to listen, for at any instant the men might reënter. He crouched in his hiding-place, the thirty-eight in his hand.

The minutes dragged interminably. More than once Clay almost made up his mind to steal out to learn what the men were doing. But his judgment told him he must avoid a brush with so many if possible.

The door opened again.

"Now beat it and do as I say if you know what's good for you," a bullying voice was ordering.

The owner of the voice came in and slammed the door behind him. He sat down at the desk, his back to the closet. Through the chink Clay saw that the man was Jerry Durand.

From his vest pocket he took a fat black cigar, struck a match and lit it. He slumped down in the swivel chair. It took no seer to divine that his mind was busy working out a problem.

Clay stepped softly from his place of refuge, but not so noiselessly that the gangman did not detect his presence. Jerry swung round in the chair and leaped up with cat-like activity. He stood without moving, poised on the balls of his feet, his deep-set eyes narrowed to shining slits. It was in his thought to hurl himself headlong on the man holding steadily the menacing revolver.

"Don't you! I've got the dead wood on you," said the Arizonan, a trenchant saltness in his speech. "I'll shoot you down sure as hell's hot."

The eyes of the men clashed, measuring each the other's strength of will. They were warily conscious even of the batting of an eyelid. Durand's face wore an ugly look of impotent malice, but his throat was dry as a lime kiln. He could not estimate the danger that confronted him nor what lay back of the man's presence.

"What you doin' here?" he demanded.

"Makin' my party call," retorted Clay easily.

Jerry cursed him with a low, savage stream of profanity. The gangman enraged was not a sight pleasing to see.

"I reckon heaven, hell, and high water could n't keep you from cussin' now. Relieve yore mind proper, Mr. Durand. Then we'll talk business," murmured Clay in the low, easy drawl that never suggested weakness.

The ex-prize-fighter's flow of language dried up. He fell silent and stood swallowing his furious rage. It had come home to him that this narrow-flanked young fellow with the close-gripped jaw and the cool, steady eyes was entirely unmoved by his threats.

"Quite through effervescing?" asked Clay contemptuously.

The gang leader made no answer. He chose to nurse his venom silently.

"Where's Kitty Mason?"

Still no answer.

"I asked you what you've done with Kitty Mason?"

"What's that to you?"

"I'm close-herdin' that li'l' girl and I'll not have yore dirty hands touch her. Where is she?"

"That's my business."

"By God, you'll tell, or I'll tear it out of you!"

Clay backed to the door, found the key, transferred it to the inner side of the lock, turned it, and put it in his pocket.

The cornered gangman took a chance. He ducked for the shelter of the desk, tore open a drawer, and snatched out an automatic.

Simultaneously the cowpuncher pressed the button beside the door and plunged the room in darkness. He side-stepped swiftly and without noise.

A flash of lightning split the blackness.

Clay dropped to his knees and crawled away. Another bolt, with its accompanying roar, flamed out.

Still the Westerner did not fire in answer, though he knew just where the target for his bullet was. A plan had come to him. In the blackness of that room one might empty his revolver and not score a hit. To wait was to take a chance of being potted, but he did not want the death of even such a ruffian as Durand on his soul.

The crash of the automatic and the rattle of glass filled the room. Jerry, blazing away at some fancied sound, had shattered the window.

Followed a long silence. Durand had changed his tactics and was resolved to wait until his enemy grew restless and betrayed himself.

The delay became a test of moral stamina. Each man knew that death was in that room lying in wait for him. The touch of a finger might send it flying across the floor. Upon the mantel a clock ticked maddeningly, the only sound to be heard.

The contest was not one of grit, but of that unflawed nerve which is so much the result of perfect physical fitness. Clay's years of clean life on the desert counted heavily now. He was master of himself, though his mouth was dry as a whisper and there were goose quills on his flesh.

But Durand, used to the fetid atmosphere of bar-rooms and to the soft living of the great city, found his nerve beginning to crack under the strain. Cold drops stood out on his forehead and his hands shook from excitement and anxiety. What kind of a man was his enemy to lie there in the black silence and not once give a sign of where he was, in spite of crashing bullets? There was something in it hardly human. For the first time in his life Jerry feared he was up against a better man.

Was it possible that he could have killed the fellow at the first shot? The comfort of this thought whispered hope in the ear of the ex-prize-fighter.

A chair crashed wildly. Durand fired again and yet again, his nerves giving way to a panic that carried him to swift action. He could not have stood another moment without screaming.

There came the faint sound of a hand groping on the wall and immediately after a flood of light filled the room.

Clay stood by the door. His revolver covered the crouching gang leader. His eyes were hard and piti-less.

"Try another shot," he advised ironically.

Jerry did. A harmless click was all the result he got. He knew now that the cowman had tempted him to waste his last shots at a bit of furniture flung across the room.

"You'll tell me what you did with Kitty Mason," said Clay in his low, persuasive voice, just as though

there had been no intermission of flying bullets since he
had mentioned the girl before.

"You can't kill me, when I have n't a loaded gun,"
Durand answered between dry lips.

The other man nodded an admission of the point.
"That's an advantage you've got of me. You could kill
me if I did n't have a gun, because you're a yellow wolf.
But I can't kill you. That's right. But I can beat hell
out of you, and I'm sure goin' to do it."

"Talk's cheap, when you've got a loaded six-gun in
your fist," jeered Jerry.

With a flirt of his hand Clay tossed the revolver to the
top of a book-case, out of easy reach of a man standing
on the floor. He ripped open the buttons of his overcoat
and slipped out of it, then moved forward with elastic
step.

"It's you or me now, Jerry Durand."

The prize-fighter gave a snort of derisive triumph.
"You damn fool! I'll eat you alive."

"Mebbeso. I reckon my system can assimilate any
whalin' you're liable to hand me. Go to it."

Durand had the heavy shoulders and swelling muscles
that come from years of training for the ring. Like most
pugilists out of active service he had taken on flesh. But
the extra weight was not fat, for Jerry kept always in
good condition. He held his leadership partly at least
because of his physical prowess. No tough in New York
would willingly have met him in rough-and-tumble
fight.

The younger man was more slightly built. He was a
Hermes rather than a Hercules. His muscles flowed.

They did not bulge. But when he moved it was with the litheness of a panther. The long lines of shoulder and loin had the flow of tigerish grace. The clear eyes in the brown face told of a soul indomitable in a perfectly synchronized body.

Durand lashed out with a swinging left, all the weight of his body behind the blow. Clay stepped back, shot a hard straight right to the cheek, and ducked the counter. Jerry rushed him, flailing at his foe blow on blow, intending to wear him out by sheer hard hammering. He butted with head and knee, used every foul trick he had learned in his rotten trade of prize-fighting. Active as a wild cat, the Arizonan side-stepped, scored a left on the eye, ducked again, and fought back the furious attack.

The gangman came out of the rally winded, perplexed, and disturbed. His cheek was bleeding, one eye was in distress, and he had hardly touched his agile opponent.

He rushed again. Nothing but his temper, the lack of self-control that made him see red and had once put him at the mercy of a first-class ring general with stamina and a punch, had kept Jerry out of a world championship. He had everything else needed, but he was the victim of his own passion. It betrayed him now. His fighting was that of a wild cave man, blind, furious, damaging. He threw away his science and his skill in order to destroy the man he hated. He rained blows on him — fought him with head and knee and fist, was on top of him every moment, controlled by one dominating purpose to make that dancing figure take the dust.

How Clay weathered the storm he did not know. Some blows he blocked, others he side-stepped, a few he took on face and body. He was cool, quite master of himself. Before the fight had gone three minutes he knew that, barring a chance blow, some foul play, or a bit of bad luck, he would win. He was covering up, letting the pugilist wear himself out, and taking only the punishment he must. But he was getting home some heavy body blows that were playing the mischief with Jerry's wind.

The New Yorker, puffing like a sea lion, came out of a rally winded and spent. Instantly Clay took the offensive. He was a trained boxer as well as a fighter, and he had been taught how to make every ounce of his weight count. Ripping in a body blow as a feint, he brought down Durand's guard. A straight left crashed home between the eyes and a heavy solar plexus shook the man to the heels.

Durand tried to close with him. An uppercut jolted him back. He plunged forward again. They grappled, knocking over chairs as they threshed across the room. When they went down Clay was underneath, but as they struck the floor he whirled and landed on top.

The man below fought furiously to regain his feet. Clay's arm worked like a piston rod with short-arm jolts against the battered face.

A wild heave unseated the Arizonan. They clinched, rolled over and bumped against the wall, Clay again on top. For a moment Durand got a thumb in his foe's eye and tried to gouge it out. Clay's fingers found the throat of the gang leader and tightened. Jerry struggled to free himself, catching at the sinewy wrist with both hands. He could not break the iron grip. Gasping for breath, he suddenly collapsed.

Clay got to his feet and waited for Durand to rise. His enemy rolled over and groaned.

"Had enough?" demanded the Westerner.

No answer came, except the heavy, irregular breathing of the man on the floor who was clawing for air in his lungs.

"I'll ask you once more where Kitty Mason is. And you'll tell me unless you want me to begin on you all over again."

The beaten pugilist sat up, leaning against the wall. He spoke with a kind of heavy despair, as though the words were forced out of him. He felt ashamed and disgraced by his defeat. Life for him had lost its savor, for he had met his master.

"She — got away."

"How?"

"They turned her loose, to duck the bulls," came the slow, sullen answer.

"Where?"

"In Central Park."

Probably this was the truth, Clay reflected. He could take the man's word or not as he pleased. There was no way to disprove it now.

He recovered his revolver, threw the automatic out of the window, and walked to the door.

"Joe's tied up in a back room," he said over his shoulder.

Thirty seconds later Clay stepped into the street. He

walked across to a subway station and took an uptown train.

Men looked at him curiously. His face was bruised and bleeding, his clothes disheveled, his hat torn. Clay grinned and thought of the old answer:

"They'd ought to see the other man."

One young fellow, apparently a college boy, who had looked upon the wine when it was red, was moved to come over and offer condolence.

"Say, I don't want to butt in or anything, but — he did n't do a thing to you, did he?"

"I hit the edge of a door in the dark," explained Clay solemnly.

"That door must have had several edges." The youth made a confidential admission. "I've got an edge on myself, sort of."

"Not really?" murmured Clay politely.

"Surest thing you know. Say, was it a good scrap?"

"I'd hate to mix in a better one."

"Wish I'd been there." The student fumbled for a card. "Did n't catch your name?"

Clay had no intention of giving his name just now to any casual stranger. He laughed and hummed the chorus of an old range ditty:

> "I'm a poor lonesome cowboy,
> I'm a poor lonesome cowboy,
> I'm a poor lonesome cowboy,
>   And a long way from home."

CHAPTER XXIII

JOHNNIE COMES INTO HIS OWN

WHEN Clay shot off at a tangent from the car and ceased to function as a passenger, Johnnie made an effort to descend and join his friend, but already the taxi was traveling at a speed that made this dangerous. He leaned out of the open door and shouted to the driver.

"Say, lemme out, doggone you. I wantta get out right here."

The chauffeur paid not the least attention to him. He skidded round a corner, grazing the curb, and put his foot on the accelerator. The car jumped forward.

The passenger, about to drop from the running-board, changed his mind. He did not want to break a bone or two in the process of alighting.

" 'F you don't lemme off right away I'll not pay you a cent for the ride," Johnnie shouted. "You got no right to pack me off thisaway."

The car was sweeping down the wet street, now and again skidding dangerously. The puncher felt homesick for the security of an outlaw bronco's back. This wild East was no place for him. He had been brought up in a country where life is safe and sane and its inhabitants have a respect for law. Tame old Arizona just now made a big appeal to one of its sons.

The machine went drunkenly up the street, zigzagging like a homeward-bound reveler. It swung into Fourth Avenue, slowing to take the curve. At the widest sweep of the arc Johnnie stepped down. His feet slid from under him and he rolled to the curb across the wet asphalt. Slowly he got up and tested himself for broken bones. He was sure he had dislocated a few hips and it took him some time to persuade himself he was all right, except for some bruises.

But Johnnie free had no idea what to do. He was as helpless as Johnnie imprisoned in the flying cab. Of what Clay's plan had been he had not the remotest idea. Yet he could not go home and do nothing. He must keep searching. But where? One thing stuck in his mind. His friend had mentioned that he would like to get a chance to call the police to find out whether Kitty had been rescued. He was anxious on that point himself. At the first cigar-store he stopped and was put on the wire with headquarters. He learned that a car supposed to be the one wanted had been driven into Central Park by the police a few minutes earlier.

Johnnie's mind carried him on a straight line to the simplest decision. He ran across to Fifth Avenue and climbed into a bus going uptown. If Kitty was in Central Park that was the place to search for her. It did not occur to him that by the time he reached there the car of the abductors would be miles away, nor did he stop to think that his chances of finding her in the wooded re- cesses of the Park would not be worth the long end of a hundred to one bet.

At the Seventy-Second Street entrance Johnnie left the bus and plunged into the Park. He threaded his way along walks beneath the dripping trees. He took a dozen shower baths under water-laden shrubbery. Sometimes he stopped to let out the wild war-whoop with which he turned cattle at the point in the good old days a month or so ago.

The gods are supposed to favor fools, children, and drunken men. Johnnie had been all of these in his day. To-night he could claim no more than one at most of these reasons for a special dispensation. He would be twenty-three "comin' grass," as he would have expressed it, and he had n't taken a drink since he came to New York, for Clay had voted himself dry years ago and just now he carried his follower with him.

But the impish gods who delight in turning upside down the best-laid plans of mice and men were working overtime to-night. They arranged it that a girl cowering among the wet bushes bordering an unfrequented path heard the "Hi — yi — yi" of Arizona and gave a faint cry for help. That call reached Johnnie and brought him on the run.

A man beside the girl jumped up with a snarl, gun in hand.

But the Runt had caught a sight of Kitty. A file of fixed bayonets could not have kept him from trying to rescue her. He dived through the brush like a football tackler.

A gun barked. The little man did not even know it. He and the thug went down together, rolled over, clawed furiously at each other, and got to their feet simultaneously. But the cowpuncher held the gun now. The crook glared at him for a moment, and bolted for the safety of the bushes in wild flight.

Johnnie fired once, then forgot all about the private

little war he had started. For his arms were full of a sobbing Kitty who clung to him while she wept and talked and exclaimed all in a breath.

"I knew you'd come, Johnnie. I knew you would — you or Clay. They left me here with him while they got away from the police. . . . Oh, I've been so scared. I did n't know — I thought —"

"'S all right. 'S all right, li'l' girl. Don't you cry, Kitty. Me 'n' Clay won't let 'em hurt you none. We sure won't."

"They said they'd come back later for me," she wept, uncertain whether to be hysterical or not.

"I wisht they'd come now," he bragged valorously, and for the moment he did.

She nestled closer, and Johnnie's heart lost a beat. He had become aware of a dull pain in the shoulder and of something wet trickling down his shoulder. But what is one little bullet in your geography when the sweetest girl in the world is in your arms?

"I ain't nothin' but a hammered-down li'l' hayseed of a cowpuncher," he told her, his voice trembling, "an' you're awful pretty an' — an' —"

A flag of color fluttered to her soft cheeks. The silken lashes fell shyly. "I think you're fine and dandy, the bravest man that ever was."

"Do you — figure you could —? I — I — I don't reckon you could ever —"

He stopped, abashed. To him this creature of soft curves was of heaven-sent charm. All the beauty and vitality of her youth called to him. It seemed to Johnnie that God spoke through her. Which is another way of saying that he was in love with her.

She made a rustling little stir in his arms and lifted a flushed face very tender and appealing. In the darkness her lips slowly turned to his.

Johnnie chose that inopportune moment to get sick at the stomach.

"I — I'm goin' to faint," he announced, and did.

When he returned to his love-story Johnnie's head was in Kitty's lap and a mounted policeman was in the foreground of the scene. His face was wet from the mist of fine rain falling.

"Don't move. Some one went for a car," she whispered, bending over him so that flying tendrils of her hair brushed his cheek. "Are you — badly hurt?"

He snorted. "I'm a false alarm. Nothin' a-tall. He jes' creased me."

"You're so brave," she cried admiringly.

He had never been told this before. He suspected it was not true, but to hear her say it was manna to his hungry soul.

The policeman helped him into a taxicab after first aid had been given and Johnnie's diagnosis verified. On the way home the cowpuncher made love. He discovered that this can be done quite well with one arm, both parties being willing.

The cab stopped at the house of a doctor and the shoulder was dressed. The doctor made one pardonable mistake.

"Get your wife to give you this sleeping powder if you find you can't sleep," he said.

"Y'betcha," answered Johnnie cheerfully.

Kitty looked at him reproachfully and blushed. She

scolded him about it after they reached the apartment where they lived.

Her new fiancé defended himself. "He's only a day or two prema-chure, honey. It was n't hardly worth while explainin'," he claimed.

"A day or two. Oh, Johnnie!"

"Sure. I ain't gonna wait. Wha's the matter with to-morrow?"

"I have n't any clothes made," she evaded, and added by way of diversion, "I always liked that kinda golden down on your cheeks."

"The stores are full of 'em. An' we ain't talkin' about my whiskers — not right now."

"You're a nice old thing," she whispered, flashing into unexpected dimples, and she rewarded him for his niceness in a way he thought altogether desirable.

A crisp, strong step sounded outside. The door opened and Clay came into the room.

He looked at Kitty. "Thank Heaven, you're safe," he said.

"Johnnie rescued me," she cried. "He got shot — in the shoulder."

The men looked at each other.

"Bad, Johnnie?"

"Nope. A plumb li'l' scratch. Wha's the matter with you?"

A gleam of humor flitted into the eyes of the cattle-man. "I ran into a door."

"Say, Clay," Johnnie burst out, "I'll betcha can't guess."

His friend laughed in amiable derision. "Oh, you

kids in the woods. I knew it soon as I opened the door."

He walked up to the girl and took her hand. "You got a good man, Kitty. I'm wishin' you all the joy in the world."

Her eyes flashed softly. "Don't I know I've got a good man, and I'm going to be happier than I deserve."

CHAPTER XXIV

CLAY LAYS DOWN THE LAW

TIM MULDOON, in his shirt-sleeves, was busy over a late breakfast when his mother opened the door of the flat to let in Clay Lindsay.

The policeman took one look at the damaged face and forgot the plate of ham and eggs that had just been put before him.

"Yuh've been at it again!" he cried, his Irish eyes lighting up with anticipatory enjoyment.

"I had a little set-to with friend Jerry last night," the Westerner explained.

"Another?"

"Now don't you blame me. I'm a peaceful citizen — not lookin' for trouble a li'l' bit. But I don't aim to let this Durand comb my hair with a rake."

"What's the trouble now?"

"You heard about the girl abducted in an auto from the Bronx?"

"Uh-huh! Was Jerry in that?"

"He was. I'll tell you the whole story, Tim."

"Meet my mother first. Mother — Mr. Lindsay. Yuh've heard me talk av him."

Mrs. Muldoon's blue Irish eyes twinkled. She was a plump and ample woman, and her handshake was firm and strong.

"I have that. Tim thinks yuh a wonder, Mr. Lindsay."

"Oh, he's prejudiced. You see he does n't like the **Big Mogul Jerry**."

"Well, he's sure a booster for yuh."

Clay told the story of his encounter with Durand on the train and of his subsequent meetings with him at the Sea Siren and on the night of the poker party. He made elisions and emendations that removed the bedroom scene from the tale.

"So that's when yuh met Annie Millikan," Tim said. "I was wonderin' how yuh knew her."

"That's when I met her. She's one fine girl, Tim, a sure-enough thoroughbred. She has fought against heavy odds all her life to keep good and honest. And she's done it."

"She has that," agreed Mrs. Muldoon heartily. "Annie is a good girrl. I always liked her."

"I'd bet my last chip on Annie. So last night I went straight to her. She would n't throw down 'Slim' Jim, but she gave me an address. I went there and met Durand."

"With his gang?" asked Tim.

"No; I waited till they had gone. I locked myself in a room alone with him. He took eight shots at me in the dark and then we mixed."

"Mother o' Moses!" exclaimed the policeman. "In the dark?"

"No. I had switched the lights on."

"You bate him! I can see it in your eye!" cried Muldoon, pounding the table so that the dishes jumped.

"You'll have to ask him about that." Clay passed to more important facts. "When I reached home Kitty was there. They had dropped her in the Park to make a safe getaway."

"That's good."

"But Tim — when Annie Millikan gave me the address where Jerry Durand was, the driver of my taxi saw her. The man was 'Slim' Jim."

Muldoon sat up, a serious look on his face. "Man, yuh spilt the beans that time. How'd you ever come to do it? They'll take it out on Annie, the dogs." The eyes of the policeman blazed.

"Unless we stand by her."

"Sure, and we'll do that. But how?"

"First we've got to get her away from there to some decent place where she'll be safe."

Mrs. Muldoon spoke up. "And that's easy. She'll just take our spare bedroom and welcome."

Tim put an arm caressingly over his mother's shoulders. "Ain't she the best little sport ever, Mr. Lindsay?" he said proudly.

Clay smiled. "She sure enough grades 'way up."

"It's blarney yuh're both talkin'," snorted Mrs. Muldoon. "Sure the girrl needs a mother and a home. An' I don't doubt she'll pay her way."

"Then that's settled. Will you see Annie, Tim? Or shall I?"

"We'll both see her. But there's another thing. Will she be safe here?"

"I'm goin' to have a talk with 'Slim' Jim and try to throw a scare into him. I'll report to you what he says."

They took a trolley to the lodging-house where Annie lived.

The girl looked pale and tired. Clay guessed she had slept little. The memory of "Slim" Jim's snarling face had stood out in the darkness at the foot of her bed.

"Is this a pinch?" she asked Tim with a pert little tilt to her chin.

"Yuh can call it that, Annie. Mother wants yuh to come and stay with us."

"And what would I do that for, Mr. Tim Muldoon?" she asked promptly, the color flushing her cheeks.

"Because you're not safe here. That gang will make yuh pay somehow for what yuh did."

"And if your mother took me in they'd make her pay. You'd maybe lose your job."

"I'd find another. I'm thinkin' of quittin' anyhow."

"Say, whadya think I am? I'll not go. I can look out for myself."

"I don't think they'd get Tim," put in Clay. "I'm goin' to see Collins and have a talk with him."

"You can't salve Jim with soft soap."

"Did I mention soft soap?"

"I heard some one most killed Jerry Durand last night," said Annie abruptly, staring at Lindsay's bruised face. "Was it you?"

"Yes," said the Arizonan simply.

"Did you get the girl?"

"They dropped her to save themselves. My friend found her with a man and took her from him."

"I hope you did up Jerry right!" cried Annie, a vindictive flash in her dark eyes.

"I haven't called him up this mo'nin' to see how he's feelin'," said Clay whimsically. "Miss Annie, we're

worried some about you. Mrs. Muldoon is right anxious
for us to get you to come and stay awhile with her. She's
honin' to have a li'l' girl to mother. Don't you reckon
you can go?"

"I — I wish yuh'd come, Annie," blurted out Tim.
looking down his nose.

Tears brimmed in Annie's eyes. To Clay it seemed
there was something hungry in the look the girl gave
Muldoon. She did not want his pity alone. She would
not have their hospitality if they were giving it to a girl
they despised and wanted to reform.

"I'm an alley cat you're offerin' to take in and feed,
Tim Muldoon," she charged suspiciously.

"Yuh're the girl — my mother loves." He choked on
the impulsive avowal he had almost made and finished
the sentence awkwardly. It was impossible for him to
escape the natural male instinct to keep his feelings out
of words.

The girl's face softened. Inside, she was a river of tenderness flowing toward the Irishman. "I'll go to your
mother, Tim, if she really wants me," she cried almost in
a murmur.

"You're shoutin' now, Miss Annie," said Clay, smiling. "She sure wants you. I'll hit the trail to have that
talk with Jim Collins."

He found "Slim" Jim at his stand. That flashily
dressed young crook eyed him with a dogged and wary
defiance. He had just come from a call at the bedside of
Jerry Durand and he felt a healthy respect for the man
who could do what this light-stepping young fellow had
done to the champion rough-houser of New York. The

story Jerry had told was of an assault from behind with a club, but this Collins did not accept at par. There were too many bruises on his sides and cuts on his face to be accounted for in any way except by a hard toe-to-toe fight.

"Mo'nin', Mr. Collins. I left you in a hurry last night and forgot to pay my bill. What's the damage?" asked Clay in his gently ironic drawl.

"Slim" Jim growled something the meaning of which was drowned in an oath.

"You say it was a free ride? Much obliged. That's sure fair enough," Clay went on easily. "Well, I did n't come to talk to you about that. I've got other business with you this mo'nin'."

The chauffeur looked at him sullenly and silently.

"Suppose we get inside the cab where we can talk comfortably," Clay proposed.

"Say, I'll stay right where I'm at," announced "Slim" Jim.

The cattleman opened the cab door. "Oh, no, we'll go inside," he said softly.

The men looked at each other and battled. The eye is a more potent weapon than the rapier. The shallow, shifty ones of the gunman fell before the deep, steady ones of the Arizonan. "Slim" Jim, with a touch of swagger to save his face, stepped into the cab and sat down. Clay followed him, closing the door.

"Have you seen Jerry Durand this sunny mo'nin'?" asked Lindsay with surface amiability.

"Wot's it to you?" demanded Collins.

"Not a thing. Nothin' a-tall," agreed Clay. "But it

may be somethin' to you. I'm kinda wonderin' whether
I'll have to do to you what I did to him."

"Slim" Jim was not a man of his hands. He could use
a gun on occasion, if the advantage was all in his favor,
but he strictly declined personal encounters at closer
quarters. Now he reached for the door hastily.

A strong, sinewy hand fell on his arm and tightened,
slightly twisting the flesh as the fingers sank deeper.

Collins let out a yell. "Gawd! Don't do that. You're
killin' me."

"Beg yore pardon. An accident. If I get annoyed
I'm liable to hurt without meanin' to," apologized
Clay suavely. "I'll come right down to brass tacks,
Mr. Collins. You're through with Annie Millikan. Under-
stand?"

"Say, wot t'ell's this stuff you're pipin'? Who d' you
t'ink youse are?"

"Never mind who I am. You'll keep away from Annie
from now on — absolutely. If you bother her — if anything happens to her — well, you go and take a good
long look at Durand before you make any mistakes."

"You touch me an' I'll croak you. See!" hissed Collins. "It won't be rough-house stuff with me. I'll fix
youse so the gospel sharks'll sing gather-at-the-river for
you."

"A gun-play?" asked Clay pleasantly. "Say, there's
a shootin'-gallery round the corner. Come along. I
wantta show you somethin'."

"Aw, go to hell!"

The sinewy hand moved again toward the aching

muscles of the gunman. Collins changed his mind hurriedly.

"All right. I'll come," he growled.

Clay tossed a dollar down on the counter, took a .22, and aimed at the row of ducks sailing across the gallery pool. Each duck went down as it appeared. He picked up a second rifle and knocked over seven or eight mice as they scampered across the target screen. With a third gun he snuffed the flaming eye from the right to the left side of the face that grinned at him, then with another shot sent it back again. He smashed a few clay pipes by way of variety. To finish off with he scored six center shots in a target and rang a bell each time. Not one single bullet had failed to reach its mark.

The New York gunman had never seen such speed and accuracy. He was impressed in spite of the insolent sneer that still curled his lip.

"Got a six-shooter — a fohty-five?" asked Clay of the owner of the gallery.

"No."

"Sorry. I'm not much with a rifle, but I'm a good average shot with a six-gun. I kinda take to it natural."

They turned and walked back to the cab. Collins fell into the Bowery strut.

"'Tryin' to throw a scare into me," he argued feebly.

"Me? Oh, no. You mentioned soft music and the preacher. Mebbeso. But it's liable to be for you if you monkey with the buzz-saw. I'm no gun-sharp, but no man who can't empty a revolver in a shade better than two seconds and put every bullet inside the rim of a cup at fifteen yards wants to throw lead at me. You see, I hang up my hat in Arizona. I grew up with a six-gun by my side."

"I should worry. This is little old New York, not Arizona," the gangman answered.

"That's what yore boss Durand thought. What has it brought him but trouble? Lemme give you something to chew on. New York's the biggest city of the biggest, freest country on God's green footstool. You little sewer rats pull wires and think you run it. Get wise, you poor locoed gink. You run it about as much as that fly on the wheel of yore taxi drives the engine. Durand's the whole works by his way of it, but when some one calls his bluff see where he gets off."

"He ain't through with you yet," growled "Slim" Jim sulkily.

"Mebbe not, but you — you're through with Annie." Clay caught him by the shoulder and swung him round. His eyes bored chilly into the other man. "Don't you forget to remember not to forget that. Let her alone. Don't go near her or play any tricks to hurt her. Lay off for good. If you don't — well, you'll pay heavy. I'll be on the job personal to collect."

Clay swung away and strode down the street, light-heeled and lithe, the sap of vital youth in every rippling muscle.

"Slim" Jim watched him, snarling hatred. If ever he got a good chance at him it would be curtains for the guy from Arizona, he swore savagely.

CHAPTER XXV

JOHNNIE SAYS HE IS MUCH OBLIGED

BEATRICE, just back from riding with Bromfield, stood on the steps in front of the grilled door and stripped the gloves from her hands.

"I'm on fire with impatience, Bee," he told her. "I can hardly wait for that three weeks to pass. The days drag when I'm not with you."

He was standing a step or two below her, a graceful, well-groomed figure of ease, an altogether desirable catch in the matrimonial market. His dark hair, parted in the middle, was beginning to thin, and tiny crow's-feet radiated from the eyes, but he retained the light, slim figure of youth. It ought not to be hard to love Clarendon Bromfield, his fiancée reflected. Yet he disappointingly failed to stir her pulses.

She smiled with friendly derision. "Poor Clary! You don't *look* like a Vesuvius ready to erupt. You have such remarkable self-control."

His smile met hers. "I can't go up and down the street ringing a bell like a town crier and shouting it out to everybody I meet."

Round the corner of the house a voice was lifted in tuneless song.

> "Oh, I'm goin' home
> Bull-whackin' for to spurn;
> I ain't got a nickel,
> And I don't give a dern.

> 'T is when I meet a pretty girl,
> You bet I will or try,
>   I'll make her my little wife,
> Root hog or die."

"You see Johnnie is n't ashamed to shout out his good intentions," she said.

"Johnnie is n't engaged to the loveliest creature under heaven. He does n't have to lie awake nights for fear the skies will fall and blot him out before his day of bliss."

Beatrice dropped a little curtsy. She held out her hand in dismissal. "Till to-morrow, Clary."

As Bromfield turned away, Johnnie came round a corner of the house dragging a garden hose. He was attacking another stanza of the song:

> "There's hard times on old Bitter Creek
>   That never can be beat.
> It was root hog or die
> Under every wagon sheet.
> We cleared up all the Indians,
> Drank . . . "

The puncher stopped abruptly at sight of his mistress.

"What did you drink that has made you so happy this morning, Johnnie?" she asked lightly.

The cowpuncher's secret burst from him. "I done got married, Miss Beatrice."

"You — what?"

"I up and got married day before yesterday," he beamed.

"And who's the happy girl?"

"Kitty Mason. We jes' walked to the church round

the corner. Clay he stood up with us and give the bride away. It's me 'n' her for Arizona *poco pronto*."

Beatrice felt a queer joyous lift inside her as of some weight that had gone. In a single breath Johnnie had blown away the mists of misunderstanding that for weeks had clouded her vision. Her heart went out to Clay with a rush of warm emotion. The friend she had distrusted was all she had ever believed him. He was more — a man too stanch to desert under pressure any one who had even a slight claim on him.

"I want to meet her. Will you bring her to see me this afternoon, Johnnie?" she asked.

His face was one glad grin. "I sure will. Y'betcha, by jollies."

He did.

To Beatrice, busy writing a letter, came Jenkins some hours later.

"A young — person — to see you, Miss Whitford." He said it with a manner so apologetic that it stressed his opinion of the social status of the visitor.

"What kind of a person?"

"A young woman, Miss. From the country, I tyke it."

"She did n't give you a card?"

"No, Miss. She came with the person Mr. Whitford took on to 'elp with the work houtside."

"Oh! Show them both up. And have tea sent in, Jenkins."

Kitty's shy eyes lifted apprehensively to those of this slim young patrician so beautifully and simply gowned. Instantly her fears fled. Beatrice moved swiftly to her with both hands outstretched.

"I'm so glad to meet you."

She kissed the young wife with unaccustomed tenderness. For the Colorado girl had about her a certain
modesty that was disarming, an appeal of helplessness
Beatrice could not resist.

Kitty, in the arms of her hostess, wept a few tears.
She had been under a strain in anticipating the ordeal of
meeting Johnnie's mistress, and she had discovered her
to be a very sweet, warm-hearted girl.

As for Johnnie, he had a miserably happy half-hour.
He had brought his hat in with him and he did not know
how to dispose of it. What he did do was to keep it
revolving in his hands. This had to be abandoned when
Miss Whitford handed him a quite unnecessary cup of
tea and a superfluous plate of toasted English muffins.
He wished his hands had not been so big and red and
freckled. Also he had an uncomfortable suspicion that
his tow hair was tousled and uncombed in spite of his
attempts at home to plaster it down.

He declined sugar and cream because for some reason
it seemed easier to say "No'm" than "Yes," though he
always took both with tea. And he disgraced himself by
scalding his tongue and failing to suppress the pain.
Finally the plate, with his muffin, carefully balanced on
his knee, from some devilish caprice plunged over the
precipice to the carpet and the bit of china broke.

Whereupon Kitty gently reproved him, as was her
wifely duty.

"I ain't no society fellow," the distressed puncher
explained to his hostess, tiny beads of perspiration on
his forehead.

Beatrice had already guessed as much, but she did not admit it to Johnnie. She and Kitty smiled at each other in that common superiority which their sex gives them to any mere man upon such an occasion. For Mrs. John Green, though afternoon tea was to her too an alien custom, took to it as a duck does to water.

Miss Whitford handed Johnnie an envelope. "Would it be too much trouble for you to take a letter to Mr. Lindsay?" she asked very casually as they rose to go.

The bridegroom said he was much obliged and he would be plumb tickled to take a message to Clay.

When Clay read the note his blood glowed. It was a characteristic two-line apology:

I've been a horrid little prig, Clay [so the letter ran]. Won't you come over to-morrow and go riding with me?

BEATRICE

CHAPTER XXVI

A LOCKED GATE

COLIN WHITFORD had been telling Clay the story of how a young cowpuncher had snatched Beatrice from under the hoofs of a charging steer. His daughter and the Arizonan listened without comment.

"I've always thought I'd like to explain to that young man I did n't mean to insult him by offering money for saving Bee. But you see he did n't give me any chance. I never did learn his name," concluded the mining man.

"And of course we'd like him to know that we appreciate what he did for me," Beatrice added. She looked at Clay, and a pulse beat in her soft throat.

"I reckon he knows that," Lindsay suggested. "You must 'a' thought him mighty rude for to break away like you say he did."

"We could n't understand it till afterwards. Mr. Bromfield had slipped him a fifty-dollar bill and naturally he resented it." Miss Whitford's face bubbled with reminiscent mirth. She looked a question at Clay. "What do you suppose that impudent young scalawag did with the fifty?"

"Got drunk on it most likely."

"He fed it to his horse. Clary was furious."

"He would be," said the cattleman dryly, in spite of the best intentions to be generous to his successful rival. "But I reckon I know why yore grand-stand friend in chaps pulled such a play. In Arizona you can't square

such things with money. So far as I can make out the
puncher did n't do anything to write home about, but
he did n't want pay for it anyhow."

"Of course, Bromfield does n't understand the West,"
said Whitford. "I would n't like that young puncher half
so well if he 'd taken the money."

"He did n't need to spoil a perfectly good fifty-dollar
bill, though," admitted Clay.

"Yes, he did," denied Beatrice. "That was his protest
against Clarendon's misjudgment of him. I've always
thought it perfectly splendid in its insolence. Some day
I'm going to tell him so."

"It happened in your corner of Arizona, Lindsay. If
you ever find out who the chap was I wish you 'd let us
know," Whitford said.

"I'll remember."

"If you young people are going riding —"

" — We 'd better get started. Quite right, Dad. We 're
off. Clarendon will probably call up. Tell him I 'll be in
about four-thirty."

She pinched her father's ear, kissed him on one ruddy
cheek, then on the other, and joined Clay at the door.

They were friends again, had been for almost half an
hour, even though they had not yet been alone together,
but their friendship was to hold reservations now. The
shadow of Clarendon Bromfield rode between them.
They were a little stiff with each other, not so casual as
they had been. A consciousness of sex had obtruded into
the old boyish *camaraderie*.

After a brisk canter they drew their horses together
for a walk.

Beatrice broke the ice of their commonplaces. She looked directly at him, her cheeks flushing. "I don't know how you're going to forgive me, Clay. I've been awf'ly small and priggish. I hate to think I'm ungenerous, but that's just what I've been."

"Let's forget it," he said gently.

"No, I don't want to forget — not till I've told you how humble I feel to-day. I might have trusted you. Why did n't I? It would have been easy for me to have taken your little friend in and made things right for her. That's what I ought to have done. But, instead of that — Oh, I hate myself for the way I acted."

Her troubled smile, grave and sweet, touched him closely. It was in his horoscope that the spell of this young Diana must be upon him.

He put his hand on hers as it rested on the pommel of the saddle and gave it a slight pressure. "You're a good scout, li'l' pardner."

But it was Beatrice's way to step up to punishment and take what was coming. As a little girl, while still almost a baby, she had once walked up to her mother, eyes flashing with spirit, and pronounced judgment on herself. "I've tum to be spanked. I broke Claire's doll an' I'm glad of it, mean old fing. So there!" Now she was not going to let the subject drop until she had freed her soul.

"No, Clay, I've been a poor sportsman. When my friend needed me I failed him. It hurts me, because — oh, you know. When the test came I was n't there. One hates to be a quitter."

Her humility distressed him, though he loved the spirit of her apology.

"It's all right, Bee. Don't you worry. All friends mis-understand each other, but the real ones clear things up."

She had not yet told him the whole truth and she meant to make clean confession.

"I've been a miserable little fool." She stopped with a little catch of the breath, flamed red, and plunged on. Her level eyes never flinched from his. "I've got to out with it, Clay. You won't misunderstand, I know. I was jealous. I wanted to keep your friendship to myself — did n't want to share it with another girl. That's how mean I am."

A warm smile lit his face. "I've sure enough found my friend again this mo'nin'."

Her smile met his. Then, lest barriers fall too fast between them, she put her horse to a gallop.

As they moved into the Park a snorting automobile leaped past them with muffler open. The horse upon which Beatrice rode was a young one. It gave instant signals of alarm, went sunfishing on its hind legs, came down to all fours, and bolted.

Beatrice kept her head. She put her weight on the reins with all the grip of her small, strong hands. But the horse had the bit in its teeth. She felt herself helpless, flying wildly down the road at incredible speed. Bushes and trees, the reeling road, a limousine, a mounted po-liceman, all flew by her with blurred detail.

She became aware of the rapid thud of hoofs behind, of a figure beside her riding knee to knee, of a brown hand taking hold of the rein close to the bit. The speed slackened. The horses pounded to a halt.

The girl found herself trembling. She leaned back in a haze of dizziness against an arm which circled her shoulder and waist. Memory leaped across the years to that other time when she had rested in his arms, his heart beating against hers. In that moment of deep understanding of herself, Beatrice knew the truth beyond any doubt. A new heaven and a new earth were waiting for her, but she could not enter them. For she herself had closed the gate and locked it fast.

His low voice soothed and comforted her.

"I'm all right," she told him.

Clay withdrew his arm. "I'd report that fellow if I had his number," he said. "You stick to yore saddle fine. You're one straight-up rider."

"I'll ask Mr. Bromfield to give you fifty dollars again," she laughed nervously.

That word *again* stuck in his consciousness.

"You've known me all along," he charged.

"Of course I've known you — knew you when you stood on the steps after you had tied the janitor."

"I knew you, too."

"Why did n't you say so?"

"Did you expect me to make that grand-stand play on the *parada* a claim on yore kindness? I did n't do a thing for you that day any man would n't have done. I happened to be the lucky fellow that got the chance. That's all. Come to that, it was up to you to do the recognizing if any was done. I had it worked out that you did n't know me, but once or twice from things you said I almost thought you did."

"I meant to tell you sometime, but — well, I wanted

to see how long you could keep from telling me. Now you've done it again."

"I'd like to ride with you the rest of yore life," he said unexpectedly.

They trembled on the edge of self-revelation. It was the girl who rescued them from the expression of their emotions.

"I'll speak to Clary about it. Maybe he'll take you on as a groom," she said with surface lightness.

As soon as they reached home Beatrice led the way into the library. Bromfield was sitting there with her father. They were talking over plans for the annual election of officers of the Bird Cage Mining Company. Whitford was the largest stockholder and Bromfield owned the next biggest block. They controlled it between them.

"Dad, Rob Roy bolted and Mr. Lindsay stopped him before I was thrown."

Whitford rose, the color ebbing from his cheeks. "I've always told you that brute was dangerous. I'll offer him for sale to-day."

"And I've discovered that we know the man who saved me from the wild steer in Arizona. It was Mr. Lindsay."

"Lindsay!" Whitford turned to him. "Is that right?"

"It's correct."

Colin Whitford, much moved, put a hand on the younger man's shoulder. "Son, you know what I'd like to tell you. I reckon I can't say it right."

"We'll consider it said, Mr. Whitford," answered Clay with his quick, boyish smile. "No use in spillin' a lot of dictionary words."

"Why did n't you tell us?"

"It was nothin' to brag about."

Bromfield came to time with a thin word of thanks. "We're all greatly in your debt, Mr. Lindsay."

As the days passed the malicious jealousy of the New York clubman deepened to a steady hatred. A fellow of ill-controlled temper, his thin-skinned vanity writhed at the condition which confronted him. He was engaged to a girl who preferred another and a better man, one against whom he had an unalterable grudge. He recognized in the Westerner an eager energy, a clean-cut resilience, and an abounding vitality he would have given a great deal to possess. His own early manhood had been frittered away in futile dissipations and he resented bitterly the contrast between himself and Lindsay that must continually be present in the mind of the girl who had promised to marry him. He had many adventitious things to offer her — such advantages as modern civilization has made desirable to hothouse women — but he could not give the clean, splendid youth she craved. It was the price he had paid for many sybaritic pleasures he had been too soft to deny himself.

With only a little more than two weeks of freedom before her, Beatrice made the most of her days. For the first time in her life she became a creature of moods. The dominant ones were rebellion, recklessness, and repentance. While Bromfield waited and fumed she rode and tramped with Clay. It was not fair to her affianced lover. She knew that. But there were times when she wanted to shriek as dressmakers and costumers fussed over her and wore out her jangled nerves with multitudinous details. The same hysteria welled up in her occasionally at the luncheons and dinners that were being given in honor of her approaching marriage.

It was not logical, of course. She was moving toward the destiny she had chosen for herself. But there was an instinct in her, savage and primitive, to hurt Bromfield because she herself was suffering. In the privacy of her room she passed hours of tearful regret for these bursts of fierce insurrection.

Ten days before the wedding Beatrice wounded his vanity flagrantly. Clarendon was giving an informal tea for her at his rooms. Half an hour before the time set, Beatrice got him on the wire and explained that her car was stalled with engine trouble two miles from Yonkers.

"I'm awf'ly sorry, Clary," she pleaded. "We ought not to have come so far. Please tell our friends I've been delayed, and — I won't do it again."

Bromfield hung up the receiver in a cold fury. He restrained himself for the moment, made the necessary explanations, and went through with the tea somehow. But as soon as his guests were gone he gave himself up to his anger. He began planning a revenge on the man who no doubt was laughing in his sleeve at him. He wanted the fellow exposed, discredited, and humiliated.

But how? Walking up and down his room like a caged panther, Bromfield remembered that Lindsay had other enemies in New York, powerful ones who would be eager to coöperate with him in bringing about the man's downfall. Was it possible for him to work with them under cover? If so, in what way?

Clarendon Bromfield was not a criminal, but a conventional member of society. It was not in his mind or in his character to plot the murder or mayhem of his rival. What he wanted was a public disgrace, one that would blare his name out to the newspapers as a lawbreaker. He wanted to sicken Beatrice and her father of their strange infatuation for Lindsay.

A plan began to unfold itself to him. It was one which called for expert assistance. He looked up Jerry Durand, got him on the telephone, and made an appointment to meet him secretly.

CHAPTER XXVII

"NO VIOLENCE"

THE ex-pugilist sat back in the chair, chewing an unlighted black cigar, his fishy eyes fixed on Bromfield. Scars still decorated the colorless face, souvenirs of a battle in which he had been bested by a man he hated. Durand had a capacity for silence. He waited now for this exquisite from the upper world to tell his business.

Clarendon discovered that he had an unexpected repugnance to doing this. A fastidious sense of the obligations of class served him for a soul and the thing he was about to do could not be justified even in his loose code of ethics. He examined the ferule of his Malacca cane nervously.

"I've come to you, Mr. Durand, about — about a fellow called Lindsay."

The bulbous eyes of the other narrowed. He distrusted on principle all kid gloves. Those he had met were mostly ambitious reformers. Furthermore, any stranger who mentioned the name of the Arizonan became instantly an object of suspicion.

"What about him?"

"I understand that you and he are not on friendly terms. I've gathered that from what's been told me. Am I correct?"

Durand thrust out his salient chin. "Say! Who the hell are you? What's eatin' you? Whatta you want?"

"I'd rather not tell my name."

"Nothin' doin'. No name, no business. That goes."

"Very well. My name is Bromfield. This fellow Lind-say — gets in my way. I want to — to eliminate him."

"Are you askin' me to croak him?"

"Good God, no! I don't want him hurt — physically," cried Bromfield, alarmed.

"Whatta you want, then?" The tight-lipped mouth and the harsh voice called for a showdown.

"I want him discredited — disgraced."

"Why?"

"Some friends of mine are infatuated by him. I want to unmask him in a public way so as to disgust them with him."

"I'm hep. It's a girl."

"We'll not discuss that," said the clubman with a touch of hauteur. "As to the price, if you can arrange the thing as I want it done, I'll not haggle over terms."

The ex-pugilist listened sourly to Bromfield's proposition. He watched narrowly this fashionably dressed visitor. His suspicions still stirred, but not so actively. He was inclined to believe in the sincerity of the fellow's hatred of the Westerner. Jealousy over a girl could easily account for it. Jerry did not intend to involve himself until he had made sure.

"Whatta you want me to do? Come clean."

"Could we get him into a gambling-house, arrange some disgraceful mixup with a woman, get the place raided by the police, and have the whole thing come out in the papers?"

Jerry's slitted eyes went off into space. The thing could be arranged. The trouble in getting Lindsay was to draw him into a trap he could not break through. If Bromfield could deliver his enemy into his hands, Durand thought he would be a fool not to make the most of the chance. As for this soft-fingered swell's stipulation against physical injury, that could be ignored if the opportunity offered.

"Can you bring this Lindsay to a gambling-dump? Will he come with you?" demanded the gang politician.

"I think so. I'm not sure. But if I do that, can you fix the rest?"

"It'll cost money."

"How much will you need?"

"A coupla thousand to start with. More before I've finished. I've got to salve the cops."

Bromfield had prepared for this contingency. He counted out a thousand dollars in bills of large denominations.

"I'll cut that figure in two. Understand. He's **not** to be hurt. I won't have any rough work."

"Leave that to me."

"And you've got to arrange it so that when the house is raided I escape without being known."

"I'll do that, too. Leave your address and I'll send a man up later to wise you as to the scheme when I get one fixed up."

On a sheet torn from his memorandum book Bromfield wrote the name of the club which he most frequented.

"Don't forget the newspapers. I want them **to get** the story," said the clubman, rising.

"I'll see they cover the raid."

Bromfield, massaging a glove on to his long fingers, added another word of caution. "Don't slip up on this thing. Lindsay's a long way from being a soft mark."

"Don't I know it?" snapped Durand viciously. "There'll be no slip-up this time if you do your part. We'll get him, and we'll get him right."

"Without any violence, of course."

"Oh, of course."

Was there a covert but derisive jeer concealed in that smooth assent? Bromfield did not know, but he took away with him an unease that disturbed his sleep that night.

Before the clubman was out of the hotel, Jerry was snapping instructions at one of his satellites.

"Tail that fellow. Find where he goes, who he is, what girl he's mashed on, all about him. See if he's hooked up with Lindsay. And how? Hop to it! Did you get a slant at him as he went out?"

"Sure I did. He's my meat."

The tailer vanished.

Jerry stood at the window, still sullenly chewing his unlighted cigar, and watched his late visitor and the tailer lose themselves in the hurrying crowds.

"White-livered simp. 'No violence, Mr. Durand.' Hmp! Different here."

An evil grin broke through on the thin-lipped, cruel face.

CHAPTER XXVIII

IN BAD

WHEN Bromfield suggested to Clay with a touch of stiffness that he would be glad to show him a side of New York night life probably still unfamiliar to him, the cattleman felt a surprise he carefully concealed. He guessed that this was a belated attempt on the part of Miss Whitford's fiancé to overcome the palpable dislike he had for her friend. If so, the impulse that inspired the offer was a creditable one. Lindsay had no desire to take in any of the plague spots of the city with Bromfield. Something about the society man set his back up, to use his own phrase. But because this was true he did not intend to be outdone in generosity by a successful rival. Promptly and heartily he accepted the invitation. If he had known that a note and a card from Jerry Durand lay in the vest pocket of his cynical host while he was holding out the olive branch, it is probable the Arizonan would have said, "No, thank you, kind sir."

The note mentioned no names. It said, "Wednesday, at Maddock's, 11 P.M. Show this card."

And to Maddock's, on Wednesday, at an hour something earlier than eleven, the New Yorker led his guest after a call at one or two clubs.

Even from the outside the place had a dilapidated look that surprised Lindsay. The bell was of that brand you keep pulling till you discover it is out of order.

Decayed gentility marked the neighborhood, though the blank front of the houses looked impeccably respectable.

As a feeble camouflage of its real reason for being, Maddock's called itself the "Omnium Club." But when Clay found how particular the doorkeeper was as to those who entered he guessed at once it was a gambling-house.

From behind a grating the man peered at them doubtfully. Bromfield showed a card, and after some hesitation on the part of his inquisitor, passed the examination. Toward Clay the doorkeeper jerked his head inquiringly.

"He's all right," the clubman vouched.

Again there was a suspicious and lengthy scrutiny.

The door opened far enough to let them slide into a scantily furnished hall. On the first landing was another guard, a heavy, brutal-looking fellow who was no doubt the "chucker-out." He too looked them over closely, but after a glance at the card drew aside to let them pass.

Through a door near the head of the stairs they moved into a large room, evidently made from several smaller ones with the partitions torn down and the ceilings pillared at intervals.

Clay had read about the magnificence of Canfield's in the old days, and he was surprised that one so fastidious as Bromfield should patronize a place so dingy and so rough as this. At the end of one room was a marble mantelpiece above which there was a defaced, gilt-frame mirror. The chandeliers, the chairs, the wall-paper, all suggested the same note of one-time opulence worn to shabbiness.

A game of Klondike was going. There were two rou-
lette wheels, a faro table, and one circle of poker
players.

The cold eyes of a sleek, slippery man sliding cards
out of a faro-box looked at the Westerner curiously.
Among the suckers who came to this den of thieves to
be robbed were none of Clay's stamp. Lindsay watched
the white, dexterous hands of the dealer with an honest
distaste. All along the border from Juarez to Calexico
he had seen just such soft, skilled fingers fleecing those
who toiled. He knew the bloodless, impassive face of
the professional gambler as well as he knew the anxious,
reckless ones of his victims. His knowledge had told him
little good of this breed of parasites who preyed upon
a credulous public.

The traffic of this room was crooked business by day
as well as by night. A partition ran across the rear of
the back parlor which showed no opening but two small
holes with narrow shelves at the bottom. Back of that
was the paraphernalia of the pool-room, another device
to separate customers from their money by playing the
"ponies."

As Clay looked around it struck him that the per-
sonnel of this gambling-den's patrons was a singularly
depressing one. All told there were not a dozen re-
spectable-looking people in the room. Most of those
present were derelicts of life, the failures of a great city
washed up by the tide. Some were pallid, haggard
wretches clinging to the vestiges of a prosperity that
had once been theirs. Others were hard-faced ruffians
from the underworld. Not a few bore the marks of the

drug victim. All of those playing had a manner of furtive suspicion. They knew that if they risked their
money the house would rob them. Yet they played.

Bromfield bought a small stack of chips at the rou-
lette table.

"Won't you take a whirl at the wheel?" he asked
Lindsay.

"Thanks, no, I believe not," his guest answered.

The Westerner was a bit disgusted at his host's lack
of discrimination. "Does he think I'm a soft mark
too?" he wondered. "If this is what he calls high life
I've had more than enough already."

His disgust was shared by the clubman. Bromfield
had never been in such a dive before. His gambling had
been done in gilded luxury. While he touched shoulders
with this motley crew his nostrils twitched with fastidious disdain. He played, but his interest was not in the
wheel. Durand had promised that there would be women
and that one of them should be bribed to make a claim
upon Clay at the proper moment. He had an unhappy
feeling that the gang politician had thrown him down
in this. If so, what did that mean? Had Durand some
card up his sleeve? Was he using him as a catspaw to
rake in his own chestnuts?

Clarendon Bromfield began to weaken. He and Clay
were the only two men in the room in evening clothes.
His questing eye fell on tough, scarred faces that offered
his fears no reassurance. Any one or all of them might
be agents of Durand.

He shoved all of his chips out, putting half of them
on number eight and the rest on seventeen. His object

was to lose his stack immediately and be free to go. To his annoyance the whirling ball dropped into the pocket labeled eight.

"Let's get out of this hole," he said to Lindsay in a low voice. "I don't like it."

"Suits me," agreed the other.

As Bromfield was cashing his chips Clay came rigidly to attention. Two men had just come into the room. One of them was "Slim" Jim Collins, the other Gorilla Dave. As yet they had not seen him. He did not look at them, but at his host. There was a question in his mind he wanted solved. The clubman's gaze passed over both the newcomers without the least sign of recognition.

"I did n't know what this joint was like or I'd never have brought you," apologized Clarendon. "A friend of mine told me about it. He's got a queer fancy if he likes this frazzled dive."

Clay acquitted Bromfield of conspiracy. He must have been tailed here by Durand's men. His host had nothing to do with it. What for? They could not openly attack him.

"Slim" Jim's eyes fell on him. He nudged Dave. Both of them, standing near the entrance, watched Lindsay steadily.

Some one outside the door raised the cry, "The bulls are comin'."

Instantly the room leaped to frenzied excitement. Men dived for the doors, bets forgotten and chips scattered over the floor. Chairs were smashed as they charged over them, tables overturned. The unwary were trodden underfoot.

Bromfield went into a panic. Why had he been fool enough to trust Durand? No doubt the fellow would ruin him as willingly as he would Lindsay. The raid was fifteen minutes ahead of schedule time. The ward politician had betrayed him. He felt sure of it. All the carefully prepared plans agreed upon he jettisoned promptly. His sole thought was to save himself, not to trap his rival.

Lindsay caught him by the arm. "Let's try the back room."

He followed Clay, Durand's gangmen at his heels.

The lights went out.

The Westerner tried the window. It was heavily barred outside. He turned to search for a door.

Brought up by the partition, Bromfield was whimpering with fear as he too groped for a way of escape. A pale moon shone through the window upon his evening clothes.

In the dim light Clay knew that tragedy impended. "Slim" Jim had his automatic out.

"I've got you good," the chauffeur snarled.

The gun cracked. Bromfield bleated in frenzied terror as Clay dashed forward. A chair swung round in a sweeping arc. As it descended the spitting of the gun slashed through the darkness a second time.

"Slim" Jim went down, rolled over, lay like a log.

Some one dived for Lindsay and drove him against the wall, pinning him by the waist. A second figure joined the first and caught the cattleman's wrist.

Then the lights flashed on again. Clay saw that the man who had flung him against the partition was Gorilla Dave. A plain-clothes man with a star had twisted his wrist and was clinging to it. Bromfield was nowhere to be seen, but an open door to the left showed that he had found at least a temporary escape.

A policeman came forward and stooped over the figure of the prostrate man.

"Some one's croaked a guy," he said.

Gorilla Dave spoke up quickly. "This fellow did it. With a chair. I seen him."

There was a moment before Lindsay answered quietly. "He shot twice. The gun must be lying under him where he fell."

Already men had crowded forward to the scene of the tragedy, moved by the morbid curiosity a crowd has in such sights. Two policemen pushed them back and turned the still body over. No revolver was to be seen.

"Anybody know who this is?" one of the officers asked.

"Collins — 'Slim' Jim," answered big Dave.

"Well, he's got his this time," the policeman said. "Skull smashed."

Clay's heart sank. In that noise of struggling men and crashing furniture very likely the sound of the shots had been muffled. The revolver gone, false testimony against him, proof that he had threatened Collins available, Clay knew that he was in desperate straits.

"There was another guy here with him in them glad rags," volunteered one of the gamblers captured in the raid.

"Who was he?" asked the plain-clothes man of his prisoner.

Clay was silent. He was thinking rapidly. His enemies had him trapped at last with the help of circumstance. Why bring Bromfield into it? It would mean trouble and worry for Beatrice.

"Better speak up, young fellow, me lad," advised the detective. "It won't help you any to be sulky. You're up against the electric chair sure."

The Arizonan looked at him with the level, unafraid eyes of the hills.

"I reckon I'll not talk till I'm ready," he said in his slow drawl.

The handcuffs clicked on his wrists.

CHAPTER XXIX

BAD NEWS

COLIN WHITFORD came into the room carrying a morning paper. His step was hurried, his eyes eager. When he spoke there was the lift of excitement in his voice.

"Bee, I've got bad news."

"Is the Bird Cage flooded?" asked Beatrice. "Or have the miners called a strike again?"

"Worse than that. Lindsay's been arrested. For murder."

The bottom fell out of her heart. She caught at the corner of a desk to steady herself. "Murder! It can't be! Must be some one of the same name."

"I reckon not, honey. It's Clay sure enough. Listen." He read the headlines of a front-page story.

"It *can't* be Clay! What would he be doing in a gambling-dive?" She reached for the paper, but when she had it the lines blurred before her eyes. "Read it, please."

Whitford read the story to the last line. Long before he had finished, his daughter knew the one arrested was Clay. She sat down heavily, all the life stricken from her young body.

"It's that man Durand. He's done this and fastened it on Clay. We'll find a way to prove Clay did n't do it."

"Maybe, in self-defense —"

Beatrice pushed back her father's hesitant suggestion, and even while she did it a wave of dread swept over her. The dead man was the same criminal "Slim" Jim Collins whom the cattleman had threatened in order to protect the Millikan girl. The facts that the man had been struck down by a chair and that her friend claimed, according to the paper, that the gunman had fired two shots, buttressed the solution offered by Whitford. But the horror of it was too strong for her. Against reason her soul protested that Clay could not have killed a man. It was too horrible, too ghastly, that through the faults of others he should be put in such a situation.

And why should her friend be in such a place unless he had been trapped by the enemies who were determined to ruin him? She knew he had a contempt for men who wasted their energies in futile dissipations. He was too clean, too much a son of the wind-swept desert, to care anything about the low pleasures of indecent and furtive vice. He was the last man she knew likely to be found enjoying a den of this sort.

"Dad, I'm going to him," she announced with crisp decision.

Her father offered no protest. His impulse, too, was to stand by the friend in need. He had no doubt Clay had killed the man, but he had a sure conviction it had been done in self-defense.

"We'll get the best lawyers in New York for him, honey," he said. "Nobody will slip anything over on Lindsay if we can help it."

"Will they let us see him? Or shall we have to get permission from some one?"

"We'll have to get an order. I know the district attorney. He'll do what he can for me, but maybe it'll take time."

Beatrice rose, strong again and resilient. Her voice was vibrant with confidence. "Then after you've called up the district attorney, we'll drive to Clay's flat in Harlem and find out from Johnnie what he can tell us. Perhaps he knows what Clay was doing in that place they raided."

It was not necessary to go to the Runt. He came to them. As Beatrice and her father stepped into the car Johnnie and Kitty appeared round the corner. Both of them had the news of a catastrophe written on their faces. A very little encouragement and they would be in tears.

"Ain't it tur'ble, Miss Beatrice? They done got Clay at last. After he made 'em all look like plugged nickels they done fixed it so he'll mebbe go to the electric chair and —"

"Stop that nonsense, Johnnie," ordered Miss Whitford sharply, a pain stabbing her heart at his words. "Don't begin whining already. We've got to see him through. Buck up and tell me what you know."

"That's right, Johnnie," added the mining man. "You and Kitty quit looking like the Atlantic Ocean in distress. We've got to endure the grief and get busy. We'll get Lindsay out of this hole all right."

"You're dawg-goned whistlin'. Y'betcha, by jollies!" agreed the Runt, immensely cheered by Whitford's confidence. "We been drug into this an' we'll sure hop to it."

"When did you see Clay last? How did he come to
be in that gambling-house? Did he say anything to you
about going there?" The girl's questions tumbled over
each other in her hurry.

"Well, ma'am, it must 'a' been about nine o'clock that
Clay he left last night. I recollect because —"

"It does n't matter why. Where was he going?"

"To meet Mr. Bromfield at his club," said Kitty.

"Mr. Bromfield!" cried Beatrice, surprised. "Are
you sure?"

"Tha's what Clay said," corroborated the husband. "Mr. Bromfield invited him. We both noticed it
because it seemed kinda funny, him and Clay not
bein'—"

"Johnnie," his wife reproved, mindful of the relationship between this young woman and the clubman.

"Did he say which club?"

"Seems to me he did n't, not as I remember. How
about that, Kitty?"

"No, I 'm sure he did n't. He said he would n't be
back early. So we went to bed. We s'posed after we
got up this mo'nin' he was sleepin' in his room till the
paper come and I looked at it." Johnnie gave way to
lament. "I told him awhile ago we had orto go back to
Arizona or they 'd git him. And now they 've gone and
done it sure enough."

Keen as a hawk on the hunt, Beatrice turned to her
father quickly. "I 'm going to get Clarendon on the
'phone. He 'll know all about it."

"Why will he know all about it?"

"Because he was with Clay. He 's the man the paper

says the police are looking for — the man with **Clay**
when it happened."

Her father's eyes lit. "That's good guessing, Bee."

It was her fiancé's man who answered the girl's call.
She learned that Clarendon was still in his room.

"He's quite sick this morning, Miss," the **valet**
added.

"Tell him I want to talk with him. It's important."

"I don't think, Miss, that he's able —"

"Will you please tell him what I say?"

Presently the voice of Bromfield, thin and worried,
came to her over the wire. "I'm ill, Bee. Absolutely
done up. I — I can't talk."

"Tell me about Clay Lindsay. Were you with **him**
when — when it happened?"

There was a perceptible pause before the answer
came.

"With him?" She could feel his terror throbbing **over**
the wire. Though she could not see him, she knew **her**
question had stricken him white. "With him where?"

"At this gambling-house — Maddock's?"

"No, I — I — Bee, I tell you I'm ill."

"He went out last night to join you at your club. **I**
know that. When did you see him last?"

"I — we did n't — he did n't come."

"Then did n't you see him at all?"

There was another pause, significant and telling,
followed by a quavering "No-o."

"Clary, I want to see you — right away."

"I'm ill, I tell you — can't leave my bed." He gave
a groan too genuine to doubt.

Beatrice hung up the receiver. Her eyes sparked. For all her slimness, she looked both competent and dangerous.

"What does he say?" her father asked.

"Says he did n't meet Clay at all — that he did n't show up. Dad, there's something wrong about it. Clary's in a panic about something. I'm going to see him, no matter whether he can leave his room or not."

Whitford looked dubious. "I don't see — "

"Well, I do," his daughter cut him off decisively. "We're going to his rooms — now. Why not? He says he's ill. All right. I'm engaged to be married to him and I've a right to see how ill he is."

"What's in your noodle, honey? You've got some kind of a suspicion. What is it?"

"I think Clary knows something. My notion is that he was at Maddock's and that he's in a blue funk for fear he'll be found and named as an accessory. I'm going to find out all he can tell me."

"But — "

She looked at her father directly, a deep meaning in the lovely eyes. A little tremor ran through her body. "Dad, I'm going to save Clay. That's the only thing that counts."

Her words were an appeal, a challenge. They told him that her heart belonged to the friend in prison, and they carried him back somehow to the hour when the nurse first laid her, a tiny baby, in his arms.

His heart was very tender to her. "Whatever you say, sweetheart."

CHAPTER XXX

BEE MAKES A MORNING CALL

THEIR chauffeur broke the speed laws getting them to the apartment house for bachelors where Bromfield lived.

His valet for once was caught off guard when he opened the door to them. Beatrice was inside before he could quite make up his mind how best to meet this frontal attack.

"We came to see Mr. Bromfield," she said.

"Sorry, Miss. He's really quite ill. The doctor says —"

"I'm Miss Whitford. We're engaged to be married. It's very important that I see him."

"Yes, Miss, I know."

The man was perfectly well aware that his master wanted of all things to avoid a meeting with her. For some reason or other, Bromfield was in a state of collapse this morning the valet could not understand. The man's business was to protect him until he had recovered. But he could not flatly turn his master's fiancée out of the apartment. His eye turned to Whitford and found no help there. He fell back on the usual device of servants.

"I don't really think he can see you, Miss. The doctor has specially told me to guard against any excitement. But I'll ask Mr. Bromfield if — if he feels up to it."

The valet passed into what was evidently a bedroom and closed the door behind him. There was a faint murmur of voices.

"I'm going in now," Beatrice announced abruptly to her father.

She moved forward quickly, before Whitford could stop her, whipped open the door, and stepped into the room. Her father followed her reluctantly.

Clarendon, in a frogged dressing-gown, lay propped up by pillows. Beside the bed was a tray, upon which was a decanter of whiskey and a siphon of soda. His figure seemed to have fallen together and his seamed face was that of an old man. But it was the eyes that held her. They were full of stark terror. The look in them took the girl's breath. They told her that he had undergone some great shock.

He shivered at sight of her.

"What is it, Clary?" she cried, moving toward him. "Tell me — tell me all about it."

"I — I'm ill." He quaked it from a burning throat.

"You were all right, yesterday. Why are you ill now?"

He groaned unhappily.

"You're going to tell me everything — *everything.*"

His fascinated, frightened eyes clung to this straight, slim girl whose look stabbed into him and shook his soul. Why had she come to trouble him this morning while he was cowering in fear of the men who would break in to drag him away to prison?

"Nothing to tell," he got out with a gulp.

"Oh, yes, you have. Are you ill because of what happened at Maddock's?"

He tried to pull himself together, to stop the chattering of his teeth.

"N-nonsense, my dear. I'm done up completely. Delighted to see you and all that, but — Won't you go home?" His appealing eyes passed to Whitford. "Can't you take her away?"

"No, I won't go home — and he can't take me away." Her resolution was hard as steel. It seemed to crowd inexorably upon the shivering wretch in the frogged gown. "What is it you're so afraid to tell me, Clarendon?"

He quailed at her thrust. "What — what do you mean?"

She knew now, beyond any question or doubt, that he had been present when "Slim" Jim Collins had been killed. He had seen a man's life snuffed out, was still trembling for fear he might be called in as a party to the crime.

"You'd better tell me before it's too late. How did you and Clay Lindsay come to go to that den?"

"We went out to — to see the town."

"But why to that place? Are you in the habit of going there?"

He shuddered. "Never was there before. I had a card. Some one gave it to me. So we went in for a few minutes — to see what it was like. The police raided the place." He dropped his sentences reluctantly, as though they were being forced from him in pain.

"Well?"

"Everybody tried to escape. The lights went out. I found a back door and got away. Then I came home."

"What about Clay?"

Bromfield told the truth. "I did n't see him after the lights went out, except for a moment. He was running at the man with the gun."

"You saw the gun?"

He nodded, moistened his dry lips with the tip of his tongue.

"And the — the shooting? Did you see that?"

Twice the words he tried to say faded on his lips. At last he managed a "No."

"Why not?"

"I — found a door and escaped."

"You must have heard shooting."

"I heard shots as I ran down the stairs. This morning I read that — that a man was — " He swallowed down a lump and left the sentence unfinished.

"Then you know that Clay is accused of killing this man, and that the police are looking for you because you were with him."

"Yes." His answer was a dry whisper.

"Did you see this man Collins in the room?"

"No. I should n't know him if I saw him."

"But you heard shots. You 're sure of that!" cried Beatrice.

"Y-yes."

The girl turned triumphantly to her father. "He saw the gun and he heard shots. That proves self-defense at the worst. They were shooting at Clay when he struck with the chair — if he did. Clarendon's testimony will show that."

"My testimony!" screamed Bromfield. "My God,

do you think I'm going to — to — go into court? They would claim I — I was — "

She waited, but he did not finish. "Clay's life may depend upon it, and of course you'll tell the truth," she said quietly.

"Maybe I did n't hear shots," he hedged. "Maybe it was furniture falling. There was a lot of noise of people stamping and fighting."

"You — heard — shots."

The eyes of the girl were deadly weapons. They glittered like unscabbarded steel. In them was a contained fire that awed him.

He threw out his hand in a weak, impotent gesture of despair. "My God, how did I ever come to get into such a mix-up? It will ruin me."

"How *did* you come to go?" she asked.

"He wanted to see New York. I suppose I had some notion of taking him slumming."

Beatrice went up to him and looked straight into his eyes. "Then testify to that in court. It won't hurt you any. Go down to the police and say you have read in the paper that they want you. Tell the whole truth. And Clary — don't weaken. Stick to your story about the shots." Her voice shook a little. "Clay's life is at stake. Remember that."

"Do you think it would be safe to go to the police?" he asked doubtfully.

Whitford spoke up. "That's the only square and safe thing to do, Bromfield. They'll find out who you are, of course. If you go straight to them you draw the sting from their charge that you were an accomplice of Clay. Don't lose your nerve. You'll go through with flying colors. When a man has done nothing wrong he need n't be afraid."

"I dare say you 're right," agreed Bromfield miserably.

The trouble was that Whitford was arguing from false premises. He was assuming that Clarendon was an innocent man, whereas the clubman knew just how guilty he was. Back of the killing lay a conspiracy which might come to light during the investigation. He dared not face the police. His conscience was not clean enough.

"Of course Dad's right. It's the only way to save your reputation," Beatrice cried. "I'm not going to leave you till you promise to go straight down there to headquarters. If you don't you'll be smirched for life — and you'd be doing something absolutely dishonorable."

He came to time with a heart of heavy dread. "All right, Bee. I'll go," he promised. "It's an awful mess, but I've got to go through with it, I suppose."

"Of course you have," she said with complete conviction. "You 're not a quitter, and you can't hide here like a criminal."

"We'll have to be moving, Bee," her father reminded her. "You know we have an appointment to meet the district attorney."

Beatrice nodded. With a queer feeling of repulsion she patted her fiancé's cheek with her soft hand and whispered a word of comfort to him.

"Buck up, old boy. It won't be half as bad as you think. Nobody is going to blame you."

They were shown out by the valet.

"You don't want to be hard on Bromfield, honey," Whitford told his daughter after they had reëntered their car. "He's a parlor man. That's the way he's been brought up. Never did a hard day's work in his life. Everything made easy for him. If he'd ever ridden out a blizzard like Clay or stuck it out in a mine for a week without food after a cave-in, he would n't balk on the job before him. But he's soft. And he's afraid of his reputation. That's natural, I suppose."

Beatrice knew he was talking to save her feelings. "You don't need to make excuses for him, Dad," she answered gently, with a wry smile. "I've got to give up. I don't think I can go through with it."

"You mean — marry him?"

"Yes." She added, with a flare of passionate scorn of herself: "I deserve what I've got. I knew all the time I did n't love him. It was sheer selfishness in me to accept him. I wanted what he had to give me."

Her father drew a deep breath of relief. "I'm glad you see that, Bee. I don't think he's good enough for you. But I don't know anybody that is, come to that."

"That's just your partiality. I'm a mean little bounder or I never should have led him on," the girl answered in frank disgust.

Both of them felt smirched. The behavior of Bromfield had been a reflection on them. They had picked him for a thoroughbred, and he had failed them at the first test.

"Well, I have n't been proud of you in that affair," conceded Colin. "It did n't seem like my girl to — "

He broke off in characteristic fashion to berate her environment. "It's this crazy town. The spirit of it gets into a person and he accepts its standards. Let's get away from here for a while, sweetheart."

"After Clay is out of trouble, Dad, I'll go with you back to Denver or to Europe or anywhere you say."

"That's a deal," he told her promptly. "We'll stay till after the annual election of the company and then go off on a honeymoon together, Bee."

CHAPTER XXXI

INTO THE HANDS OF HIS ENEMY

DURAND waited alone for word to be flashed him that the debt he owed Clay Lindsay had been settled in full. A telephone lay on the desk close at hand and beside it was a watch. The second-hand ticked its way jerkily round and round the circle. Except for that the stillness weighed on him unbearably. He paced up and down the room chewing nervously the end of an unlit cigar. For the good tidings which he was anxious to hear was news of the death of the strong young enemy who had beaten him at every turn.

Why did n't Collins get to the telephone? Was it possible that there had been a slip-up, that Lindsay had again broken through the trap set for him? Had "Slim's" nerve failed him? Or had Bromfield been unable to bring the victim to the slaughter?

His mind went over the details again. The thing had been well planned even to the unguarded door through which Collins was to escape. In the darkness "Slim" could do the job, make his getaway along with Dave, and be safe from any chance of identification. Bromfield, to save his own hide, would keep still. If he did n't, Durand was prepared to shift the murder upon his shoulders.

The minute-hand of the watch passed down from the quarter to the half and from the half to the three quarters. Still the telephone bell did not ring. The gang leader began to sweat blood. Had some one bungled after all the care with which he had laid his plans?

A door slammed below. Hurried footsteps sounded on the stair treads. Into the room burst a man.

"'Slim' 's been croaked," he blurted.

"What!" Durand's eyes dilated.

"At Maddock's."

"Who did it?"

"De guy he was to gun."

"Lindsay."

"Dat's de fellow."

"Did the bulls get Lindsay?"

"Pinched him right on de spot."

"Gun 'Slim,' did he?"

"Nope. Knocked him cold wit' a chair. Cracked his skull."

"Is he dead?"

"He'll never be deader. Dave grabbed this sucker Lindsay and yelled that he done it. The bulls pinched him like I said right there."

"Did it happen in the dark?"

"Sure as you're a foot high. My job was dousin' the glims, and I done it right."

"What about 'Slim'? Was he shooting when he got it?"

The other man shook his head. "This Lindsay man claims he was. I talked wit' a bull afterward. Dey did n't find no gun on 'Slim.' The bull says there was no gun-play."

"What became of 'Slim's' gun?"

"Search me."

Durand slammed a big fist exultantly down on the desk. "Better than the way I planned it. If the gun's gone, I'll frame Lindsay for the chair. It's Salt Creek for his."

He lost no time in getting into touch with Gorilla Dave, who was under arrest at the station house. From him he learned the story of the killing of Collins. One whispered detail of it filled him with malicious glee.

"The boob! He'll go to the death chair sure if I can frame him. We're lucky Bromfield ran back into the little room. Up in front a dozen guys might have seen the whole play even in the dark."

Durand spent the night strengthening the web he had spun to destroy his enemy. He passed to and fro among those who had been arrested in the raid and he arranged the testimony of some of them to suit his case. More than one of the men caught in the dragnet of the police was willing to see the affray from the proper angle in exchange for protection from prosecution.

After breakfast Durand went to the Tombs, where Clay had been transferred at daybreak.

"You need n't bring the fellow here," he told the warden. "I'll go right to his cage and see him. I wantta have a talk with him."

CHAPTER XXXII

MR. LINDSAY RECEIVES

BETWEEN two guards Clay climbed the iron steps to an upper tier of cages at the Tombs. He was put into a cell which held two beds, one above the other, as in the cabin of an ocean liner. By the side of the bunks was a narrow space just long enough for a man to take two steps in the same direction.

An unshaven head was lifted in the lower bunk to see why the sleep of its owner was being disturbed.

"I've brought you a cell mate, Shiny," explained one of the guards. "You want to be civil to him. He's just croaked a friend of yours."

"For de love o' Gawd. Who did he croak?"

"'Slim' Jim Collins. Cracked him one on the bean and that was a-plenty. Hope you'll enjoy each other's society, gents." The guard closed the door and departed.

"Is that right? Did youse do up 'Slim,' or was he kiddin' me?"

"I don't reckon we'll discuss that subject," said Clay blandly, but with a note of finality in his voice.

"No offense, boss. It's an honor to have so distinguished a gent for a cell pal. For that matter I ain't no cheap rat myself. Dey pinched me for shovin' de queer. I'd ought to get fifteen years," he said proudly.

This drew a grin from Lindsay, though not exactly

a merry one. "If you're anxious for a long term you can have some of mine," he told the counterfeiter.

"Maybe youse'll go up Salt Creek," said Shiny hopefully.

Afraid the allusion might not be understood, he thoughtfully explained that this was the underworld term for the electric chair.

Clay made no further comment. He found the theme a gruesome one.

"Anyhow, I'm glad dey did n't put no hoister nor damper-getter wit' me. I'm partickler who I meet. De whole profesh is gettin' run down at de heel. I'm dead sick of rats who can't do nothin' but lift pokes," concluded the occupant of the lower berth with disgust.

Though Clay's nerves were of the best he did very little sleeping that night. He was in a grave situation. Even if he had a fair field his plight would be serious enough. But he guessed that during the long hours of darkness Durand was busy weaving a net of false evidence from which he could scarcely disentangle himself. Unless Bromfield came forward at once as a witness for him, his case would be hopeless — and Clay suspected that the clubman would prove only a broken reed as a support. The fellow was selfish to the core. He had not, in the telling Western phrase, the guts to go through. He would take the line of least resistance.

Beatrice was in his thoughts a great deal. What would she think of him when the news came that he was a murderer, caught by the police in a den of vice where he had no business to be? Some deep instinct of his soul told him that she would brush through the evidence to the essential truth. She had failed him once. She would never do it again. He felt sure of that.

The gray morning broke, and brought with it the steaming smell of prison cooking, the sounds of the caged underworld, the sense of life all around him dwarfed and warped to twisted moral purposes. A warden came with breakfast — a lukewarm, muddy liquid he called coffee and a stew in which potatoes and bits of fat beef bobbed like life buoys — and Clay ate heart· ily while his cell mate favored him, between gulps, with a monologue on ethics, politics, and the state of society, as these related especially to Shiny the Shover. Lindsay was given to understand that the whole world was "on de spud," but the big crooks had fixed the laws so that they could wear diamonds instead of stripes.

Presently a guard climbed the iron stairway with a visitor and led the way along the deck outside the tier of cells where Clay had been put.

"He's in seventy-four, Mr. Durand," the man said as he approached. "I'll have to beat it. Come back to the office when you're ready."

The ex-pugilist had come to gloat over him. Clay knew it at once. His pupils narrowed.

He was lying on the bed, his supple body stretched at graceful ease. Not by the lift of an eyelid did he recognize the presence of his enemy.

Durand stood in front of the cell, hands in pockets, the inevitable unlit black cigar in his mouth. On his face was a sneer of malevolent derision.

Shiny the Shover bustled forward, all complaisance. "Pleased to meet youse, Mr. Durand."

The gang politician's insolent eyes went up and down him. "I did n't come to see *you*."

" 'S all right. Glad to see youse, anyhow," the counterfeit passer went on obsequiously. "Some day, when you've got time I'd like to talk wit' youse about gettin' some fall money."

"Nothin' doin', Shiny. I'm not backin' you," said Jerry coldly. "You've got to go up the river."

"Youse promised — "

"Aw, what the hell's eatin' you?"

Shiny's low voice carried a plaintive whine. "If you'd speak to de judge —"

"Forget it." Durand brushed the plea away with a motion of his hand. "It's your cell pal I've come to take a look at — the one who's goin' to the chair."

With one lithe movement Clay swung down to the floor. He sauntered forward to the grating, his level gaze full on the ward boss.

"Shiny, this fellow's rotten," he said evenly and impersonally. "He's not only a crook, but he's a crooked crook. He'd throw down his own brother if it paid him."

Durand's cruel lips laughed. "Your pal's a little worried this mornin', Shiny. He ain't slept much. You see the bulls got him right. It's the death chair for him and no lifeboat in sight."

Clay leaned against the bars negligently. He spoke with a touch of lazy scorn. "See those scars on his face, Shiny — the one on the cheek bone and the other above the eye. Ask him where he got 'em and how."

Jerry cursed. He broke into a storm of threats, anger sweeping over him in furious gusts. He had come to make sport of his victim and Lindsay somehow took the upper hand at once. He had this fellow where he wanted him at last. Yet the man's soft voice still carried the note of easy contempt. If the Arizonan was afraid, he gave no least sign of it.

"You'll sing another tune before I'm through with you," the prize-fighter prophesied savagely.

The Westerner turned away and swung back to his upper berth. He knew, what he had before suspected, that Durand was going to "frame" him if he could. That information gained, the man no longer interested him.

Sullenly Jerry left. There was no profit in jeering at Lindsay. He was too entirely master of every situation that confronted him.

Within the hour Clay was wakened from sleep by another guard with word that he was wanted at the office of the warden. He found waiting him there Beatrice and her father. The girl bloomed in that dingy room like a cactus in the desert.

She came toward him with hands extended, in her eyes gifts of friendship and faith.

"Oh, Clay!" she cried.

"Much obliged, little pardner." Her voice went to his heart like water to the thirsty roots of prickly pears. A warm glow beat through his veins. The doubts that had weighed on him during the night were gone. Beatrice believed in him. All was well with the world.

He shook hands with Whitford. "Blamed good of you to come, sir."

"Why wouldn't we come?" demanded the mining

man bluntly. "We're here to do what we can for
you."

Little wells of tears brimmed over Beatrice's lids.
"I've been so worried."

"Don't you. It'll be all right." Strangely enough
he felt now that it would. Her coming had brought rippling sunshine into a drab world.

"I won't now. I'm going to get evidence for you.
Tell us all about it."

"Why, there isn't much to tell that you haven't
read in the papers probably. He came a-shootin' and
was hit by a chair."

"Was it you that hit him?"

"Wouldn't I be justified?" he asked gently.

"But did you?"

For a moment he hesitated, then made up his mind
swiftly. "Yes," he told her gravely.

She winced. "You couldn't help it. How did you come
to be there?"

"I just dropped in."

"Alone?"

"Yes."

He had burned the bridges behind him and was lying
glibly. Why bring Bromfield into it? She was going to
marry him in a few days. If her fiancé was man enough
to come forward and tell the truth he would do so
anyhow. It was up to him. Clay was not going to betray
him to Beatrice.

"The paper says there was some one with you."

"Sho! Reporters sure enough have lively imaginations."

"Johnnie told me you had an engagement with Mr. Bromfield."

"Did you ever know Johnnie get anything right?"

"And Clarendon says he was with you at Maddock's."

Clay had not been prepared for this cumulative evidence. He gave a low laugh of relief. "I'm an awful poor liar. So Bromfield says he was with me, does he?"

"Yes."

He intended to wait for a lead before showing his hand. "Then you know all about it?" he asked carelessly.

Their eyes were on each other, keen and watchful. She knew he was concealing something of importance. He had meant not to tell her that Bromfield had been with him. Why? To protect the man to whom she was engaged. She jumped to the conclusion that he was still shielding him.

"Yes, you're a poor liar, Clay," she agreed. "You stayed to keep back Collins so as to give Clarendon a chance to escape."

"Did I?"

"Can you deny it? Clarendon heard the shots as he was running downstairs."

"He told you that, did he?"

"Yes."

"That ought to help a lot. If I can prove Collins was shootin' at me I can plead self-defense."

"That's what it was, of course."

"Yes. But Durand does n't mean to let it go at that. He was here to see me this mo'nin'." Clay turned to the mining man, his voice low but incisive. His brain was working clear and fast. "Mr. Whitford, I have a hunch he's going to destroy the evidence that's in my favor. There must be two bullet holes in the partition of the rear room where Collins was killed. See if you can't find those bullet holes and the bullets in the wall behind."

"I'll do that, Lindsay."

"And hire me a good lawyer. Send him to me. I won't use a smart one whose business is to help crooks escape. If he doesn't believe in me, I don't want him. I'll have him get the names of all those pulled in the raid and visit them to see if he can't find some one who heard the shots or saw shooting. Then there's the gun. Some one's got that gun. It's up to us to learn who."

"That's right."

"Tim Muldoon will do anything he can for me. There's a girl lives with his mother. Her name's Annie Millikan. She has ways of finding out things. Better talk it over with her too. We've got to get busy in a hurry."

"Yes," agreed Whitford. "We'll do that, boy."

"Oh, Clay, I'm sure it's going to be all right!" cried Beatrice, in a glow of enthusiasm. "We'll give all our time. We'll get evidence to show the truth. And we'll let you know every day what we are doing."

"How about my going bail for you?" asked her father.

Clay shook his head. "No chance just yet. Let's make our showing at the coroner's inquest. I'll do fine and dandy here till then."

He shook hands with them both and was taken back

to his cell. But hope was in his heart now. He knew his friends would do their best to get the evidence to free him. It would be a battle royal between the truth and a lie.

CHAPTER XXXIII

BROMFIELD MAKES AN OFFER

A YOUTH with a face like a fox sidled up to Durand in the hotel lobby and whispered in his ear. Jerry nodded curtly, and the man slipped away as furtively as he had come.

Presently the ex-prize-fighter got up, sauntered to the street, and hailed a taxi. Twenty minutes later he paid the driver, turned a corner, and passed into an apartment house for bachelors. He took the elevator to the third floor and rang an electric bell at a door which carried the name "Mr. Clarendon Bromfield."

From the man who came to the door Mr. Bromfield's visitor learned that he was not well and could receive no callers.

"Just mention the Omnium Club, and say I'm here on very important business," said Jerry with a sour grin.

The reference served as a password. Jerry was admitted to meet a host quite unable to control his alarm. At sight of his visitor Bromfield jumped up angrily. As soon as his man had gone he broke out in a subdued scream.

"You rotten traitor! Get out of my room, or I'll call the police."

Durand found a comfortable chair, drew a case from his pocket, and selected a cigar. He grinned with evil mirth.

"You will, eh? Like hell you will. You're hidin' from the cops this blessed minute. I've just found out myself where you live."

"You took my money and threw me down. You hired a gunman to kill me."

"Now, what would I do that for? I had n't a thing in the world against you, an' I have n't now."

"That damned ruffian shot at me. He was still shooting when I struck him with the chair," cried Bromfield, his voice shaking.

"He did n't know it was you — mistook you for Lindsay in the darkness."

"My God, I did n't mean to kill him. I had to do something."

"You did it all right."

"I told you there was n't to be any violence. It was explicitly stated. You promised. And all the time you were planning murder. I'll tell all I know. By God, I will."

"Go easy, Mr. Bromfield," snarled Jerry. "If you do, where do ye think you'll get off at?"

"I'll go to the police and tell them your hired gunman was shooting at us."

"Will you now? An' I'll have plenty of good witnesses to swear he was n't." Durand bared his teeth in a threat. "That's not all either. I'll tie you up with the rube from the West and send you up to Sing Sing as accessory. How'd you like that?"

"If I tell the truth — "

"You'll be convicted of murder in place of him and he'll go up as accessory. I don't care two straws how it is. But you'd be a damned fool. I'll say that for you."

"I'm not going to let an innocent man suffer in my place. It would n't be playing the game."

Durand leaned forward and tapped the table with his finger-tips. His voice rasped like a file. "You can't save him. He's goin' to get it right. But you can hurt yourself a hell of a lot. Get out of the country and stay out till it's over with. That's the best thing you can do. Go to the Hawaiian Is'ands, man. That's a good healthy climate an' the hotel cooking's a lot better than it is at Sing Sing."

"I can't do it," moaned the clubman. "My God, man, if it ever came out — that I'd paid you money to — to — ruin his reputation, and that I'd run away when I could have saved an innocent man — I'd be done for. I'd be kicked out of every club I'm in."

"It won't ever come out if you're not here. But if you force my hand — well; that's different." Again Jerry's grin slit his colorless face. He had this poor devil where he wanted him, and he was enjoying himself.

"What do you want me to do, then?" cried Bromfield, tiny beads of perspiration on his forehead.

"You'll do as I say — beat it outa the country till the thing's over with."

"But Lindsay will talk."

"The boob's padlocked his mouth. For some fool reason he's protectin' you. Get out, an' you're safe."

Bromfield sweated blood as he walked up and down the room looking for a way out of his dilemma. He had come to the parting of the road again. If he did this thing he would be a yellow cur. It was one thing to destroy Lindsay's influence with Beatrice by giving her a false impression. From his point of view their friendship was pernicious anyhow and ought to be wiped out. At most the cattleman would have gone back unhurt to the Arizona desert he was always talking about. Nobody there would care about what had happened to him in New York. But to leave him, an innocent man, to go to his death because he was too chivalrous to betray his partner in an adventure — this was something that even Bromfield's atrophied conscience revolted at. Clay was standing by him, according to Durand's story. The news of it lifted a weight from his soul. But it left him too under a stronger moral obligation to step out and face the music.

The clubman made the only decision he could, and that was to procrastinate, to put off making any choice for the present.

"I'll think it over. Give me a day to make up my mind," he begged.

Jerry shrugged his heavy shoulders. He knew that every hour counted in his favor, would make it more difficult for the tortured man to come forward and tell the truth. "Sure. Look it over upside and down. Don't hurry. But, man, what's there to think about? I thought you hated this guy — wanted to get rid of him."

"Not that way. God, no! Durand, I'll give you any sum in reason to let him go without bringing me into it. You can arrange it."

Jerry slammed down a fist heavily on the table. "I can, but I won't. Not if you was to go fifty-fifty with

me to your last cent. I'm goin' to get this fellow. See?
I'm goin' to get him good. He'll be crawlin' on his hands
and knees to me before I'm through with him."

"What good will that do you? I'm offering you cold
cash just to let the truth get out — that Collins was
trying to kill him when he got hit."

"Nothin' doin'. I've been layin' for this boob. I've
got him now. I'm goin' to turn the screws on and listen
to him holler."

Bromfield's valet stepped into the room. "Mr. and
Miss Whitford to see you, sir."

CHAPTER XXXIV

ANNIE MILLIKAN nodded her wise little head. "Jerry's gonna frame him if he can. He's laid the wires for it. That's a lead pipe."

"Sure," agreed Muldoon. "I'll bet he's been busy all night fixin' up his story. Some poor divvles he'll bully-rag into swearin' lies an' others he'll buy. Trust Jerry for the crooked stuff."

"We've got to get the truth," said Beatrice crisply, pulling on her gloves. "And we'll do it too. A pack of lies can't stand against four of us all looking for the truth."

Annie looked curiously at this golden-haired girl with the fine rapture of untamed youth, so delicate and yet so silken strong. By training and tradition they were miles apart, yet the girl who had lived on the edge of the underworld recognized a certain kinship. She liked the thorough way this young woman threw herself into the business of the day. The wireless telegraphy of the eyes, translated through the medium of her own emotions, told her that no matter whose ring Beatrice Whitford was wearing Clay Lindsay held her happiness in the cup of his strong brown hand.

"You're shoutin', Miss." Annie rose briskly. "I'll get busy doin' some sleuthin' myself. I liked your friend from the minute he stepped through — from the minute. I set me peepers on him. He's one man, if anybody asks you. I'm soitainly for him till the clock strikes twelve.

And say, listen! Jerry's liable not to get away with it. I'm hep to one thing. The gang's sore on him. He rides the boys too hard. Some of 'em will sure t'row him down hard if they think they'll be protected."

"The district attorney will stand by us," said Whitford. "He told me himself Durand was a menace and that his days as boss were numbered. Another thing, Miss Millikan. If you need to spend any money in a legitimate way, I'm here to foot the bills."

Muldoon, who was on night duty this month and therefore had his days free, guided Whitford and his daughter to Maddock's. As they reached the house an express wagon was being driven away. Automatically the license number registered itself in Tim's memory.

The policeman took a key from his pocket and unlocked the door. The three went up the stairs to the deserted gambling-hall and through it to the rear room.

"From what Lindsay says the bullet holes ought to be about as high as his arm pits," said Whitford.

"'Slim' must 'a' been standin' about here," guessed Muldoon, illustrating his theory by taking the position he meant. "The bullets would hit the partition close to the center, would n't they?"

Beatrice had gone straight to the plank wall. "They're not here," she told them.

"Must be. According to Lindsay's story the fellow was aiming straight at it."

"Well, they're not here. See for yourself."

She was right. There was no evidence whatever that any bullets had passed through the partition. They covered every inch of the cross wall in their search.

"Lindsay must have been mistaken," decided Whitford, hiding his keen disappointment. "This man Collins could n't have been firing in this direction. Of
course everything was confusion. No doubt they shifted
round in the dark and — "

He stopped, struck by an odd expression on the face
of his daughter. She had stooped and picked up a small
fragment of shaving from the floor. Her eyes went from
it to a plank in the partition and then back to the thin
crisp of wood.

"What is it, honey?" asked Whitford.

The girl turned to Muldoon, alert in every quivering
muscle. "That express wagon — the one leaving the
house as we drove up — Did you notice it?"

"Number 714," answered Tim promptly.

"Can you have it stopped and the man arrested?
Don't you see? They've rebuilt this partition. They
were taking away in that wagon the planks with the
bullet holes."

Muldoon was out of the room and going down the
stairs before she had finished speaking. It was a quarter
of an hour later when he returned. Beatrice and her
father were not to be seen.

From back of the partition came an eager, vibrant
voice. "Is that you, Mr. Muldoon? Come here quick.
We've found one of the bullets in the wall."

The policeman passed out of the door through which
Bromfield had made his escape and found another small
door opening from the passage. It took him into the
cubby-hole of a room in which were the wires and in-
struments used to receive news of the races.

"What about the express wagon?" asked Whitford.

"We'll get it. Word is out for those on duty to keep an eye open for it. Where's the bullet?"

Beatrice pointed it out to him. There it was, safely embedded in the plaster, about five feet from the ground.

"Durand wasn't thorough enough. He quit too soon," said the officer with a grin. "Crooks most always do slip up somewhere and leave evidence behind them. Yuh'd think Jerry would have remembered the bullet as well as the bullet hole."

They found the mark of the second bullet too. It had struck a telephone receiver and taken a chip out of it.

They measured with a tape-line the distance from the floor and the side walls to the place where each bullet struck. Tim dug out the bullet they had found.

They were back in the front room again when a huge figure appeared in the doorway and stood there blocking it.

"Whatta youse doin' here?" demanded a husky voice.

Muldoon nodded a greeting. "'Lo, Dave. Just lookin' around to see the scene of the scrap. How about yuh?"

"Beat it," ordered Gorilla Dave, his head thrust forward in a threat. "Youse got no business here."

"Friends av mine." The officer indicated the young woman and her father. "They wanted to see where 'Slim' was knocked out. So I showed 'em. No harm done."

Dave moved to one side. "Beat it," he ordered again.

In the pocket of Muldoon was a request of the district attorney for admission to the house for the party, with an O.K. by the captain of police in the precinct, but Tim did not show it. He preferred to let Dave think that he had been breaking the rules of the force for the sake of a little private graft. There was no reason whatever for warning Durand that they were aware of the clever trick he had pulled off in regard to the partition.

CHAPTER XXXV

TWO AND TWO MAKE FOUR

From Maddock's the Whitfords drove straight to the apartment house of Clarendon Bromfield. For the third time that morning the clubman's valet found himself overborne by the insistence of visitors.

"We're coming in, you know," the owner of the Bird Cage told him in answer to his explanation of why his master could not be seen. "This is important business and we've got to see Bromfield."

"Yes, sir, but he said — "

"He'll change his mind when he knows why we're here." Whitford pushed in and Beatrice followed him. From the adjoining room came the sound of voices.

"I thought you told us Mr. Bromfield had gone to sleep and the doctor said he wasn't to be wakened," said Beatrice with a broad, boyish smile at the man's discomfiture.

"The person inside wouldn't take no, Miss, for an answer."

"He was like us, wasn't he? Did he give his name?" asked the young woman.

"No, Miss. Just said he was from the Omnium Club."

Whitford and his daughter exchanged glances. "Same business we're on. Announce us and we'll go right in."

They were on his heels when he gave their names. Bromfield started up, too late to prevent their entrance. He stood silent for a moment, uncertain what to do, disregarding his fiancée's glance of hostile inquiry lifted toward the other guest.

The mining man forced his hand. "Won't you introduce us, Clarendon?" he asked bluntly.

Reluctantly their host went through the formula. He was extremely uneasy. There was material for an explosion present in this room that would blow him sky-high if a match should be applied to it. Let Durand get to telling what he knew about Clarendon and the Whitfords would never speak to him again. They might even spread a true story that would bar every house and club in New York to him.

"We've heard of Mr. Durand," said Beatrice

Her tone challenged the attention of the gang leader. The brave eyes flashed defiance straight at him. A pulse of anger was throbbing in the soft round throat.

Inscrutably he watched her. It was his habit to look hard at attractive women. "Most people have," he admitted.

'Mr. Lindsay is our friend," she said. "We've just come from seeing him."

The man to whom she was engaged had been put through so many flutters of fear during the last twelve hours that a new one more or less did not matter. But he was still not shock-proof. His fingers clutched a little tighter the arm of the chair.

"W-what did he tell you?"

Beatrice looked into his eyes and read in them once more stark fear. Again she had a feeling that there was something about the whole affair she had not yet fathomed — some secret that Clay and Clarendon and perhaps this captain of thugs knew.

She tried to read what he was hiding, groped in her mind for the key to his terror. What could it be that he was afraid Clay had told her? What was it they all knew except Lindsay's friends? And why, since Clarendon was trembling lest it be discovered, should the Arizonan too join the conspiracy of silence? At any rate she would not uncover her hand.

"He told us several things," she said significantly. "You've got to make open confession, Clary."

The ex-pugilist chewed his cigar and looked at her.

"What would he confess? That the man with him murdered Collins?"

"That's not true," said the girl quickly.

"So Lindsay's your friend, eh? Different here, Miss." Jerry pieced together what the clubman had told him and what he had since learned about her. He knew that this must be the girl to whom his host was engaged. "How about you, Bromfield?" he sneered.

The clubman stiffened. "I've nothing against Mr. Lindsay."

"Thought you had."

"Of course he has n't. Why should he?" asked Beatrice, backing up Clarendon.

Durand looked at her with a bold insolence that was an insult. His eyes moved up and down the long, slim curves of her figure. "I expect he could find a handsome reason if he looked around for it, Miss."

The girl's father clenched his fist. A flush of anger

swept his ruddy cheeks. He held himself, however, to the subject.

"You forget, Mr. Durand, that Lindsay was his guest last night."

Jerry's laugh was a contemptuous jeer. "That's right. I'd forgot that. He was your guest, was n't he, Bromfield?"

"What's the good of discussing it here?" asked the tortured host.

"Not a bit," admitted Whitford. "Actions talk, not words. Have you seen the police yet, Bromfield?"

"N-not yet."

"What's he gonna see the police about?" Jerry wanted to know, his chin jutting out.

"To tell them that he saw Collins draw a gun and heard shots fired," retorted the mining man instantly.

"Not what he's been tellin' me. He'll not pull any such story — not unless he wants to put himself in a cell for life."

"Talk sense. You can't frighten Bromfield. He knows that's foolishness."

"Does he?" The crook turned derisive eyes on the victim he was torturing.

Certainly the society man did not look a picture of confidence. The shadow of a heavy fear hung over him.

The telephone rang. Bromfield's trembling fingers picked up the transmitter. He listened a moment, then turned it over to Beatrice.

"For you."

Her part of the conversation was limited. It consisted of the word "Yes" repeated at intervals and a concluding, "Oh, I'm so glad. Thank you." Her eyes were sparkling when she hung up.

"Good news, Dad," she said. "I'll tell you later."

Durand laughed brutally as he rose. "Good news, eh? Get all you can. You'll need it. Take that from me. It's straight. Your friend's in trouble up to the neck." He swaggered to the door and turned. "Don't forget, Bromfield. Keep outa this or you'll be sorry." His voice was like the crack of a trainer's whip to animals in a circus.

For once Bromfield did not jump through the hoop. "Oh, go to the devil," he said in irritation. flushing angrily.

"Better not get gay with me," advised Durand sourly.

After the door had closed on him there was a momentary pause. The younger man spoke awkwardly. "You can tell me now what it was Mr. Lindsay told you."

"We'd like to know for sure whether you're with us or with Durand," said Whitford mildly. "Of course we know the answer to that. You're with us. But we want to hear you say it, flat-foot."

"Of course I'm with you. That is, I'd like to be. But I don't want to get into trouble, Mr. Whitford. Can you blame me for that?"

"You wouldn't get into trouble," argued the mine owner impatiently. "I keep telling you that."

Beatrice, watching the younger man closely, saw as in a flash the solution of this mystery — the explanation of the tangle to which various scattered threads had been leading her.

"Are you sure of that, Dad?"

"How could he be hurt, Bee?"

The girl let Bromfield have it straight from the shoulder. "Because Clay did n't kill that man Collins. Clarendon did it."

"My God, you know!" he cried, ashen-faced. "He told you."

"No, he did n't tell us. For some reason he's protecting you. But I know it just the same. You did it."

"It was in self-defense," he pleaded.

"Then why did n't you say so? Why did you let Clay be accused instead of coming forward at once?"

"I was waiting to see if he could n't show he was innocent without — "

"Without getting you into it. You wanted to be shielded at any cost." The scorn that intolerant youth has for moral turpitude rang in her clear voice.

"I thought maybe we could both get out of it that way," he explained weakly.

"Oh, you thought! As soon as you saw this morning's paper you ought to have hurried to the police station and given yourself up."

"I was ill, I keep telling you."

"Your man could telephone, could n't he? He was n't ill, too, was he?"

Whitford interfered. "Hold on, honey. Don't rub it in. Clarendon was a bit rattled. That's natural. The question is, what's he going to do now?"

Their host groaned. "Durand 'll see I go to the chair — and I only struck the man to save my own life. I was n't trying to kill the fellow. He was shooting at me, and I had to do it."

"Of course," agreed Whitford. "We 've got proof of

that. Lindsay is one witness. He must have seen it all. I've got in my pocket one of the bullets Collins shot. That's more evidence. Then —"

Beatrice broke in excitedly. "Dad, Mr. Muldoon just told me over the 'phone that they've got the express wagon. The plank with the bullet holes was in it. And the driver has confessed that he and a carpenter, whose name he had given, changed the partition for Durand."

Whitford gave a subdued whoop. "We win. That lets you out, Clarendon. The question now is n't whether you or Clay will go to the penitentiary, but whether Durand will. We can show he's been trying to stand in the way of justice, that he's been cooking up false evidence."

"Let's hurry! Let's get to the police right away!" the girl cried, her eyes shining with excitement. "We ought not to lose a minute. We can get Clay out in time to go home to dinner with us."

Bromfield smiled wanly. He came to time as gallantly as he could. "All right. I'm elected to take his place, I see."

"Only for a day or two, Clarendon," said the older man. "As soon as we can get together a coroner's jury we'll straighten everything out."

"Yes," agreed the clubman lifelessly.

It was running through his mind already that if he should be freed of the murder charge, he would only have escaped Scylla to go to wreck on Charybdis. For it was a twenty to one bet that Jerry would go to Whitford with the story of his attempt to hire the gang leader to smirch Lindsay's reputation.

CHAPTER XXXVI

A BOOMERANG

IT must be admitted that when Bromfield made up his mind to clear Lindsay he did it thoroughly. His confession to the police was quiet and businesslike. He admitted responsibility for the presence of the Westerner at the Omnium Club. He explained that his guest had neither gambled nor taken any liquors, that he had come only as a spectator out of curiosity. The story of the killing was told by him simply and clearly. After he had struck down the gunman, he had done a bolt downstairs and got away by a back alley. His instinct had been to escape from the raid and from the consequences of what he had done, but of course he could not let anybody else suffer in his place. So he had come to give himself up.

The late afternoon papers carried the story that Clarendon Bromfield, well-known man about town, had confessed to having killed "Slim" Collins and had completely exonerated Lindsay. It was expected that the latter would be released immediately.

He was. That evening he dined at the home of the Whitfords. The mine owner had wanted to go on the bond of Bromfield, but his offer had been rejected.

"We'll hear what the coroner's jury has to say," the man behind the desk at headquarters had decided. "It'll not hurt him to rest a day or two in the cooler."

After dinner the committee of defense met in the Red

Room and discussed ways and means. Johnnie and his bride were present because it would have been cruel to exclude them, but for the most part they were silent members. Tim Muldoon arrived with Annie Millikan, both of them somewhat awed by the atmosphere of the big house adjoining the Drive. Each of them brought a piece of information valuable to the cause.

The man in charge of the blotter at the station had told Tim that from a dip called Fog Coney, one of those arrested in the gambling-house raid, an automatic gun with two chambers discharged had been taken and turned in by those who searched him. It had required some maneuvering for Tim to get permission to see Fog alone, but he had used his influence on the force and managed this.

Fog was a sly dog. He wanted to make sure on which side his bread was buttered before he became communicative. At first he had been willing to tell exactly nothing. He had already been seen by Durand, and he had a very pronounced respect for that personage. It was not until he had become convinced that Jerry's star was on the wane that he had "come through" with what Muldoon wanted. Then he admitted that he had picked the automatic up from the floor where Collins had dropped it when he fell. His story still further corroborated that of the defense. He had seen "Slim" fire twice before he was struck by the chair.

Through an admirer Annie had picked up a lead that might develop into something worth while. Her friend had told her that Durand had made a flat offer to one of the dope fiends caught in the raid to look after him if he would swear that "Slim" had not drawn a gun. Though the story had not come at first hand, she believed it was true, and thought from her knowledge of him that the man would weaken under a mild third degree.

Clay summed up in a sentence the result of all the evidence they had collected. "It's not any longer a question of whether Bromfield goes to prison, but of Durand. The fellow has sure overplayed his hand."

Before twelve hours more had passed Durand discovered this himself. He had been too careless, too sure that he was outside of and beyond the law. At first he had laughed contemptuously at the advice of his henchmen to get to cover before it was too late.

"They can't touch me," he bragged. "They dare n't."

But it came to him with a sickening realization that the district attorney meant business. He was going after him just as though he were an ordinary crook.

Jerry began to use his "pull." There reached him presently that same sinking at the pit of the stomach he had known when Clay had thrashed him. He learned that when a lawbreaker is going strong, friends at court who are under obligations to him are a bulwark of strength, but when one's power is shaken politicians prefer to take no risks. No news spreads more rapidly than that of the impending fall of a chieftain. The word was passing among the wise that Jerry Durand was to be thrown overboard.

The active center of the attack upon him was the group around Clay Lindsay. To it was now allied the office of the district attorney and all the malcontent subordinates of the underworld who had endured his domination so long only because they must. The campaign was gathering impetus like a snowslide. Soon it would be too late to stop it even if he could call off the friends of the Westerner.

Durand tried to make an appointment with Whitford. That gentleman declined to see him. Jerry persisted. He offered to meet him at one of his clubs. He telephoned to the house, but could not get any result more satisfactory than the cold voice of a servant saying, "Mr. Whitford does not wish to talk with you, sir." At last he telegraphed.

The message read:

I'll come to your house at eight this evening. Better see me for Missie's sake.

It was signed by Durand.

When Jerry called he was admitted.

Whitford met him with chill hostility. He held the telegram in his hand. "What does this message mean?" he asked bluntly.

"Your daughter's engaged to Bromfield, ain't she?" demanded the ex-prize-fighter, his bulbous eyes full on his host.

"That's our business, sir."

"I got a reason for asking. She is or she ain't. Which is it?"

"We'll not discuss my daughter's affairs."

"All right, since you're so damned particular. We'll discuss Bromfield's. I warned him to keep his mouth shut or he'd get into trouble."

"He was released from prison this afternoon."

"Did I say anything about prison?" Durand asked. "There's other kinds of grief beside being in stir. I've got this guy right."

"Just what do you mean, Mr. Durand?"

"I mean that he hired me to get Lindsay in bad with you and the girl. He was to be caught at the Omnium Club with a woman when the police raided the place, and it was to get into the papers."

"I don't believe it," said Whitford promptly.

"You will. I had a dictagraph in the room when Bromfield came to see me. You can hear it all in his own voice."

"But there was n't any woman with Lindsay at Maddock's when the raid was pulled off."

"Sure there was n't. I threw Bromfield down."

"You arranged to have Lindsay killed instead."

"Forget that stuff. The point is that if you don't call off the district attorney, I'll tell all I know about son-in-law Bromfield. He'll be ruined for life."

"To hear you tell it."

"All right. Ask him."

"I shall."

"Conspiracy is what the law calls it. Maybe he can keep outa stir. But when his swell friends hear it they'll turn their backs on Bromfield. You *know* it."

"I'll not know it unless Mr. Bromfield tells me so himself. I don't care anything for your dictagraph. I'm no eavesdropper."

"You tell him what he's up against and he'll come through all right. I'll see that every newspaper in New

York carries the story if you don't notify me to-day that this attack on me is off. I'll learn you silk stockings you can't make Jerry Durand the goat."

"You can't implicate him without getting yourself into trouble — even if your story is true, and I still don't believe it."

"You believe it all right," jeered the crook. "And the story don't hurt me a bit. I pretended to fall in with his plans, but I did n't do it. The results show that."

"They show me that you tried to do murder instead."

"That's all bunk. The evidence won't prove it."

Whitford announced his decision sharply. "If you'll leave me your telephone number, I'll let you know later in the day what we'll do."

He had told Durand that he did not believe his story. He had tried to reject it because he did not want to accept it, but after the man had gone and he thought it over, his judgment was that it held some germ of truth. If so, he was bound to protect Bromfield as far as he could. No matter what Clarendon had done, he could not throw overboard to the sharks the man who was still engaged to his daughter. He might not like him. In point of fact he did not. But he had to stand by him till he was out of his trouble.

Colin Whitford went straight to his daughter.

"Honey, this man Durand has just brought me a story about Clarendon. He says he paid him to get Clay into trouble at the Omnium Club in order to discredit him with us."

"Oh, Dad!"

"I'm going to see Clarendon. If it's true I don't want

you to see him again. Authorize me to break the engagement for you."

They talked it over for a few minutes. Beatrice slipped the engagement ring from her finger and gave it to her father with a sigh.

"You can't do wrong without paying for it, Dad."

"That's right. Bromfield — "

"I'm not thinking of Clarendon. I'm thinking about me. I feel as if I had been dragged in the dust," she said wearily.

CHAPTER XXXVII

ON THE CARPET

THE question at issue was not whether Beatrice would break with her fiancé, but in what way it should be done. If her father found him guilty of what Durand had said, he was to dismiss him brusquely; if not, Beatrice wanted to disengage herself gently and with contrition.

Whitford summoned Bromfield to his office where the personal equation would be less pronounced. He put to him plainly the charge made by Jerry and demanded an answer.

The younger man was between the devil and the deep sea. He would have lied cheerfully if that would have availed. But a denial of the truth of Durand's allegations would be a challenge for him to prove his story. He would take it to the papers and spread it broadcast. From that hour Clarendon Bromfield would be an outcast in the city. Society would repudiate him. His clubs would cast him out. All the prestige that he had built up by a lifetime of effort would be swept away.

No lie could save him. The only thing he could do was to sugarcoat the truth. He set about making out a case for himself as skillfully as he could.

"I'm a man of the world, Mr. Whitford," he explained. "When I meet an ugly fact I look it in the face. This man Lindsay was making a great impression on you and Bee. Neither of you seemed able quite to realize his — his deficiencies, let us say. I felt myself at a disadvantage with him because he's such a remarkably virile young man and he constantly reminded you both of the West you love. It seemed fair to all of us to try him out — to find out whether at bottom he was a decent fellow or not. So I laid a little trap to find out."

Bromfield was sailing easily into his version of the affair. It was the suavest interpretation of his conduct that he had been able to prepare, one that put him in the rôle of a fair-minded man looking to the best interests of all.

"Not the way Durand tells it," answered the miner bluntly. "He says you paid him a thousand dollars to arrange a trap to catch Lindsay."

"Either he misunderstood me or he's distorting the facts," claimed the clubman with an assumption of boldness.

"That ought to be easy to prove. We'll make an appointment with him for this afternoon and check up by the dictagraph."

Bromfield laughed uneasily. "Is that necessary, Mr. Whitford? Surely my word is good. I have the honor to tell you that I did nothing discreditable."

"It would have been good with me a week ago," replied the Coloradoan gravely. "But since then — well, you know what's happened since then. I don't want to hurt your feelings, Clarendon, but I may as well say frankly that I can't accept your account without checking up on it. That, however, isn't quite the point. Durand has served notice that unless we call off the prosecution of him he's going to ruin you. Are you satisfied to have us tell him he can go to the devil?"

"I would n't go that far." Bromfield felt for his words carefully. "Maybe in cold type what I said might be misunderstood. I would n't like to push the fellow too far."

Whitford leaned back in his swivel chair and looked steadily at the man to whom his daughter was engaged. "I'm going to the bottom of this, Bromfield. That fellow Durand ought to go to the penitentiary. We're gathering the evidence to send him there. Now he tells me he'll drag you down to ruin with him if he goes. Come clean. Can he do it?"

"Well, I would n't say — "

"Don't evade, Bromfield. Yes or no."

"I suppose he can." The words came sulkily after a long pause.

"You did hire him to destroy Lindsay's reputation."

"Lindsay had no business here in New York. He was disturbing Bee's peace of mind. I wanted to get rid of him and send him home."

"So you paid a crooked scoundrel who hated him to murder his reputation."

"That's not what I call it," defended the clubman.

"It does n't matter what you call it. The fact stands."

"I told him explicitly — again and again — that there was to be no violence. I intended only to show him up. I had a right to do it."

Whitford got up and walked up and down the room. He felt like laying hands on this well-dressed scamp and throwing him out of the office. He tasted something of his daughter's sense of degradation at ever having been connected with a man of so little character. The experience was a bitterly humiliating one to him. For Bee was, in his opinion, the cleanest, truest little thoroughbred under heaven. The only questionable thing he had ever known her to do was to engage herself to this man.

Colin came to a halt in front of the other.

"We've got to protect you, no matter how little you deserve it. I can't have Bee's name dragged into all the papers of the country. The case against Durand will have to be dropped. He's lost his power anyhow and he'll never get it back."

"Then it does n't matter much whether he's tried or not."

That phase of the subject Whitford did not pursue. He began to feel in his vest pocket for something.

"Of course you understand that we're through with you, Bromfield. Neither Beatrice nor I care to have anything more to do with you."

"I don't see why," protested Bromfield. "As a man of the world — "

"If you don't see the reason I'm not able to explain it to you." Whitford's fingers found what they were looking for. He fished a ring from his pocket and put it on the desk. "Beatrice asked me to give you this."

"I don't think that's fair. If she wants to throw me over she ought to tell me her reasons herself."

"She's telling them through me. I don't want to be more explicit unless you force me."

"Of course I'm not good enough. I know that. No man's good enough for a good woman. But I'm as good as other fellows. We don't claim to be angels. New York does n't sprout wings."

"I'm not going to argue this with you. And I'm not going to tell you what I think of you beyond saying that we're through with you. The less said about it the better. Man, don't you see I don't want to have any more talk about it? The engagement was a mistake in the first place. Bee never loved you. Even if you'd been what we thought you, it would n't have done. She's lucky to have found out in time."

"Is this a business rupture, too, Mr. Whitford?"

"Just as you say about that, Bromfield. As an investor in the Bird Cage you're entitled to the same consideration that any other stockholder is. Since you're the second largest owner you've a right to recognition on the board of directors. I'm not mixing my private affairs with business."

"Good of you, Mr. Whitford." The younger man spoke with a hint of gentle sarcasm. He flicked a speck of dirt from his coat-sleeve and returned to the order of the day. "I understand then that you'll drop the case against Durand on condition that he'll surrender anything he may have against me and agree to keep quiet."

"Yes. I think I can speak for Lindsay. So far most of the evidence is in our hands. It is not yet enough to convict him. We can probably arrange it with the district attorney to have the thing dropped. You can make your own terms with Durand. I'd rather not have anything to do with it myself."

Bromfield rose, pulled on the glove he had removed, nodded good-bye without offering to shake hands, and sauntered out of the office. There was a look on his face the mining man did not like. It occurred to Whitford that Clarendon, now stripped of self-respect by the knowledge of the regard in which they held him, was in a position to strike back hard if he cared to do so. The right to vote the proxies of the small stockholders of the Bird Cage Company had been made out in his name at the request of the president of the corporation.

CHAPTER XXXVIII

A CONVERSATION ABOUT STOCK

THE case against Durand was pigeon-holed by the district attorney without much regret. All through the underworld where his influence had been strong, it was known that Jerry had begged off. He was discredited among his following and was politically a down-and-outer. But he knew too much to permit him to be dragged into court safely. With his back to the wall he might tell of many shady transactions implicating prominent people. There were strong influences which did not want him pressed too hard. The charge remained on the docket, but it was set back from term to term and never brought to trial.

Colin Whitford found his attention pretty fully absorbed by his own affairs. Bromfield had opened a fight against him for control of the Bird Cage Company. The mine had been developed by the Coloradoan from an unlikely prospect into a well-paying concern. It was the big business venture of his life and he took a strong personal interest in running it. Now, because of Bromfield's intention to use for his own advantage the proxies made out in his name, he was likely to lose control. With Bromfield in charge the property might be wrecked before he could be ousted.

"Dad's worrying," Beatrice told Lindsay. "He's afraid he'll lose control of the mine. There's a fight on against him."

"What for? I thought yore father was a mighty competent operator. Don't the stockholders know when
they're well off?"

She looked at him enigmatically. "Some one he
trusted has turned out a traitor. That happens occasionally in business, you know."

It was from Colin himself that Clay learned the name
of the traitor.

"It's that fellow Bromfield," he explained. "He's the
secretary and second largest stockholder in the company. The annual election is to be to-morrow afternoon.
He's got me where the wool's short. I was fool enough
to ask the smaller stockholders to make out their proxies in his name. At that time he was hand in glove with
us. Now I'm up against it. He's going to name the board
of directors and have himself made president."

Clay ventured on thin ice. The name of Bromfield
had not been mentioned to him before in the last twenty-
four hours by either Beatrice or her father. "Surelv
Bromfield would n't want to offend you."

"That's exactly what he would want to do."

"But — "

"He's got his reasons."

"Is n't there some way to stop him, then?"

"I've been getting a wrinkle trying to figure out one.
I'd certainly be in your debt if you could show me a way."

"When is the election?"

"At three o'clock."

"Where?"

"At the company offices."

"Perhaps if I talked with Bromfield — "

Whitford laughed shortly. "I'd talk an arm off him if it would do any good. But it won't. He's out for revenge."

Clay's eyes alighted swiftly on the older man. They asked gravely a question and found an answer that set his heart singing. Beatrice had broken her engagement with Bromfield.

"He won't do, Clay. He's off color." Whitford did a bit of mental acrobatics. "Why do you suppose he took you to Maddock's?"

Again Lindsay's appraising gaze rested on his friend. "I've never worked that out to my satisfaction. It wasn't the kind of place he would be likely to go for pleasure. But I don't think he'd arranged a trap for me, if that's what you mean. It doesn't look reasonable that he would want me killed."

Whitford told him all he knew about the affair. The story told him banished any doubts Clay may have had about a certain step he had begun during the last few minutes to hold in consideration. It did more. It hardened a fugitive impulse to a resolution. Bromfield was fair game for him.

It was a little after eleven o'clock next morning when the cattleman walked into an apartment house for bachelors, took the elevator, and rang the bell at Bromfield's door.

Clarendon, fresh from the hands of his valet, said he was glad to see Lindsay, but did not look it. He offered his guest a choice of liquors and selected for himself a dry martini. Cigars and cigarettes were within reach on a tabouret.

Clay discovered that one difficulty he had expected to meet did not complicate the problem. The valet had left to select the goods for half a dozen custom-made shirts, Bromfield explained apologetically, apropos of the lack of service. He would not return till late in the afternoon.

"I've come to see about that Bird Cage business, Mr. Bromfield," his visitor explained. "I've been millin' it over in my mind, and I thought I'd put the proposition up to you the way it looks to me."

Bromfield's eyebrows lifted. His face asked with supercilious politeness what the devil business it was of his.

"Mr. Whitford has put in twenty years of his life building up the Bird Cage into a good property. It's a one-man mine. He made it out of a hole in the ground, developed it, expanded it, gave it a market value. He's always protected the stockholders and played the game square with them. Don't it look like he ought to stay in control of it?"

"Did he send you here to tell me that?"

"No, he didn't. But he's gettin' along in years, Bromfield. It don't look hardly right to me for you to step in and throw him out. What do you think about it, yourself?"

The clubman flushed with anger. "I think that it's damned impertinent of you to come here meddling in my business. I might have expected it. You've always been an impertinent meddler."

"Mebbeso," agreed Clay serenely, showing no surprise at this explosion. "But I'm here. And I put a question. Shall I ask it again?"

"No need. I'm going to take what the law allows me — what I and my friends have bought and paid for in the open market. The more it hurts Whitford the better I'll be pleased," answered Bromfield, his manner of cynical indifference swept away by gathering rage. The interference of this "bounder" filled him with a passion of impotent hate.

"Is that quite correct? Did you buy control in the market? In point of fact, are n't you holdin' a bunch of proxies because Whitford wrote and asked the stockholders to sign them for you to vote? What you intend doing is a moral fraud, no matter what its legal aspect is. You'd be swindling the very stockholders you claim to represent, as well as abusing the confidence of Whitford."

"What you think is n't of the least importance to me, Mr. Lindsay. If you're here merely to offer me your advice, I suppose I shall now have regretfully to say goodday." The New Yorker rose, a thin lip smile scarcely veiling his anger at this intruder who had brought his hopes to nothing.

"I reckon I'll not hurry off, Mr. Bromfield," Clay replied easily. "You might think I was mad at you. I'll stick around awhile and talk this over."

"Unfortunately I have an engagement," retorted the other icily.

"When?"

"I really think, Mr. Lindsay, that is my business."

"I'm makin' it mine," said Clay curtly.

Bromfield stared. "I beg your pardon?"

"I said it was mine too. You see I bought a coupla

shares of Bird Cage stock yesterday. I'd hate to see Whitford ousted from control. I've got confidence in him."

"It's your privilege to vote that stock this afternoon. At least it would be if it had been transferred to you on the books. I'll vote my stock according to my own views."

"I wonder," murmured Clay aloud.

"What's that?" snapped Bromfield.

"I was just figurin' on what would happen if you got sick and could n't attend that annual meeting this afternoon," drawled the Westerner. "I reckon mebbe some of the stockholders you've got lined up would break away and join Whitford."

The New Yorker felt a vague alarm. What idea did this fellow have in the back of his head. Did he intend to do bodily violence to him? Without any delay Bromfield reached for the telephone.

The large brown hand of the Westerner closed over his.

"I'm talkin' to you, Mr. Bromfield. It's not polite for you to start 'phoning, not even to the police, whilst we're still engaged in conversation."

"Don't you try to interfere with me," said the man who paid the telephone bill. "I'll not submit to such an indignity."

"I'm not the only one that interferes. You fixed up quite an entertainment for me the other night, did n't you? Would n't you kinda call that interferin' some? I sure ought to comb yore hair for it."

Bromfield made a hasty decision to get out. He started

for the door. Clay traveled in that direction too. They arrived simultaneously. Clarendon backed away. The Arizonan locked the door and pocketed the key.

His host grew weakly violent. From Whitford he had heard a story about two men in a locked room that did not reassure him now. One of the men had been this cattleman. The other — well, he had suffered. "Let me out! I'll not stand this! You can't bully me!" he cried shrilly.

"Don't pull yore picket-pin, Bromfield," advised Lindsay. "I've elected myself boss of the *rodeo*. What I say goes. You'll save yorese'f a heap of worry if you make up yore mind to that right away."

"What do you want? What are you trying to do? I'm not a barroom brawler like Durand. I don't intend to fight with you."

"You've ce'tainly relieved my mind," murmured Clay lazily. "What's yore own notion of what I ought to do to you, Bromfield? You invited me out as a friend and led me into a trap after you had fixed it up. Would n't a first-class thrashin' with a hawsswhip be about right?"

Bromfield turned pale. "I've got a weak heart," he faltered.

"I'll say you have," agreed Clay. "It's pumpin' water in place of blood right now, I'll bet. Did you ever have a real honest-to-God lickin' when you was a boy?"

The New Yorker knew he was helpless before this clear-eyed, supple athlete who walked like a god from Olympus. One can't lap up half a dozen highballs a day for an indeterminate number of years without getting flabby, nor can he spend himself in feeble dissipations and have reserves of strength to call upon when needed. The tongue went dry in his mouth. He began to swallow his Adam's apple.

"I'm not well to-day," he said, almost in a whisper.

"Let's look at this thing from all sides," went on Clay cheerfully. "If we decide by a majority of the voting stock — and I'm carryin' enough proxies so that I've got control — that you'd ought to have a whalin', why, o' course, there's nothin' to it but get to business and make a thorough job."

"Maybe I did n't do right about Maddock's."

"No mebbe about that. You acted like a yellow hound."

"I'm sorry. I apologize."

"I don't reckon I can use apologies. I might make a bargain with you."

"I'll be glad to make any reasonable bargain."

"How'd this do? I'll vote my stock and proxies in the Bromfield Punishment Company, Limited, against the whalin', and you vote yore stock and proxies in the Bird Cage Company to return the present board and directorate."

"That's coercion."

"Well, so it is."

"The law — "

"Did you go hire a lawyer for an opinion before you paid Durand to do me up?"

"You've got no right to hold me a prisoner here to help Whitford."

"All right, I won't. I'll finish my business with you

and when I'm through, you can go to the annual meetin' — if you feel up to travelin' that far."

"I'll give you a thousand dollars to let me alone."

"That'd be a thousand and fifty you had given me,
would n't it?" returned Lindsay gayly.

Tears of vexation stood in Bromfield's eyes. "All
right. Let me go. I'll be fair to Whitford and arrange
a deal with him."

"Get the stockholders who're with you on the 'phone
and tell 'em to vote their stock as Whitford thinks best.
Get Whitford and tell him the fight's off."

"If I do, will you let me go?"

"If you don't, we'll return to the previous question —
the annual meeting of the Bromfield Punishment Company, Limited."

Bromfield got busy with the telephone.

When he had finished, Clay strolled over to a book-
case, cast his eyes over the shelves, and took out a book.
It was "David Harum." He found an easy-chair, threw
a leg over one arm, and presently began to chuckle.

"Are you going to keep me here all day?" asked his
host sulkily.

"Only till about four o'clock. We're paired, you and
me, so we'll both stay away from the election. Why
don't you pick you a good book and enjoy yoreself?
There's a lot of A 1 readin' in that case over there. It'll
sure improve yore mind."

Clarendon ground his teeth impotently.

His guest continued to grin over the good stories of
the old horse-trader. When he closed the book at last,
he had finished it. His watch told him that it was twenty

minutes to five. Bromfield's man was at the door trying
to get in. He met Lindsay going out.

"No, I can't stay to tea to-day, Mr. Bromfield," the
Arizonan was saying, a gleam of mirth in his eyes. "No
use urging me. Honest, I've really got to be going. Had
a fine time, did n't we? So long."

Bromfield used bad language.

CHAPTER XXXIX

IN CENTRAL PARK

JOHNNIE burst into the kitchen beaming. "We're gonna p'int for the hills, Kitty. Clay he's had a letter callin' him home."

"When are you going?"

"Thursday. Ain't that great?"

She nodded, absently. Her mind was on another tack already. "Johnnie, I'm going to ask Miss Whitford here for dinner to-night."

"Say, you ce'tainly get the best notions, honeybug," he shouted.

"Do you think she'll come?"

"Sure she'll come."

"I'll fix up the bestest dinner ever was, and maybe — "

Her conclusion wandered off into the realm of unvoiced hopes, but her husband knew what it was as well as if she had phrased it.

When Clay came home that evening he stopped abruptly at the door. The lady of his dreams was setting the table in the dining-room and chatting gayly with an invisible Kitty in the kitchen. Johnnie was hovering about her explaining some snapshots of Clay he had gathered.

"Tha's the ol' horn-toad winnin' the ropin' championship at Tucson. He sure stepped some that day," the Runt boasted.

The delicate fragrance of the girl's personality went

to Clay's head like wine as he stepped forward and shook
hands. To see her engaged in this intimate household
task at his own table quickened his pulse and sent a
glow through him.

"You did n't know you had invited me to dinner, did
you?" she said, little flags a-flutter in her cheeks.

They had a gay dinner, and afterward a pleasant hour
before Clay took her home.

Neither of them was in a hurry. They walked through
Central Park in the kindly darkness, each acutely sensitive to the other's presence.

Her gayety and piquancy had given place to a gentle
shyness. Clay let the burden of conversation fall upon
her. He knew that he had come to his hour of hours and
his soul was wrapped in gravity.

She had never before known a man like him, a personality so pungent, so dynamic. He was master of himself. He ran a clean race. None of his energy was wasted
in futile dissipation. One could not escape from his
strength, and she had already discovered that she did
not want to escape it. If she gave herself to him, it
might be for her happiness or it might not. She must
take her chance of that. But it had come to her that a
woman's joy is to follow her heart — and her heart answered "Here" when he called.

She too sensed what was coming, and the sex instinct
in her was on tiptoe in flight. She was throbbing with
excitement. Her whole being longed to hear what he had
to tell her. Yet she dodged for a way of escape. Silences
were too significant, too full-pulsed. She made herself
talk. It did not much matter about what.

"Why did n't you tell us that it was **Mr. Bromfield**
who struck down that man Collins? Why did you let
us think you did it?" she queried.

"Well, folks in New York don't know me. What was
the use of gettin' him in bad?"

"You know that was n't the reason. You did it because — " She stopped in the midst of the sentence. It
had occurred to her that this subject was more dangerous even than silence.

"I did it because he was the man you were goin' to
marry," he said.

They moved side by side through the shadows. In the
faint light he could make out the fine line of her exquisite throat. After a moment she spoke. "You're a good
friend, Clay. It was a big thing to do. I don't know anybody else except Dad that would have done it for me."

"You don't know anybody else that loves you as
much as I do."

It was out at last, quietly and without any dra-
matics. A flash of soft eyes darted at him, then veiled
the shining tenderness beneath long lashes. She paced
a little faster, chin up, nerves taut.

"I've had an attack of common sense," he went on,
and in his voice was a strength both audacious and pa-
tient. "I thought at first I could n't hope to win you
because of your fortune and what it had done for you.
Even when I knew you liked me I felt it would n't
be fair for me to ask you. I could n't offer you the advantages you'd had. But I've changed my mind. I've
been watching what money does to yore friends. It
makes them soft. They flutter around like butterflies.

They're paupers — a good many of them — because they don't pay their way. A man's a tramp if he does n't saw wood for his breakfast. I don't want you to get like that, and if you stay here long enough you sure will. It's in my heart that if you'll come with me we'll live."

In the darkness she made a rustling movement toward him. A little sob welled up in her throat as her hands lifted to him. "Oh, Clay! I've fought against it. I did n't want to, but — I love you. Oh, I do love you!"

He took her lissom young body in his arms. Her lips lifted to his.

Presently they walked forward slowly. Clay had never seen her more lovely and radiant, though tears still clung to the outskirts of her joy.

"We're going to live — oh, every hour!" she cried to the stars, her lover's hand in hers.

CHAPTER XL

CLAY PLAYS SECOND FIDDLE

JOHNNIE felt that Kitty's farewell dinner had gone very well. It was her first essay as a hostess, and all of them had enjoyed themselves. But, so far as he could see, it had not achieved the results for which they had been hoping.

Clay came home late and next morning was full of plans about leaving. He discussed the packing and train schedules and affairs at the B-in-a-Box. But of Beatrice Whitford he made not even a casual mention.

"Two more days and we'll hit the trail for good old Tucson," he said cheerfully.

"Y'betcha, by jollies," agreed his bandy-legged shadow.

None the less Johnnie was distressed. He believed that his friend was concealing an aching heart beneath all this attention to impending details. As a Benedict he considered it his duty to help the rest of the world get married too. A bachelor was a boob. He didn't know what was best for him. Same way with a girl. Clay was fond of Miss Beatrice, and she thought a heap of him. You couldn't fool Johnnie. No, sirree! Well, then?

Mooning on the sad plight of these two friends who were too coy or too perverse to know what was best for them, Johnnie suddenly slapped himself a whack on the thigh. A brilliant idea had flashed into his cranium. It proceeded to grow until he was like to burst with it.

When Lindsay rose from breakfast he was mysteriously beckoned into another room. Johnnie outlined sketchily and with a good deal of hesitation what he had in mind. Clay's eyes danced with that spark of mischief his friends had learned to recognize as a danger signal.

"You're some sure-enough wizard, Johnnie," he admitted. "I expect you're right about girls not knowin' their own minds. You've had more experience with women than I have. If you say the proper thing to do is to abduct Miss Whitford and take her with us, why — "

"That's whatever. She likes you a heap more than she lets on to you. O' course it would be different if I was n't married, but Kitty she can chaperoon Miss Beatrice. It'll be all accordin' to Hoyle."

The cattleman gazed at the puncher admiringly. "Don't rush me off my feet, old-timer," he said gayly. "Gimme a coupla hours to think of it, and I'll let you know what I'll do. This is real sudden, Johnnie. You must 'a' been a terror with the ladies when you was a bachelor. Me, I never kidnaped one before."

"Onct in a while you got to play like you're gonna treat 'em rough," said Mr. Green sagely, blushing a trifle nevertheless.

"All right. I'll let you engineer this if I can make up my mind to it after I've milled it over. I can see you know what you're doin'."

When Johnnie returned from a telephone call at the office two hours later, Kitty had a suspicion he was up to something. He bubbled mystery so palpably that her curiosity was piqued. But the puncher for once was silent as a clam. He did not intend to get Kitty into trouble if his plan miscarried. Moreover, he had an intuition that if she knew what was under way she would put her small, competent foot through the middle of the project.

The conspirators arranged details. Johnnie was the brains of the kidnaping. Clay bought the tickets and was to take charge of the prisoner after the train was reached. They decided it would be best to get a stateroom for the girl.

"We wantta make it as easy as we can for her," said Johnnie. "O' course it's all for her own good, but we don't figure to treat her noways but like the princess she is."

"Yes," agreed Clay humbly.

According to programme, carefully arranged by Johnnie, Beatrice rode down to the train with him and Kitty in their taxicab. She went on board for the final goodbyes and chatted with them in their section.

The chief conspirator was as easy as a toad in a hot skillet. Now that it had come down to the actual business of taking this young woman with them against her will, he began to weaken. His heart acted very strangely, but he had to go through with it.

"C-can I see you a minute in the next car, Miss Beatrice?" he asked, his voice quavering.

Miss Whitford lifted her eyebrows, but otherwise expressed no surprise.

"Certainly, Johnnie."

"What do you want to see Miss Whitford about, Johnnie?" his spouse asked. There were times when

Kitty mistrusted Johnnie's judgment. She foresaw that he might occasionally need a firm hand.

"Oh, nothin' much. Tell you about it later, honey." The kidnaper mopped the perspiration from his forehead. At that moment he wished profoundly that this brilliant idea of his had never been born.

He led the way down the aisle into the next sleeper and stopped at one of the staterooms. Shakily he opened the door and stood aside for her to pass first.

"You want me to go in here?" she asked.

"Yes'm."

Beatrice stepped in. Johnnie followed.

Clay rose from the lounge and said, "Glad to see you, Miss Whitford."

"Did you bring me here to say good-bye, Johnnie?" asked Beatrice.

The Runt's tongue stuck to the roof of his mouth. His eyes appealed dumbly to Clay.

"Better explain to Miss Whitford," said Clay, passing the buck.

"It's for yore good, Miss Beatrice," stammered the villain who had brought her. "We — we — I — I done brought you here to travel home with us."

"You — what?"

Before her slender, outraged dignity Johnnie wilted. "Kitty, she — she can chaperoon you. It's all right, ma'am. I — we — I did n't go for to do nothin' that was n't proper. We thought — "

"You mean that you brought me here expecting me to go along with you — without my consent — without a trunk — without — "

Clay took charge of the kidnaping. "Johnnie, if I were you I'd light a shuck back to the other car. I see I'll have to treat this lady rough as you advised."

Johnnie wanted to expostulate, to deny that he had ever given such counsel, to advise an abandonment of the whole project. But his nerve unexpectedly failed him. He glanced helplessly at Clay and fled.

He was called upon the carpet immediately on joining Kitty.

"What are you up to, Johnnie? I'm not going to have you make a goose of yourself if I can help it. And where's Mr. Lindsay? You said he'd meet us here."

"Clay, he's in the next car."

"You took Miss Beatrice in there to say good-bye to him?"

"No — she — she's goin' along with us."

"Going along with us? What do you mean, Johnnie Green?"

He told her his story, not at all cheerfully. His bold plan looked very different now from what it had two days before.

Already the chant of the wheels had begun. The train was in the sub-Hudson darkness of the tunnel.

Kitty rose with decision. "Well, of all the foolishness I ever heard, Johnnie, this is the limit. I'm going right to that poor girl. You've spoiled everything between you. She'll hate Mr. Lindsay for the rest of her life. How could he be so stupid?"

Her husband followed her, crestfallen. He wanted to weep with chagrin.

Beatrice opened the door of the stateroom. She

had taken off her hat and Clay was hanging it on a hook.

"Come in," she said cordially, but faintly.

Kitty did not quite understand. The atmosphere was less electric than she had expected. She stopped, taken aback at certain impressions that began to register themselves on her brain.

"Johnnie was tellin' me — "

"About how he abducted me. Yes. Was n't it dear of him?"

"But — "

"I've decided to make the best of it and go along."

"I — your father, Mr. Whitford — " Kitty bogged down.

Beatrice blushed. Little dimples came out with her smile. "I think I'd better let Clay explain."

"We were married two days ago, Kitty."

"What!" shouted the Runt.

"We intended to ask you both to the wedding, but when Johnnie proposed to abduct Miss Whitford, I thought it a pity not to let him. So we — "

Johnnie fell on him and beat him with both fists. "You daw-goned ol' scalawag! I never will help you git married again!" he shouted gleefully.

Clay sat down on the seat and gave way to mirth. He rocked with glee. Beatrice began to chuckle. She, too, yielded to laughter. Kitty, and then Johnnie, added to the chorus.

"Oh, Johnnie — Johnnie — you'll be the death of me!" cried Clay. "It'll never be a dull old world so long as you stay a bandit."

"Did you really advise him to beat me, Johnnie?" asked Beatrice sweetly. "I never would have guessed you were such a cave man."

Johnnie flamed to the roots of his hair. "Now, ma'am, if you're gonna believe that — "

Beatrice repented and offered him her hand.

"We'll not believe anything of you that isn't good, even if you did want to kidnap me," she said.

CHAPTER XLI

THE NEW DAY

THE slapping of the wind against the tent awakened Beatrice. She could hear it soughing gently through the branches cf the live oaks. An outflung arm discovered Clay missing.

Presently she rose, sleep not yet brushed fully from her eyes, drew the tent flaps together modestly under her chin, and looked out upon a world which swam in the enchanted light of a dawn primeval. The eastern sky was faintly pink with the promise of a coming sun. The sweet, penetrating lilt of the lark flung greeting at her.

Her questing glance found Clay, busy over the mesquite fire upon which he was cooking breakfast. She watched him move about, supple and light and strong, and her heart lifted with sheer joy of the mate she had chosen. He was such a man among men, this clear-eyed, bronzed husband of a week. He was so clean and simple and satisfying. As she closed the flaps she gave a deep sigh of content.

Every minute till she joined him was begrudged. For Beatrice had learned the message of her heart. She knew that she was wholly and completely in love with what life had brought her.

The hubbub of the city seemed to her now so small and so petty. Always she had known a passionate love of things fine and good. But civilization had thwarted her purposes, belittled her expression of them. Environment had driven her into grooves of convention. Here at last she was free.

And she was amazingly, radiantly happy. What did motor-cars or wine-suppers or Paris gowns matter? They were the trappings that stressed her slavery. Here she moved beside her mate without fear or doubt in a world wonderful. Eye to eye, they spoke the truth to each other after the fashion of brave, simple souls.

Glowing from the ice-cold bath of water from a mountain stream, she stepped down the slope into a slant of sunshine to join Clay. He looked up from the fire and waved a spoon gayly at her. For he too was as jocund as the day which stood tiptoe on the misty mountain-tops. They had come into the hills to spend their honeymoon alone together, and life spoke to him in accents wholly joyous.

The wind and sun caressed her. As she moved toward him, a breath of the morning flung the gown about her so that each step modeled anew the slender limbs.

Her husband watched the girl streaming down the slope. Love swift as old wine flooded his veins. He rose, caught her to him, and looked down into the deep, still eyes that were pools of happiness.

"Are you glad — glad all through, sweetheart?" he demanded.

A little laugh welled from her throat. She gave him a tender, mocking smile.

"I hope heaven's like this," she whispered.

"You don't regret New York — not a single, hidden longing for it 'way down deep in yore heart?"

She shook her head. "I always wanted to be rescued from the environment that was stifling me, but I did n't know a way of escape till you came," she said.

"Then you knew it?"

"From the moment I saw you tie the janitor to the hitching-post. You remember I was waiting to go riding with Mr. Bromfield. Well, I was bored to death with correct clothes and manners and thinking. I knew just what he would say to me and how he would say it and what I would answer. Then you walked into the picture and took me back to nature."

"It was the hitching-post that did it, then?"

"The hitching-post began it, anyhow." She slipped her arms around his neck and held him fast. "Oh, Clay, is n't it just too good to be true?"

A ball of fire pushed up into the crotch between two mountain-peaks and found them like a searchlight, filling their little valley with a golden glow.

The new day summoned them to labor and play and laughter, perhaps to tears and sorrow too. But the joy of it was that the call came to them both. They moved forward to life together.

THE END